Troublemakers

The

John

Simmons

Short

Fiction

Award

University of

Iowa Press

Iowa City

*John
McNally*

Troublemakers

University of Iowa Press, Iowa City 52242

Printed in the United States of America

http://www.uiowa.edu/~uipress

The publication of this book is supported by a grant
from the National Endowment for the Arts in
Washington, D.C., a federal agency.

Printed on acid-free paper

Library of Congress Cataloging-in-Publication Data
McNally, John, 1965–
Troublemakers / by John McNally.
p.   cm.—(The John Simmons short fiction award)
Contents: The vomitorium—The new year—The end of
romance—Smoke—The first of your last chances—The
politics of correctness—The grand illusion—The greatest
goddamn thing—Roger's new life—Torture—Limbs.
ISBN 0-87745-727-1 (pbk.)
1. United States—Social life and customs—20th century—
Fiction.   I. Title.   II. Series.
PS3563.C38813 T76   2000
813'.6—dc21   00-039247

00   01   02   03   04   P   5   4   3   2   1

For Amy Knox Brown

(and for Beth, Yogi, Chloe, and Lucille)

Contents

ACKNOWLEDGMENTS

The following troublemakers need to be
properly thanked, once and for all: Rodney Jones, James
Solheim, and Rick Russo (my first three creative writing
teachers); and Gerry Shapiro, Judy Slater, and Marly Swick
(my last three). Tireless readers, supporters, friends, and
thugs include Ted Genoways, Mary Anne Andrei, Brian Fitch,
Jenny Brantley, Gregg and Leslie Palmer, Scott M. Smith, Troy
Steinmacher, Kip Kotzen, Eric T. Lindvall, Christine Aguila,
Darrel Simmons, Paul and Ellen Eggers, Michael Honch, and
Dan Gutstein. *That's right.* Among the praiseworthy Wisconsin
riffraff are Jesse Lee, Ron W., Ron K., Lorrie M., Allison G.,
Kathy W., Judy M., and my pool-playing buddy, Stephen
Schottenfeld. A warm thanks to Alice K. Turner of *Playboy*
for giving me my first boost. A big bear hug to Paul Ingram of
Prairie Lights bookstore for offering me the most interesting
job in town, and, in doing so, helping me to buy a bit more
writing time. Kudos to David Sherwin at AWP. My wonderful
agent, Frances M. Kuffel, has worked tirelessly on my behalf and
deserves, well, more money than I'm making for her, but this
heartfelt *thank you* will just have to suffice in the meantime.
Boundless appreciation to everyone at the University of Iowa
Press and the Iowa Writers' Workshop. To my oldest and dearest
troublemaking friend, Joseph Salvatore Caccamisi, that notable
alumnus of Jacqueline Bouvier Kennedy Grade School (located
in beautiful downtown Burbank, Illinois), I owe years of
gratitude.

Thanks to the Browns, Larry and Carol, of
Lincoln, Nebraska.

Also, thanks to my brother, Gerald, and
his wife, Anne. My father deserves sainthood for years of
unwavering moral and financial support. Finally, this book
could not have been written without the influence of my
mother, who died at much too young an age, but whose own
tales about her childhood instilled in me a love for storytelling
and a respect for its craft.

Special thanks to the following individuals,
organizations, and magazines for awards and fellowships, which

provided money and, in turn, time to write some of these stories: the late James Michener and the Copernicus Society of America; Carl Djerassi and the Wisconsin Institute for Creative Writing; Margaret Bridgman and the Bread Loaf Writers' Conference; *Columbia: A Magazine of Poetry and Prose* for choosing "The Greatest Goddamn Thing" for an Editors' Award; *Sonora Review* for choosing "The End of Romance" as the winner of their annual Short Story Contest; and *Prairie Schooner* and the University of Nebraska-Lincoln for the Mari Sandoz Award, also for "The End of Romance."

The following stories in this collection have previously appeared elsewhere and in somewhat different versions: "The Vomitorium," the *Sun*; "The New Year," the *North American Review*; "The End of Romance," *Sonora Review*; "Smoke," *Sun Dog: The Southeast Review*; "The First of Your Last Chances," *Open City*; "The Politics of Correctness," *Colorado Review*; "The Grand Illusion," *Chelsea*; "The Greatest Goddamn Thing," *Columbia: A Magazine of Poetry and Prose*; "Roger's New Life," *Crescent Review*; "Torture," *Beloit Fiction Journal*; and "Limbs," *Meridian*. A sincere thanks to the editors of these magazines for their time, support, and generosity.

Troublemakers

The Vomitorium

Ralph ran a hand up and over his head, flattening his hair before some freak combination of wind and static electricity blew it straight up and into a real-life fright wig.

We were standing at the far edge of the blacktop at Jacqueline Bouvier Kennedy Grade School, as far away from the recess monitor as we could get. It was 1978, the year we started eighth grade, though Ralph would have been in high school already if he hadn't failed both the third and fifth grades. He was nearly a foot taller than the rest of us, and every few weeks new sprigs of whiskers popped up along his cheeks and chin, scaring the girls and prompting the principal, Mr. Santoro, to drop into our homeroom unexpectedly and deliver speeches about personal hygiene.

"Boys," Mr. Santoro would say. "Some of you are starting to look like hoodlums." Though he addressed his insult to all the boys, everyone knew he meant Ralph.

Today, Ralph pulled a fat Sears catalog out of a grocery sack, shook it at me, and said, "Get a load of this." The catalog was fatter than it should have been, as if someone had dropped it into a swamp and left it there to rot.

"I don't think they sell that stuff anymore," I said. "That's a 1974 catalog, Ralph. That was four years ago."

"Quiet," Ralph said. He licked two fingers, smearing photos and words each time he touched a page to turn it. "I'll show you Patty O'Dell."

"You found it?" I said. "That's it?"

Ralph nodded.

Rumor was that Patty O'Dell had modeled panties for Sears when she was seven or eight, and for the past two years Ralph had diligently pursued the rumor. If there existed somewhere on this planet a photo of Patty O'Dell in nothing but her panties, Ralph was going to find it.

"Here she is," Ralph said. Reluctantly, he handed over the mildewed catalog. "Careful with it," he said.

Ralph stood beside me, arms crossed, guarding his treasure. His hair still stood on end, as if he had stuck the very fingers he had licked into a live socket. I looked down at the photo, then peeked up at Ralph, but he just nodded for me to keep my eyes on the catalog.

I had no idea why Ralph and I were friends. I was a B+ student, a model citizen. Ralph already had a criminal record, a string of shoplifting charges all along Chicago's southwest side. He kept mug shots of himself in his wallet. We were friends, I suppose, because he had walked up to me one day and asked if he could bum a smoke. That was three years ago. I was nine. I didn't smoke, but I didn't tell Ralph that. I said, "Sorry. Smoked the last one at recess."

The photo in the catalog was, in fact, of a girl wearing only panties. She was holding each of her shoulders so that her arms criss-crossed over her chest, and though I was starting to feel the first tremors of a boner, the girl in the photo was *not* Patty O'Dell. Not even close. After two years of fruitless searching, Ralph was starting to get desperate.

"That's not her," I said.

"Of course it's her," he said.

"You're crazy," I said.

"Give it to me," Ralph said. He snatched the catalog out of my hands.

"Ralph. Get real. All you need to do is look at Patty, then look at the girl in the photo. They look nothing alike."

Ralph and I scanned the blacktop, searching for Patty O'Dell. It was Halloween, and I couldn't help myself: I looked instead for girls dressed like cats. All year I would dream about the girls who came to school as cats—Mary Pulaski zipped up inside of a one-piece cat costume, purring, meowing, licking her paws while her stiff, curled tail vibrated behind her with each step she took. Or Gina Morales, actually down on all fours, crawling along the scuffed tile floor of our classroom: up one aisle, down the next, brushing against our legs, and letting us pet her. The very thought of it now gave my heart pause. It stole my breath. But only the younger kids dressed up these days, and all I could find on the blacktop today were Darth Vaders and Chewbaccas, C3POs and R2-D2s, the occasional Snoopy.

The seventh and eighth graders were already tired of Halloween, tired of shenanigans, slouching and yawning, waiting for the day to come to an end. Among us, only Wes Papadakis wore a costume, a full-head rubber "Creature from the Black Lagoon" mask, suctioned to his face. Next to him was Pete Elmazi, who wore his dad's Vietnam army jacket every day to school, no matter the season, and whose older brother was locked up in a home for juvenile delinquents because he'd beaten another kid to death with a baseball bat. There was Fred Lesniewski, who stood alone, an outcast for winning the science fair eight years in a row, since everyone knew his father worked at Argonne National Laboratory—where the white deer of genetic experiments loped behind a hurricane-wire fence, and where tomatoes grew to be the size of pumpkins—and that it was Fred's father (and not Fred) who was responsible for such award-winning projects as "How to Split an Atom in Your Own Kitchen" and "The Zero Gravity Chamber: Step Inside!"

There were all of these losers, plus a few hundred more, but no Patty. Then, as a sea of people parted, Ralph spotted her and pointed, and at the far end of an ever-widening path I saw her: Patty O'Dell. We stared at her, speechless, conjuring up the Patty of panty ads, a nearly naked Patty O'Dell letting a stranger snap photos of her while she stood under the hot, blinding lights in her bare feet. It was a thought so unfathomable, I might as well have been trying to grasp a mental picture of infinity, as complex and mysterious as the idea of something never coming to an end.

"You're right," Ralph said, shaking his head. "It's not her." He tossed the catalog off to the side of the blacktop, as if it were a fish too small to keep. He shook his head sadly and said, "Damn, Hank. I thought we had her."

Ralph had told me to meet him outside my house at eight, that his cousin Norm was going to pick us up and take us to a party. Norm had just started dating Patty O'Dell's older sister, Jennifer, and with Norm's help, Ralph and I hoped to get to the bottom of the panty ads, maybe even score a few mint condition catalogs from Jennifer, if at all possible.

"You got a costume?" Ralph asked.

"Of course I do," I said. "I've got all sorts of costumes. Hundreds!"

I had lied to Ralph; I didn't own any costumes. In fact, I'd had no plans of dressing up this year. But now I was trapped into scrounging up whatever I could, piecing together a costume from scratch.

My sister, Kelly—though disgusted by my choice and unable to conceal her revulsion—expertly applied the make-up.

"Of all the costumes," she said.

"What's wrong with Gene Simmons? What's wrong with KISS?" I asked.

"One day," she said, smearing grease paint from my eye, all the way up to my ear, and back. "One day you'll look back on this moment, and you'll consider shooting yourself."

"Okay," I said. "Whatever."

"Just let me know when you reach that point," Kelly said, "and I'll supply the gun."

I found hidden at the back of my parents' closet a stiff black wig hugging a Styrofoam ball. I snuck a dinner roll out to the garage, spray-painted it black, then pinned it to the top of the wig, hoping it would look like a bun of hair. My parents didn't own any leather, but I found a black Naugahyde jacket instead, along with a pair of black polyester slacks I wore to church. For the final touch, my sister gave me her clogs. She was two years older than me, and her feet were exactly my size.

In the living room, in the shifting light of the color TV, my parents stared at me with profound sadness, as if all their efforts on my behalf had proven futile. My mother looked for a moment as though she might speak, then turned away, back to the final minutes of *M*A*S*H*.

Outside, I met Ralph. As far as I could tell, his only costume was a cape. A long black cape. One look at Ralph, and I suddenly felt the weight of what I'd done to myself. Ralph said, "What're you supposed to be? A transvestite?"

"I'm Gene Simmons," I said. "From KISS."

"Jesus," Ralph said. He reached up and touched the dinner roll on top of my head. "What's that?"

"It's a bun," I said.

"I can see *that*," Ralph said. "But why would you put a hamburger bun on top of your head? And why would you paint it black?"

"It's not *that* kind of bun," I said.

"Oh."

"At least I'm wearing a costume," I said. "Look at you. Where's *your* costume? All you've got on is a cape."

Ralph smiled and pulled his left hand from his cape. Butter knives were attached to each of his fingers, including his thumb.

"Holy smoke," I said. It was the most impressive thing I'd ever seen.

"I'm an Etruscan," he said, pronouncing it carefully while rattling his knives in front of my face.

"A what?"

"An Etruscan," Ralph said. "I've been reading a lot of history lately."

"History?" I asked. This was news to me. Ralph hated school.

"Yeah," he said. "Stuff about the Romans."

"Romans," I said. I didn't tell Ralph, but I knew a little something about the Romans myself. I wrote my very first research paper in the sixth grade on them, though all I remembered now were bits and pieces: the Gallic War, the Ides of March, some creep named Brutus stabbing Caesar to death. The idea of Ralph's picking up a book and actually reading it was so preposterous, I decided to lob a few slow ones out to him, a quiz, and test what little he knew against what little I knew.

"So," I said. "What do you think about Caesar?"

"A great man," he said. "He brought a lot of people together."

"Oh really. How'd he do that?"

"Violence," Ralph said. I expected him to smile, but he didn't. His eyes, I noticed, were closer together than I had realized, and his eyebrows were connected by a swatch of fuzz. Ralph glared at me, as if he were thinking about punching me to illustrate what he'd just said. But the thought must have passed, and he said, "Etruscans were the original gladiators. Crazy, but smart. Geniuses, actually. Very artistic."

"How'd you get the knives to stick to your fingers?"

"Krazy Glue," Ralph said.

I nodded appreciatively. I had always feared Krazy Glue, scared I'd accidentally glue myself to my mother or father, or to a lamppost. I'd seen such things on the news, men and women rushed to the hospital, their fingers permanently connected to their foreheads.

"What if they don't come off?" I asked.

Ralph said, "I thought of that. That's why I glued them to my fingernails. My fingernails will grow out, see. And then I can clip them."

"You're a genius," I said.

"I'm an Etruscan," he said. "Very brilliant, but violent."

Ralph's cousin Norm eventually pulled up in a Chevy Impala and motioned with his head for us to get in. He was twenty-five years old and ghoulishly thin, but the veins in his arms were thick and bulged out to the point you'd think they were going to explode right there—a spooky guy with spooky veiny arms, but he worked at the Tootsie Roll factory on Cicero Avenue, along with Ralph's other two cousins, and he gave me and Ralph bags of Tootsie Pops each month, which made up in part for the spookiness.

I took the backseat; Ralph rode shotgun. Norm said nothing about our costumes. I reached up and made sure the bun on top of my wig was still there. Norm gunned the engine, then floored it. Blurry strings of ghosts, clowns, and pirates appeared and disappeared along the sidewalk. Pumpkins beamed at us from porch stoops.

A mile or two later, Ralph said, "Where we going, Norm?"

"I've got some business to take care of first."

"What kind of business?"

"I've got a trunk full of goods I need to unload."

Ralph cocked his head. If he were a dog, his ears would have stiffened. He loved the prospect of anything criminal. "Goods," Ralph repeated. "Are they stolen?"

"What do you think?" Norm said.

Ralph turned around and smiled at me. "What kind of goods?" Ralph asked.

Norm lifted his veiny arm and pointed at Ralph. "None of your business," he said. "The less you know, the better."

Ralph nodded; Norm was the only person who could talk to Ralph like that and get away with it. A few minutes later, Norm pulled into a White Hen Pantry parking lot.

"I need some smokes," he said, and left us alone with the engine running.

Ralph turned around in his seat. "So . . . ," he said.

"So what?"

"So what do you think's in the trunk?"

"I don't know," I said.

"Drugs," Ralph said. "That's my guess. Stolen drugs." He turned back to the White Hen to watch his cousin. He rested his hand with the knives onto the dashboard and began drumming them quickly. "Maybe guns," Ralph said. "A trunkload of semi-automatic machine guns."

Norm returned to the car, sucking on a cigarette so hard that the tip turned bright orange and whistled. Then he filled the entire car with smoke and said, "I ran into a little trouble two nights ago. Serious trouble. I'll admit, I fucked up. But hey, everyone fucks up every now and then, right? Huh? Am I right?"

"Right," Ralph said.

"Right on," I said. I lifted my fist into the air, a symbol of brotherhood, but nobody paid any attention.

"I had to get on the ball," Norm said. "Think fast. Figure out a way to come up with some money, pronto."

"What happened?" Ralph asked.

Norm looked at Ralph, then looked down at Ralph's fingers with the attached butter knives, as if he hadn't noticed them until this very second. He turned and looked at me, squinting, raising his cigarette to his mouth for another deep puff. "Just what the hell are you guys supposed to be anyway?"

Ralph said, "I'm an Etruscan."

"And I'm Gene Simmons," I said. "From KISS."

"The Etruscans," Norm said. "I never heard of those guys. They must be new. But KISS," he said and snorted. "That's sissy shit. You should've gone as Robert Plant. Or Jimmy Page. Or somebody from Blue Öyster Cult. Now *that* I'd have respected."

Then Norm put the car in drive and peeled out.

The longer we sat in the car, the more I thought of Patty O'Dell wearing nothing but panties, and the more I thought of Patty O'Dell, the more I had to cross and uncross my legs.

Norm wheeled quickly into the parking lot of a ratty complex called Royal Chateau Apartments and said, "Give me a few minutes, guys. If the deal goes through, we'll party. If not, I'm fucked. Big time," he said, opening the door and getting out. He slammed the door so hard, my ears popped.

Ralph turned around and said, "How's it going back there?"

I gave him the thumbs up.

Ralph said, "Let's take a look and see what he's got in the trunk."

"I don't think that's a good idea," I said.

"C'mon," Ralph said. "Pretend you're Gene Simmons. What would he do in a situation like this?"

I leaned my head back and stuck my tongue all the way out, but the bun on top of my wig flopped over, cutting short my impression. A pin, apparently, had fallen out.

"I got the Krazy Glue with me," Ralph said. "You want me to glue it down?"

"I'm fine," I said.

Ralph reached over, turned off the car, and jerked the keys from the ignition.

"Hey," I said. "What're you doing?" But Ralph was already outside, leaving me with no choice. I got out, too. By the time I reached the trunk, Ralph had already inserted the key into the lock.

"Ready?" he asked. He turned the key and the trunk hissed open. Slowly, he lifted the trunk's lid, as if it were the lid of a treasure chest and we were seeing if the mutiny had been worth the trouble.

"Holy shit!" Ralph said. "Would you look at that?"

"Jesus," I said.

My heart paused briefly before kicking back in, pounding harder than ever. I'd never seen anything like it. The entire trunk was packed full of bite-size Tootsie Rolls. There must have been a few thousand. I dipped my hand inside and ran my fingers through them. Ralph scraped his knives gently across the heap, as if it were a giant cat wanting to be scratched.

"Norm," Ralph said, frowning and nodding at the same time, clearly impressed with his cousin. "He's a real thinking man's man," Ralph said. "He knows when to steal and when not to. Don't you see? This is perfect. I mean, when's the only time people start thinking bulk Tootsie Rolls? Halloween, man."

"Halloween's almost over," I said.

Ralph pointed a butter knife at me and said, "That's the point exactly. People are running out of candy. They're getting desperate. Here's where Norm comes in. Bingo!"

"We better shut the trunk," I said.

"Not yet," Ralph said. "I'm hungry. Give me a hand. Start stuffing some of these babies into my pockets."

Ralph and I scooped up handfuls of Tootsie Rolls and dumped them into Ralph's cape pocket. Then Ralph shoved as many as he could into his jeans pockets. Twice, he accidentally poked my head with a butter knife.

"Watch it," I said. "You're gonna put my eye out."

"Count yourself lucky," Ralph said. "An Etruscan would've chopped off your head or thrown you to a lion by now."

We shut the trunk and waited for Norm. Using only his teeth and one hand, Ralph unrolled Tootsie Roll after Tootsie Roll, cramming one after another into his mouth, until his cheeks bulged and chocolate juice dribbled down his chin. He started talking, but his mouth was so full I couldn't understand a word he said.

"Uh-huh," I said. "Oh yeah? Really? No kidding, Ralph," I said.

When he finally swallowed the boulder of chocolate, he said, "What's your problem? You're not making any sense."

Out of the corner of my eye I spotted Norm, so I nudged Ralph. Norm was walking toward us, along with a fat guy decked out in a red-white-and-blue sweat suit. The man's hair was sticking up on one side, but flat on the other, as if Norm had woken him.

When Norm saw us, he shot us a look and said, "Get off the trunk, you punks." To the man, he said, "All I need are the keys . . ."

"I got 'em," Ralph said. "Here."

He tossed them to Norm; Norm glared at Ralph, a look that said, *We'll talk about this later.*

"Didn't want to waste gas," Ralph said. "Remember when they had that shortage?"

The fat guy said, "I ain't got all fucking day. Let's take a look."

Norm nodded, popped the trunk.

Where there had once been a mound of Tootsie Rolls was now an obvious trench. I didn't realize we'd taken that many. I looked at Ralph, but he just pulled another Tootsie Roll from his cape pocket and unrolled it with his teeth and weapon-free hand.

The fat guy said, "These are the small ones. I thought you were talking about the long ones."

"They're the same thing," Norm said. "One's just smaller than the other."

The fat guy shook his head. "Look, Slick. To make a profit I got to sell a hundred of these for every twenty of the big ones I'd've sold. You see what I'm saying? Kids want the ones they can stick in their mouths like a big cigar."

"That's true," Ralph whispered to me.

"Okay," Norm said. "All right. You want to haggle? Fine. I respect that."

But the guy was already walking away, back to his Royal Chateau, saying, "No can do, Slick. No business tonight."

After the man rounded the corner, I looked up at Norm, afraid he was going to yell at us, but he was holding two fistfuls of his own hair and yanking on it. "I'm *fucked*," he said. "Do you hear me? I . . . am . . . *fucked*."

Ralph made a move to offer Norm a few Tootsie Rolls, but when I nudged him, he thought better of it, slipping the stolen goods back into his own pocket, keeping them out of Norm's sight.

For an hour we sat in Norm's car and said nothing while Norm drove. Ralph started running his butter knives through his hair, giving himself a scalp massage. "Hey, Norm," Ralph finally said. "What do you know about Patty O'Dell posing naked for a Sears catalog?"

Norm said, "Would you mind just shutting up a minute and letting me think?"

"Sure," Ralph said. He turned back to me and said, "Hey, Hank. Quit talking. Let the man think."

"What am *I* doing?" I asked.

"Both of you," Norm said. "Shut the fuck up."

Norm drove us in circles—from 79th and Harlem to 87th and Harlem, over to 87th and Cicero, then north to 79th and Cicero—a loop that eventually took us back to 79th and Harlem, a corner Ralph and I knew well because it was the home of Haunted Trails Miniature Golf Range (where Ralph and I enjoyed chipping golf balls over the fence and into heavy traffic), and behind Haunted Trails was the Sheridan Drive-In, where we could sneak through a chopped-out part of the fence and watch women take off their clothes on a screen the size of a battleship.

My favorites were the martial arts movies, though Ralph preferred the ones about women in prison. We never heard any of the dialogue—we were too far away from the rows of cast-iron speakers—so Ralph would pass the night speculating about what was going on: "See that chick?" Ralph would say. "She probably killed her old man. That's why the warden pulled her pants down."

The seventh time Norm made the loop, I gave up any hope of ever making it to a party. When Norm finally deviated from his endless loop, he jerked a quick right into Guidish Park Mobile Homes. He stopped the car, killed the lights, and turned back to look at me.

"I need a favor," he said.

It was so dark, I couldn't even see his face. "What?" I said.

"I want you to take something to number 47—it's about a half a block up there—and I want you to give it to whoever answers the door and tell them I'll get the rest of the money tomorrow. Okay?"

I didn't want to do it—my bowels felt on the verge of collapsing—but I was awful at standing up for myself, unable to tell someone older than me no, if only because my parents had trained me too well. I was dutiful to the end. So I told Norm okay, that I'd go, and when I stepped out of the car, he unrolled his window and handed over a cardboard cylinder. It was about a foot long. I shook it but couldn't hear anything inside. Only when I passed under a streetlamp did I see what I was holding: a giant Tootsie Roll bank. It had a removable tin cap with a slit for depositing coins. I shook it again but couldn't hear any change.

At number 47, I knocked lightly on the door, two taps with a single knuckle. I was about to give up when the door creaked open and a man poked his head outside. He narrowed his eyes and inspected my costume. Without looking away, he reached off to the side and asked, "You like Butterfingers or Milk Duds?"

"Milk Duds," I said. "But actually I've got something for *you*. It's from Norm."

Before I could smile and surrender the giant Tootsie Roll, I was yanked inside the trailer by the scruff of my Naugahyde jacket. He shut the door behind us and said, "Who are you?"

"His cousin," I lied.

"Uh-huh," he said, nodding. "So you're the famous *Ralph* I've heard so much about."

"I guess so," I said.

"My name's Bob. Can you remember to tell that to Norm? *Bob.*"

"Sure," I said.

"I'm Jennifer's brother," Bob said.

"Jennifer O'Dell?" I asked.

"That's right."

"So you must be Patty's brother, too." I glanced quickly around the room for catalogs. Bob kept his eyes on me, then squeezed the giant Tootsie Roll, as if it were my neck, until the lid popped off. He emptied it onto a card table. The best I could tell, there were three tens and a twenty, along with a note folded into a tight triangle, the kind we used in homeroom as footballs.

"Maybe I should go," I said.

Bob put his hand out, as if he were a traffic cop, and said, "Not yet. Follow me." We walked down a short and narrow hallway to a door at the far end of the trailer. When Bob opened the door, he motioned for me to join him inside the room.

It was dark, almost too dark to see, the only light coming from the room we had just left. Two women were resting in bed, and at first I wanted to laugh, because one of the women was wearing Wes Papadakis's "Creature from the Black Lagoon" mask, and the thought of a grown woman lying in bed in the dark wearing a stupid rubber mask struck just the right chord in me tonight. Bob was trying to scare me, his very own Halloween prank, but I wasn't falling for it. I started snickering when Bob flipped on the light and I saw it wasn't a mask at all. It was her face. I wanted to look away, but I couldn't. It kept drawing me in, like a pinwheel or a pendulum: *eyes so puffy she could barely see out . . . lips cracked open and swollen . . . the zigzag of stitches along her nostril.*

The other woman sitting on the bed was actually just a girl, and when I realized who it was—that it was Patty O'Dell—I quit breathing. She was wearing a long white T-shirt that she kept pulling over her knees, trying to hide herself from me. I knew it was the wrong time to think about it, I knew it shouldn't have even crossed my mind, but I wanted to believe that she was naked underneath that T-shirt. I tried imagining it, too: Patty lifting the shirt up and over her head, taking it off, until she was completely naked on the bed. But each time I got to the naked part, I would glance over and look at her sister—I couldn't help it—and the nude Patty in my head would dissolve into something dark and grainy.

When I finally gave up, I raised my hand and said, "Hi, Patty," but Patty turned her head away from me and stared at the wall.

"How much did he bring?" Jennifer asked.

Bob huffed. "Fifty bucks," he said.

The woman slowly turned her head away from us.

"There's a note, too," Bob said. He unfolded the triangle and said, "Oh, this is classic. You'll love *this*. He spelled your name wrong. He doesn't even know how to spell your name. Hey. Big surprise. The man's *illiterate*." Bob laughed and shook his head. "Says here he'll try to get you the rest of the money tomorrow."

"Figures," she said.

Bob crumpled the note and said, "So what should we tell Gene Simmons? We can't keep an important man, a man of his *stature*, tied up all night."

"Tell Norm it's too late. He had his chance. That was the agreement. A thousand dollars or I'd call the police and file a complaint."

Bob looked at me. "You got that?"

I nodded.

"Good," Bob said. "Tell him to expect the police at his door in, oh, let's say an hour, two at the most. Maybe that'll teach the son of a bitch not to hit a woman."

My clogs clopped hollowly against the asphalt all the way back to the car. The night was officially ruined. I might not have been able to hold infinity in my mind, but I sure as hell knew the end of something when I saw it.

My stomach cramped up, as if it had been punctured, as if my body were somehow poisoning itself. I was angry at Norm, certainly, angry at Norm for beating up Jennifer, angry at Norm for driving us around and acting like it was nothing, a mistake, a mistake anyone could make—but I was angrier at Norm for how Patty had looked at me, then looked away, angry because I was close to something, I wasn't sure what, but each time I got within reach, I looked over at Jennifer, I saw her face, and it all disappeared. Norm had ruined it for me, whatever it was. For that I wanted to hurt Norm myself, but the closer I got to him, the more unlikely that seemed. I was twelve. Norm was twenty-five. What could I possibly do?

Near the Impala, I could hear someone gagging, trying to catch his breath. I dashed around the car and found Ralph bent over, a pool of vomit next to a tire. Ralph's door was open, and the dome light inside the car lit up half of Ralph's face. Norm was slumped down in the driver's seat, his hand drooped over the steering wheel, a cigarette smoldering between two fingers. The radio was on low. Ralph's fingers clanked together, and I thought of Brutus, his knife plunging into Caesar, again and again.

"What did he do to you?" I whispered to Ralph. "Did he punch you in the stomach?"

"Who?" Ralph asked, still bent over, not looking at me.

"Norm," I said.

Ralph peeked up now, fangs of vomit dripping from his chin. "Why would Norm punch me in the stomach?"

"You're throwing up," I said.

"I know. I ate too many Tootsie Rolls," Ralph said. "Besides, it's a Roman ritual. Eat till you puke. I wanted to see if I could do it. You should congratulate me."

After Ralph cleaned himself off with handfuls of loose dirt and the inside of his cape, we slid back into the car. Ralph said, "The first vomitorium on the South Side of Chicago. People will travel from miles around to come here and yak their brains out."

Norm revved the engine. He said, "So? What did she say?"

"She wants to talk to you," I lied.

"Oh yeah?"

"She wants you to go home," I said, thinking of the police at his door later tonight, knocking with their billy clubs. "She said she'll be there in an hour," I added.

"Really," Norm said, sticking the cigarette in the corner of his mouth and pounding the steering wheel with his palm. "What do you know about that? She's forgiven me."

"You bet," I said.

Norm shook his head and put the car in reverse. Back on Harlem Avenue, he said, "So where do you boys want to go?"

"Home," I said.

"Home it is!" Norm said. He said *home* as if it were an exotic place, like Liechtenstein or the Bermuda Triangle.

And so we drove in silence the first few miles. Then Norm said, "You think I should buy her some roses?"

"Nah," I said. "No sense wasting your money."

I could see Norm's eyes in the rearview mirror. He was watching me, but I couldn't tell if he knew that I was lying. At a stoplight he turned around and said, "Gene Simmons, huh?"

"Gene Simmons," I said.

"From KISS," Ralph added.

Norm said, "When I was in high school, I went to a costume party dressed as Jim Croce. I glued on this big hairy-ass mustache and walked around with a cigar and sang 'Operator.' Chicks dug it." He smiled nostalgically until people behind us started honking. The light had turned green. "All right!" he yelled. "Shut the fuck up! I'm *going* already!"

Not far from the junior college, a pack of men and women wearing togas trudged along a sidewalk, hooting and raising bottles of liquor above their heads. "Would you look at that," Norm said.

Ralph cranked down the window for a better view. He said, "Stop the car."

"What?"

"Stop the car, Norm. I need to join them."

"Why?"

Ralph peered out the window at the throng of bedsheets and olive wreaths, and said, "My people."

"What people?" Norm asked.

"Romans!" Ralph got out of the car and yelled to the passing crowd: "Greetings!" He raised his hand with the butter knives in salutation, and the Romans went wild. They beckoned Ralph over, and Ralph loped across the street.

Norm shook his head. "He's something else, ain't he? Half the time I forget we're related."

I had turned back to Norm, but Norm was still watching Ralph, amazed. I studied Norm but found no clues, no trace of what I was looking for, so I decided to ask him, to see what he'd say. "Why'd you do it?"

Norm's eyes moved slowly from Ralph to me, focusing, his pupils growing, adjusting to the difference in light. His brow furrowed, and he looked like he really wanted to answer me, as if the reasons were somewhere on the tip of his tongue. Then he shook his head and said, "Hell, I don't know. You lose control sometimes." He rubbed his hand up over his hair in such a way that it stood on end, the way Ralph's hair had stood on end this morning—a family gene, I suspected, a whole genealogy of screwed-up things inside him that he didn't understand, would *never* understand—and I thought, *Of course Norm doesn't know. Of course.* Not that the answer to my question was any comfort. Just the opposite, in fact.

Slowly we drove on, though a block away, as the last goblin of the night floated beside us, I couldn't resist. I turned and looked out the back window again.

The Romans were holding Ralph aloft, over their heads, and chanting his name. Ralph, floating above them, looked so content, so pleased, you could almost be fooled into believing he was leading his people into Chicago, as Caesar had gone into Gaul, to bring us all, by way of murder and pillage, together as one people, one tribe.

The New Year

At midnight, party horns blow obscenely, strangers kiss with tongues, and champagne corks fire perilously across the smoky room like a barrage of SCUD missiles. No one here has ever heard of "Auld Lang Syne," so what they do instead to celebrate the new year is blast the first few tracks off Ozzy Osbourne's *Blizzard of Ozz.*

Two hours later, half the people have gone home, fearing the approaching snowstorm. The remaining half have coupled, staking out for themselves every bedroom, hallway, and closet in the house. Here and there, men and women copulate—some, discreetly; others as if auditioning for the victim role in a slasher film: lots of panting, then moans, then a high-pitched squeal followed by a howl or scream, then nothing at all.

Dead, Gary thinks.

This is how he entertains himself: absorbing the reality around him and turning it into something other than what it is, something menacing. Only he and Linda remain among the flotsam of the party—cigarette butts rising like crooked tombstones out of bowls of salsa; a slice of pizza dangling like a limp hand over the edge of the coffee table—and Gary, lost in his own private world of the macabre, is listening for the next rising moan, the next victim, when Linda, joint in one hand, vodka tonic in the other, tells Gary that she's pregnant.

"I'm keeping it, too," she says, meeting Gary's eyes and smiling wildly, as if announcing an extravagant purchase she cannot afford, like alligator shoes or a raccoon coat, challenging Gary to tell her *No, you'll have to take it back.*

Gary dips his hand into the ice bucket, scoops out the last pitiful shards of ice, and deposits them into a tall glass. With the assortment of leftover liquor, he mixes what he thinks is a Harvey Wallbanger, a name his father uses freely for all occasions, exclamations of surprise and scathing insults alike, the way another man might say, *Great Scott!* or *Son of a bitch!* Gary sips the drink tentatively, squinting at Linda while he does so. The first concert he ever took her to was Megadeath in Omaha, and he wants to ask her if that had been the night, in a dark and cavernous loading dock at Rosenblatt Stadium, that he'd unceremoniously knocked her up, but he is having a difficult time summoning the proper words, let alone stringing them into a meaningful sentence.

"Do you mind?" he asks and picks up the four-foot bong he had packed earlier in the night but had somehow forgotten about. He holds it to his mouth as if it were a saxophone, and while Linda leans over to light the bowl, Gary sucks hard on the tube. He inhales for what seems an impossibly long time, and when he finally exhales, he tilts his head back so as not to blow smoke in the face of his girlfriend who is carrying his child.

Over their heads and scattered about the room float swollen clouds of marijuana smoke, thick as doom, and though Gary has long since run out of breath, smoke continues to leak from his nose and mouth. He's been working out daily at the gym, and he's amazed at how much his lung capacity has improved in just two short weeks.

"Wow," he says, amazed at *everything*—the pending baby, his new lungs—and it's the word *wow*, this last puff of smoke streaming from his mouth when he speaks, that triggers the smoke alarm. The alarm is deafening, piercing Gary's consciousness, one steady shriek after another, like a knife thrust repeatedly into his head, and though Gary wants nothing more than to stop the noise, he has no idea where to start looking.

Four men instantly appear from each corner of the house. They arrive like Romans, bedsheets draped around hips and torsos. One man stands on a chair, disappearing into a head of smoke, and when he rips open the smoke alarm's casing and yanks free the battery, along with the two wires the battery had been connected to, the noise mercifully stops.

The man steps off the chair, looks Gary in the eyes, and says, "What the fuck?"

Gary shrugs. He's still holding the bong, resting it against his shoulder as if it were a rifle. Then he tips the bong toward Linda, points the smoking barrel at her stomach, and says, "She's pregnant."

At this news, women emerge one by one from the darkest chambers and alcoves of the house. Some are barely dressed, wearing only underthings. Others wear long hockey jerseys or concert T-shirts that belong to the men they have chosen for the night. They surround Linda and gently prod her belly. *How far along are you?* they ask. *Is it a boy or a girl?* They move in closer and closer, confiscating her vodka tonic, relieving her of the roach pinched between her thumb and forefinger, until Linda becomes the nucleus, the Queen Bee of the party, pleasantly crushed by a circle of women who "ooooo" and "ahhhh" against her stomach and buzz with spurious tips on prenatal care.

Gary backs away from the chatter and smoke. As soon as he's outside, he bolts for his car. His coat, he realizes, is somewhere in the house, but it's too late now. If he returns, Linda will see him and want to leave as well, and what he wants now is to be alone. What he *needs* is to think.

Inside the Swinger, where everything is ice-cold to the touch, Gary starts the engine, then rubs his hands together, blowing frequently into the cave of his cupped palms. "Harvey *Wallbanger!*" he yells. "It's friggin' *cold*." He yanks the gearshift into drive and pulls quickly away from the party, heading for the unmarked road that will take him home.

Only after putting a safe distance between himself and the party does Gary allow himself to entertain the otherwise unthinkable, that Linda is pregnant. He says it aloud, trying out the feel of it. "So," he says. "You're pregnant." Then he laughs. He laughs until his throat burns and the windows fog up all around him. "Pregnant," he says, clearing a swatch of windshield. "Yow!"

Other girls he's known have called it *prego*, like the spaghetti sauce, or *preggers*, which sounds to Gary like something made by Nabisco, a new brand of snack cracker. He can't stop shivering, and the convulsions come stronger each time he thinks of Linda walking around with a smaller, mucousy version of himself inside her. *Inside her.* The very idea! A person inside of a person! Now that he really thinks about it, pregnancy makes no sense whatsoever—a horror movie where a living organism grows and grows, until, finally, it bursts through an innocent victim's stomach, a terrible surprise for everyone.

Truth is, Gary knows less than squat about the finer points of the subject. He'd slacked off in Sex Ed, unable to stop himself from laughing out loud at words like *fallopian tube* and *mons glans*. And the textbook, with its floating orbs and scary cross-sections, was like some kind of underground science fiction comic book, where body parts looked extraterrestrial, and their corresponding names, like *vas deferens*, were obviously chosen for haunting effect. The one time he ever even remotely touched on the subject of pregnancy was with a kid he knew named Jim Davis.

It had been a peculiar friendship from the start, one that had materialized between seventh and eighth grade because all of Jim's real friends had gone away for the summer, and because Gary seemed the least harmful of prospects. The subject had come up in regard to Jim's mother, who was much younger than Gary's mother, and who doted on her son in ways that Gary's mother had never doted on him. Jim and his mother played this game, acting as if Gary were not present: mother and son whispering, pinching each other, always telling the other one how cute they were. Gary never knew where to look, what to do, so he would stand off to the side, rearranging the fruit-shaped magnets and family photos on the refrigerator: a pineapple in lieu of a toddler's head, a giant banana sprouting from their schnauzer's butt.

One day, after a game of eight-ball in their basement, Jim Davis made a confession that he had once tasted an eighteen-year-old girl.

Gary imagined a fork and knife, a dash of salt. "When was this?" he asked.

"Birth," Jim said.

Gary leaned his head sideways, scratched the inside of his ear with the tip of the pool cue.

What Jim Davis was claiming was that when he was born, he kept his tongue out the whole time, and even now, twelve years later, he remembered how it tasted.

"You want to know what it's like?" he said. "Go home and lick two hot slices of liver. I'm telling you, man, that's it. I shit you not, my friend."

Gary is on the unmarked road now, and since he is driving into the storm, it's significantly worse here than it had been on the highway. Visibility is zip. The wind has picked up, and snow swirls about the highway like smoke from a fog machine, not at all unlike the opening of that Megadeath concert three months ago. *Liver*, Gary thinks. He never touches the stuff. Gary squints for better vision. For stretches as long as fifteen seconds he can see one or two car lengths ahead, whips of snow wiggling snake-like from one side of the road to the other, but soon they dissolve into dense sheets of white that repeatedly slap the windshield, and Gary cannot see more than a foot beyond his headlights. He doesn't want a child. Earlier that evening, in fact, he was devising a strategy for breaking up with Linda. Strategy is everything when it comes to breaking up, and what he always strives for is to find a way to make it look like his girlfriend's idea, and not his. You have to flip-flop the argument, twist words, drag the murky past for minor infractions. It's an ugly way to conduct business, but sometimes you have to jumpstart the end of a relationship, otherwise it'll just rot and stink up the rest of your life.

He knows he should ask for advice on this one, but he doesn't know who to turn to. Gary's father has his own problems right now: the man hasn't spoken a word to anyone in two weeks. And besides, Gary was cured years ago of asking his father anything about sex after the day his father pulled him aside to warn him about transmittable diseases.

"In the old days," his father began, "when I was your age, if you had the clap, the doctor would make you set your thing onto a stainless-steel table. You know what I'm talking about, right? Your thing. Your Howard Johnson. So you'd do what the man said. You'd slap it down for him to look at, and after you told him what was wrong, he'd reach into a drawer and pull out a giant rubber mallet, and then he'd take that mallet and hit your thing as hard as he could with it, and that would be that. Believe you me, son, you'd be *damn* particular from that point on where you went sticking man's best friend."

Gary is imagining his own thing getting whacked with a rubber hammer when someone or something steps out in front of his car. He is doing sixty or seventy miles per hour, the road is slick, and he touches his foot to the brake only after he has hit whatever it is that crossed his path. People claim that these moments always occur in slow motion, but Gary is so stoned, the opposite is true: everything speeds up. One second he is thinking about his thing getting whacked; the next, he is lying with his head on the horn of his car. He has no idea how much time passes before he lifts his head and steps outside, but it's still dark when he does so, and the falling snow, sharp as pins, has thickened.

Gary hugs his arms and limps to the front of what's left of the Swinger. What he hit was the largest deer he's ever seen: a twelve-point buck. A gem of a kill if he were a hunter, which he's not—the only nonhunter, in fact, in a long line of men who prefer oiling their rifles and shitting in the woods to smoking dope and listening to Ratt. The deer, apparently, had slid all the way up onto his hood, smashed the windshield, then slid back down after Gary, either semi- or unconscious, brought the car to a stop. It lies now in front of the Swinger, its black eyes eternally fixed on something far, far away. Clots of fur sprout from the tip of the crumpled hood, as if the car itself is in the first stages of metamorphosis.

Gary licks his lips and tastes blood. No telling the damage he did to his face when his head hit the steering wheel. For all Gary knows, his forehead is split wide open and his nose, through which he can no longer breathe, is permanently flattened. He may have a concussion, too, his brain puffy, slowly inflating with blood. But far more pressing than any physical damage is the subzero temperature. His entire body is starting to stiffen. He shuffles from foot to foot to keep warm. He rubs his bare arms and yells *fuck* over and over. "Fuck, fuck, fuck."

Years ago he read a wilderness story in which a man stuck out in the freezing cold sliced open the carcass of a dead animal and crawled inside to keep warm. It was a bear, Gary remembers, and the man stayed inside of the bear until someone discovered him in there. Gary craves warmth, he's willing to make deals with a higher power, but he'll be goddamned if he's going to hang around inside of a dead deer and wait for his worthless friends and neighbors to find him. Besides, it's a small town, word travels fast, and he can't imagine any girl ever wanting to date him after hearing where he'd been. The girls he knows, they'll overlook the fact that you've slept with the town hosebag, but there is always a line, and sleeping inside of anything dead is clearly on the other side of it. Gary's about five miles from home—walking distance, really—close enough, he decides, to make a go of it, even without a coat.

Gary starts to jog, but his legs aren't working quite right. It's as if he's running on stumps instead of feet. He suspects a bone somewhere has snapped in two, so he works on the basics of walking instead, just keeping one foot in front of the other. He hugs himself the whole way, hands secured under his armpits. He'll have to wake his father when he gets home so they can tow the car before sunrise and avoid getting a ticket. He'd prefer not bothering him at all, but he sees no way around it. Gary's mother left home a year ago, and for a while Gary thought that this was the worst thing that could possibly happen to his father. Then, two weeks ago, his mother surprised everyone and married his father's best friend, a man named Chuck Linkletter. And that's when his father quit talking. He quit going to work at the gas station he owns, and he has quit taking calls. He has, it seems to Gary, quit altogether, like an old lawnmower.

Gary's ears and fingertips throb, and the snow pelting his face temporarily blinds him. His eyebrows are starting to ice over and sag, as are the few sad whiskers on his upper lip, a mustache Gary's been closely monitoring these past few months. He wishes he had taken the bong from the party. He'd be standing in the middle of the road right now, his back to the storm, lighting a fresh bowl. And then everything wouldn't seem so bad—Linda's news, his car, the pain.

When he finally reaches his house, shivering his way inside, he collapses next to the sofa.

"Oh. My. God," he says. "*I made it.*" His voice, a croak in the dark, sounds like the voice of nobody he knows. Now that he's home and out of the cold, he's thinking maybe he won't wake his father after all—towing the car no longer seems so dire—but then the light in his father's bedroom comes on, the door swings opens, and his father appears as if from one of his own nightmares: sleepy but crazed, thin hair crooked atop his head like bad electrical wiring. This is how the man has looked ever since learning the news of the marriage, and though Gary is starting to wonder if he should seek professional help for his father, they live in a town of two hundred, and the only people around who claim to be professionals of anything either strip and refinish woodwork or groom dogs.

Gary himself holds no grudge against his mother. As far as he's concerned, she's been a good mom. When Gary was in the third grade and his father refused to bring him a cat from the pound, his mother took Gary outside with several spools of thread. "You have to use your imagination," she'd told him. It was summer, and while Gary captured a few dozen grasshoppers, holding them captive inside a Hills Brothers coffee can with holes punched in the plastic lid, his mother made several dozen miniature nooses with the thread. "Here," she said. "Let's see one of them." Gary gently pinched a grasshopper and held it up for his mother while she slid a noose over the insect's torso, then tightened it. "What's his name?" she asked.

"Fred Astaire," Gary said.

Later, while Gary walked thirty or so of his grasshoppers down the street, old man Wickersham stepped down from his front stoop, stopped Gary, and asked him what he was doing.

"I'm taking my pets for a walk."

"Oh," the old man said.

Near the end of summer Gary had caught several hundred bumblebees, and over the next month, using his mother's tweezers and suffering through one painful sting after another, Gary managed to tie each surviving bee to one of his mother's nooses, and when he finished, he took all of them out for a stroll. The bees droned overhead, following him like a dark cloud. Old Man Wickersham burst out of his house, yelling, "My God, son, they're after you," and Gary, not realizing the old man meant the bees, let go of the strings and took off running. For days after that, people in town—and as far away as North Platte—reported getting tickled by mysterious airborne threads.

"Dad," Gary says now. "I totaled the car. We should probably tow it home before the police find it." Then Gary tells his father the story, omitting the pregnant girlfriend, the endless kegs of Old Style, and the four-foot bong. What he focuses on is the deer.

"You should see this thing," he said. "It's gargantuan. A twelve-pointer. Swear to God, I thought I slammed into a bulldozer."

His father puts on a coat and disappears through a door in the kitchen that leads into the garage, reappearing seconds later carrying an ax.

Gary, unable to stop quivering, the night's deep freeze still trapped in his bones, slips on leather gloves, zips himself into his father's wool trenchcoat, and pulls on a ski mask that covers his entire head except for his eyes and mouth. They take the new pickup, Gary's father skillfully navigating the vehicle at high speeds through miles of virgin snow. Amazingly, they cover in less than ten minutes the distance it took Gary an hour and a half to travel on foot.

His father parks in front of the dead deer and the demolished car, illuminating the scene with the pickup's high beams. The deer is already dusted with snow. Outside, towering over the carcass, Gary's father reaches down, takes hold of the base of the rack, and lifts the deer's head. He jiggles the head a few times, then crouches to get a better look.

"What do you think?" Gary asks through the ski mask. "Should we drag it by the horns or just back it ass-first into the ditch?"

His father doesn't answer. He walks to the pickup. He returns with the ax, lifting it over his head and taking aim.

"Dad," Gary says. "What are you doing?"

The blade comes down hard, slamming into the deer's neck. The deer's head rises off the ground, as if looking up to Gary for help, but it's the force of the blow causing it to do this, and the head falls quickly back into the snow. His father swings a second time, then a third, each time hitting a different part of the animal, though keeping within the general vicinity of the neck. It slowly creeps up on Gary that what his father is trying to do is chop off the deer's head. "The car," Gary says. "Maybe we should, like, shift our focus?" He points at the Swinger, but his father plants his foot onto the deer's ribs, jerks free the ax, then lifts it again. Each time his father lands a blow, Gary's fingertips and ears throb, a jolt of pain pulsing through the thousands of miles of nerves that twist and wind throughout his own body. In a few weeks, when Doctor Magnabosco asks Gary why he waited until the frostbite had progressed to this point before seeking help—this *critical* point, he'll add for effect—Gary will have no idea where to begin, nor will he know how to tell the story of this night in such a way that his father won't end up looking like a madman, and so Gary will simply shrug.

Gary watches his father through the tiny slits of the ski mask, and still unable to breathe through his nose, he starts gasping for air. His father is crying. He keeps slamming the ax into the deer, each strike harder than the last, and Gary realizes that he, too, is crying. He chokes out one breath after another, large plumes of air, ghostly in the truck's headlights, spewing from his mouth. He's about to say something to his father, a word or two of consolation, when a car approaches, slowing at the sight of them. The car hits its own high beams to see what's the matter, and what they see is a wrecked car, a dead deer, a weeping man holding an ax, and another man wearing a ski mask and a trench coat, glaring back into the eyes of the driver. In this moment, seemingly frozen in time, Gary spots Linda in the backseat, mittened hands cupped over her mouth. He starts walking toward the car, but the high beams blink off and the car speeds away, disappearing into thick swirls of snow, the red glow of taillights dissolving into two pinpoints, then nothing.

When Gary turns back to his father, he sees that the deer's head has finally come detached. His father lifts the head by the rack and carries it to the pickup where he heaves it up and over, into the bed. As for the other carnage—the headless deer, the wrecked car—they leave it all behind.

Once they are inside the truck's cab and on their way home, Gary experiences a surge of adrenaline, a genuine rush, and he can't wait to call Linda. He wishes he could hug his father, he wishes he could say, *Shit, man, what the hell just happened back there?* but his father is driving more cautiously now, both hands on the steering wheel, and any impulsive move on Gary's part may cause his father to drive them into a snowdrift.

Why another man's misery—his dad's, in particular—inspires Gary to want to call Linda and make amends, he's not sure, but he feels suddenly pumped, as though he has just had a great work-out at the gym, his best workout ever. He feels almost *possessed*, but possessed by what, he doesn't know. He's still too messed up to put his finger on it, to understand how one thing in his life could possibly be connected to another, but after he gets some sleep, he's going to call Linda and tell her that he has come to a decision. He, too, wants to keep the child.

"Fuckin' A, Dad," Gary says. "We took the bull by the horns, didn't we? And now we're bringing home the head to prove it."

His father laughs. His mood has taken a dramatic turn for the better. He is chipper, even. "We'll mount it," his father says. "We'll mount it and we'll send it to your mother and that son of a bitch she married for a wedding present. What do you say? You want to give me a hand with it tonight?"

"Tonight?" Gary asks. The sun is about to rise. Tonight, as far as Gary can tell, is over. It's already tomorrow. "Don't we have to get it taxidermied first?"

"Oh no," his father says, smiling. "Not this one. They'll get it just like this, nailed to a sheet of plywood. And I want to ship it off, lickety-split. I want to FedEx this baby right to their front porch. I'll show those two Harvey Motherfucking Wallbangers I mean business."

Gary removes his ski mask and touches his face experimentally. His flesh is disconcertingly spongy, and each time he presses down on his cheek or forehead, he leaves behind the soft imprint of his fingertip. "I think I'll pass," he says. "I'm sort of beat."

"Suit yourself," his father says. "But mark my words, this is going to be the highlight of the year. You can bet your ass on that."

Gary nods. He reassures himself that all of this is a good sign. At least his dad's talking again. Surely that's a step in the right direction.

They drive the rest of the way home in silence, the deer's head rolling around behind them, antlers clawing the truck's bed. Though the storm has ended and the sun is peeking over the tree line, the wind is still fierce, and Gary stares blankly at the snow whirling across the highway. His surge of adrenaline is on the wane now, the rush of exhilaration over. He's falling asleep, slipping into that precarious crack between consciousness and unconsciousness, but for a moment, before he drifts completely away, Gary pretends that he and his father have been in a fatal collision, and that although dead, they are still puttering along in the pickup, maneuvering it through swirling clouds instead of snow, and they are having the best time they've ever had together, father and son floating high above the rural roads and farms, two men no longer of this earth.

The End of Romance

Squeaky Fromme came to Roger Wood in the night, in a dream, and when he awoke, Roger could still feel the weight of Squeaky, a whisper in his head coaxing him back to sleep. She had orange eyelashes, difficult to see in direct light. Her hair was naturally curly and red, her nose thin. She was covered in freckles, too—across her face, along her back, up and down her sun-blistered arms and legs. She told Roger how much she liked him. She baked hash brownies for him, mushroom pie, and cookies laced with LSD. She spoke incessantly about Charlie Manson, her savior. *You've got to meet him*, she kept saying, and each time she said so, Roger nodded.

Roger awoke alone in bed. It was true then: his wife had left him. He didn't have the slightest idea where she'd gone or how long she'd be there. She'd given no indication, only a general sense that she was disgusted enough to leave him for good.

It had happened last night, on Christmas Eve, Tracy pacing the living room and reciting what struck Roger as a well-rehearsed list of complaints, "things," she called them, *things* she couldn't live with anymore: the way Roger left his half-empty Coke cans all over the house; his relentless diet of red meat; his unwillingness to try Chinese food; his toenails, always in need of clipping; the way he combed his thin hair to the side instead of straight back; how he never tucked in his shirts except at work; how the balance of their checking account was always a mystery; his refusal to throw away socks with holes or briefs once the elastic had gone bad; the way he looked at people when they spoke to him, as if they were speaking Zulu; the way he filled the sink with warm water, dish soap, and filthy dishes, then left everything to soak, apparently forgetting it all, never touching any of it again, the water turning gray while water-logged hunks of tomato, spaghetti, or green beans floated to the surface; the fact that he wore his T-shirt when they made love. The fact, it seemed to Roger, that he existed.

After she had gone away for the night, Roger stood in the bathroom, peering into the medicine chest, lifting smoky, orangish brown cylinders of pills and shaking them. He found Tracy's Valium and took four, chasing them down with a coffee mug full of Hungarian port. On the couch, flat on his back, he watched CNN, the same news stories repeating over and over, hour after hour: Libya building a chemical weapons factory; Israel bearing down on protesters; Squeaky Fromme escaping from the women's prison in Alderson, West Virginia. When he couldn't stomach it anymore, the yawn of sleep becoming too strong, he hit the remote and dragged himself to the bedroom. He slid open a drawer where Tracy kept her underclothes, swept everything to one side, and picked up her diaphragm case. He opened the pink box and removed the diaphragm, and for a good minute he stared at the orb, holding it up and turning it this way and that in the light as if it were the Hope diamond or a lunar rock, and not the stiff, rubber sperm-catcher that it was. At least she hadn't taken the diaphragm with her, he thought. He was, for the time being, safe.

That night, Roger dreamed about Squeaky Fromme—the Squeaky of his childhood, the way she had looked back in the late 1960s. And in his dream, she was taking Roger around the ranch, introducing him one by one to the Family—Linda Kasabian, Leslie Van Houten, Patricia Krenwinkle, and Susan Atkins—women who touched him with their warm palms while Squeaky whispered into his ear, *You've got to meet him. You've got to meet Charlie.* Even in deep sleep, Roger knew she meant Charlie Manson—a man she trusted with her life, the man she honestly believed was Jesus Christ.

Zach and June charged the Christmas tree, searching for their presents. They shook each box carefully, then violently shredded away the wrapping paper. Neither noticed that their mother was gone—or *if* they noticed, they didn't say anything. Each time Zach opened one of the presents he had asked for, he glanced back over his shoulder and smiled at his father; June, on the other hand, looked sullen, searching for something that wasn't there, a gift Roger had forgotten or didn't know she wanted. He kept waiting for her to smile at him, as Zach had, but she continued searching, no longer shaking boxes, merely peeling away the paper before moving on to the next gift.

Groggy, hungover, Roger stared blankly at a crumpled pattern of Santa Clauses, each one returning the stare and waving at him. He shifted his focus to a hangnail jutting from his thumb. Too tired to get up and find the clippers, he decided to pull on it. He yanked it twice, his eyes beginning to tear up, but the hangnail remained. It pointed now at an even more dangerous angle. He pushed the wound back together and said, "Don't forget to check your stockings, kids."

Then Tracy came home. She pulled her Mustang into the drive, and the kids stopped what they were doing. They could see her through the large living room window. She was revving the engine too hard, her car disappearing in swirls of exhaust; and with one final rev—her foot evidently pressed all the way down on the accelerator—she cut the ignition.

"Sweetie," Roger said when the front door creaked open.

Tracy walked over to him slowly, cautiously, as though he were a small but dangerous rodent. She said, "I'm back." Wads of wrapping paper surrounded her feet. Her hair was flat on one side. "For the time being," she added.

"Mom!" Zach yelled. "Look at this!" He lifted a high-powered squirt gun the length of his leg above his head; but June was already running away, back upstairs, pulling her hair and screaming, unable, Roger thought, to weigh this day against all the others, to accept the promise of failure, especially today, on Christmas morning.

On the day that Squeaky Fromme was apprehended by the authorities and returned to the penitentiary, Tracy told Roger that she was going to start spending more time with the women she worked with.

"The girls," Tracy called them, though *which* girls, Roger didn't know. The women from the PTA? The women she volunteered with at the Salvation Army?

"I need my own life," she said.

Roger watched the headlights of Tracy's car illuminate the semidark living room, then swirl along the wall as she backed out of the drive. Roger got off the couch, walked into the bedroom, and opened the second drawer of their clothes chest. He pushed aside abandoned panties and hose crumpled into a ball of static cling. He slid everything from one side of the drawer to the other.

Had she moved it?

He checked the other drawers, pulling everything out and throwing it onto the floor. He jerked the drawers one by one from the chest and shook them, even after each drawer proved to be empty. Roger rubbed his face, then scratched it hard. It was gone. Tracy had taken the diaphragm with her.

Sitting on the edge of the bed, Roger stared at the naked drawers piled on the floor. That was all he could stand to do—stare, remain motionless, lose himself to inertia—but then he became aware that his shirt was moving. It was *twitching*. *Odd*, he thought. He watched it closely, listening, finally deducing the cause: his heart, beating. It was pounding harder than he thought possible for so little movement. And then he heard a clicking noise. At first he thought it was a bird tapping on his bedroom window, until he noticed a rhythm to it, a pattern, how it clicked only between the beats of his heart. It was getting harder to breathe, and the clicking got louder: it was, he realized, the sound of his windpipe opening and closing.

Roger felt as though his heart had floated up to his neck and lodged itself, cutting off his breath. He was certain he would die if he didn't stand up at that moment, so he did. With his children asleep upstairs, he left the house. He walked for several blocks, losing track not only of time but direction as well, just moving, moving, until, at long last, a wave of exhaustion swept over him, and when he got home, he cleaned the bedroom and put everything back to how it had been. He took four Valium and lay in bed thinking, *It's nothing, nothing at all*, but hoping he would fall asleep long before his wife came back home and slipped into bed beside him.

Roger ate breakfast and thought of Squeaky Fromme coming to him on Christmas Eve: her droopy eyelids, the downward curl of her mouth, the way she tilted her head back and off to the side when she smiled.

He decided not to say anything to Tracy about the diaphragm. If she was, in fact, having an affair, he would find out soon enough. If she wasn't, why make false accusations? Why bring it up? Instead, he sat at the table and pulled on his hangnail—that same hangnail—though the pain had sharpened since Christmas, and a red blotch had begun to form around the point where the hangnail intersected with his thumb.

"What's wrong?" Tracy asked.

"Hangnail," Roger said.

"Don't pick at it," she said. "You should get the clippers."

Roger shrugged. He opened a fat paperback and carefully examined the *chilling 64 pages of photos!* in the middle. Then he flipped back to the front of the book and read aloud the only words on the first page: *The story you are about to read will scare the hell out of you.*

"Yikes," Tracy said. She was chopping onions on the cutting board, her eyes beginning to water. "What're you reading?"

"*Helter Skelter*," Roger said. He'd found a copy at the Paperback Trader on Spruce, the front cover torn off, the pages wavy and bloated from having been submerged in water. A flooded basement, Roger thought. Or perhaps someone had fallen asleep in the tub, dropping the paperback into a warm bubble bath in December.

"Is it any good?" Tracy asked.

"I don't know yet," Roger said, then he held the book toward her and said, "Look. It's bloated."

The next time he glanced up from reading, he saw his kids, Zach and June, sitting in the living room, watching cartoons. They seemed startlingly taller and older since the last time he'd really looked at them. They spent a lot of time in their bedrooms, or they were outside, pedaling their bikes at dangerously high speeds, heading nowhere. They were like cats, disappearing for what seemed like weeks at a time, then showing up just when you'd begun to think they'd been hit by a car or taken in by strangers. Though maybe, in truth, they were around more than Roger realized, and somehow—he wasn't sure how this was possible—he'd simply overlooked them, much as he'd quit noticing certain pieces of furniture or clothes he never wore anymore. He considered joining them on the floor, sprawling out in front of the TV as he had when he was ten years old. Back then, the television set was always on the blink—rolling, fuzzy images; only one antenna, bent and wrapped in aluminum foil; needle-nose pliers resting on top for turning the channels. That was 1969, and Roger would stare intently for hours at the images flickering across the screen, his brain compensating for the slow flip, the greenish tint, and the blurry heads, until what he saw became as clear as life: bald women with carvings on their foreheads, sitting every night in groups of four, five, or six. They were the Manson girls, camping out on the corner of Temple and Broadway, in front of the Hall of Justice.

Roger's mother had watched the news religiously, absorbed by the relentless details, always sitting in her recliner in front of the Motorola, feet propped up, a cigarette resting in the ashtray or between her fingers. Whenever Roger spoke, she shushed him.

"Shhhhh," she said. "Listen."

After the news, later in the night, they watched *Rowan and Martin's Laugh-In*, though Roger's mother didn't think *Laugh-In* was all that funny. Instead, she talked about those poor bald girls on the corner.

"It takes a lot of dedication," she said, "to take a pocketknife and carve something on your forehead. You've got to be careful, Roger."

Night after night, they watched the vigil, and Roger began playing a game: pretending the Manson girls were speaking directly to him—that somehow they, too, could see him as he saw them. And what they told him was that Charlie was Jesus Christ, that the murder trial was Charlie's crucifixion. They warned Roger of Judgment Day, which was near, just around the corner.

Roger's mother had read a magazine article about the X's they'd put on their foreheads—how the girls had used knives the first time, but when the scar tissue began to fade, they branded themselves instead, heating the side of a screwdriver, then pressing it firmly into their skin.

"Could you imagine!" his mother said. Then she lifted her purse and rifled around inside for a pack of cigarettes. Chain-smoking, leaning back in her recliner, she began developing theories about each of the girls, and she had decided that it was Squeaky who'd been hurt the most by what was happening to Charlie, that she was the girl who most needed "*real* love," as Roger's mother put it, "*real* affection," that it was Squeaky who had been drawn deepest into Manson's spell, his ruse.

"Poor Squeaky," she said, and Roger nodded.

Roger played with his Hot Wheels for hours at a time. He created towns and mountain valleys out of a half-dozen pillows and the blankets on his bed, and he used the names he'd heard so often to give life to the characters who drove his little cars. Manson owned a fire truck. Leslie Van Houten and Patricia Krenwinkle shared a forest green Ferrari. For Susan Atkins, a cement truck. But Roger gave Squeaky a junkyard of cars to choose from, whatever she wanted: a Corvette, an ambulance, a Rolls Royce.

In school, during recess, Roger stayed at the edge of the black-top, off to the side, and he watched the girls play in groups of four, five, or six. Hopscotch, mostly. Or jump rope. Certain boys could tease the girls and get away with it. They could step into a game, ruin it, then lure the girls back toward them again, and the girls would no longer be angry. They spoke with their eyes, these boys. They understood the give and take of play and danger. Roger wasn't one of those boys. It took Roger years to come to grips with the fact that he would never be one of these boys, that he was incapable of that sort of control. With boys like that, there was another force at work—a spirit or a demon—another presence altogether invading their souls.

At night, in bed, as Roger inched his way into sleep, he began seeing girls with large, smooth heads moving closer and closer, surrounding him at the corner of the playground, their skin tinted green and fuzzy like TV static, all of them holding hands and circling Roger, chanting, "*Charlie, Charlie.*"

And now the dreams were coming back, years later, and what Roger saw in his sleep were women, not girls. They lured him with drugs and food and sex; and on a particularly cold night in January, Susan Atkins came to Roger, rubbing herself against him, brushing her lips gently across the lobe of an ear, whispering, always whispering; and even in sleep Roger knew that she was the worst, the one who had done the unthinkable. But here, alone, just the two of them, Roger could let it slide. She was rubbing herself against him, and Roger knew his weakness—the weakness of all men, it seemed—and though Roger knew full well what Susan had done, it didn't make a difference. He was willing, for the moment, to give her the benefit of the doubt.

Roger Wood worked for UPS, picking up and delivering packages. He drove a huge, solar-heated, chocolate-colored truck. Lately, while driving across town, he pretended that he was behind the wheel of Manson's famous VW Van. The van had been spray-painted black, and Manson drove it up and down the California highways, picking up hippies along the way, luring them back to Death Valley, to the Spahn Movie Ranch, where the Family lived, took drugs, had sex, and drove dune buggies. The year 1968 struck Roger as the sort of moment in history that happened only once to a nation—a country's adolescence—and for awhile, Charlie Manson reaped its rewards. Charlie'd had it all. Roger couldn't even begin to imagine what having it all would feel like. The Ford administration loomed over his own adolescence. Then Carter and disco.

Often, while working, Roger saw hitchhikers standing near the exit ramps—young men mostly, or middle-aged drifters. Today, though, while on his way to a Radio Shack delivery, Roger noticed a woman at the side of the road, her feet sunk all the way into the snow, so he eased his truck onto the shoulder. He got out, walked to the passenger's side, and opened the truck's door. She was tall and gawky, much younger than he'd thought at first glance. She told him that her radiator had blown out. Her car, she said, was at least a mile back. Roger shut the door for her, the way he might if they had been dating, going home after a long dinner in a nice restaurant.

Merging back onto the highway, Roger said, "There's not a pay phone for another five miles."

"I know," the woman said, and that was the end of their conversation.

The silence made Roger's head feel extraordinarily heavy. The longer he kept silent, the harder it was to speak. What would Manson have said? Would he have offered a joint? A snort of coke? A hit of acid? Would he've told her about the ranch? Would he have mentioned the Family in passing, gauging her interest? Sooner or later, sex would have come up—but those days were long gone. You had to be careful now. You had to watch what you said to strangers.

Roger listened for signs of his kids moving around upstairs, but he heard nothing. They had gone to bed or were silently rough-housing, the way they did some nights. Roger couldn't remember the last time he'd actually been up there. For all he knew, they'd switched bedrooms or drilled holes in their walls.

While brushing his teeth, he opened the medicine chest, and to his surprise, Tracy's diaphragm case was inside, wedged between cinnamon floss and Mercurochrome. For the first time in weeks he felt the pressure that had been building in the center of chest lift. It was possible he'd been imagining things, that he'd been jumping to hasty conclusions. He pulled the case out and shook it, though shaking wasn't necessary: it was empty. This was a code, and Roger knew all too well what it meant, that Tracy was waiting for him to come to bed.

He slid in next to her and whispered her name: *Tracy*. She was facing a window, her back to him, the crook of her arm blocking her face. Touching her thigh, Roger said her name again, louder than he meant to: "Tracy!"

"Don't shout at me," she said. She looked over her shoulder at him and said, "What?"

Roger smiled, but Tracy looked away. "Not tonight," she said. "I'm beat."

"What do you mean, *not tonight*?"

"I mean, *not tonight*. What else does *not tonight* mean?"

Roger's throat tightened. He kept his voice even and said, "Were you in the mood *earlier*?"

Tracy rolled onto her stomach and said, "Not particularly. No."

Roger had a sudden and violent impulse: to reach up inside her, touch the diaphragm he knew was there, and say, *What's this?* But the impulse passed, and Roger, exhausted by the probability of his wife's deception, turned over and tried willing himself to sleep.

——— ———

That night Roger had what he thought was a dream, that he called his boss, Lou Delahanty, in the dead of night. He needed to talk to the man, a matter that couldn't wait until morning, so he reached over and dialed the number. Fifteen rings later, Lou's wife answered.

It's Roger, he said, whispering into the mouthpiece. *Can I speak to Lou?*

Mrs. Delahanty said, *Who is this? It's late. Do you know what time it is?*

No, I don't.

It's four in the morning, she said. *Lou's still asleep. Who did you say you were?*

Roger.

Roger who?

Roger Wood.

Well, she said. *I'm not going to wake up my husband, Roger Wood. You can talk to him in the morning.*

My wife, Roger said.

What did you say?

I think my wife is having an affair, Roger said. *I think she's cheating on me.*

Mrs. Delahanty didn't respond. Then Roger began crying. He felt utterly helpless, whispering to a woman he didn't know, asking to speak to his boss, a man he *barely* knew. But he had to tell *someone*; he'd been holding it inside, hoping it wasn't true. *I'm sorry,* Roger said, and he returned the phone to the cradle.

Roger carefully backed his truck down into the sloped loading dock at the Dutch Boy warehouse. The dock had been designed for tractor trailers, not delivery trucks, which meant Roger would do a lot of lifting, handing one box at a time to a man standing high above him on the dock who, in turn, would hand it to another man, and so on, each box passed fireman-style until it reached a plywood desk where a teenager smoking a cigarette took inventory. Roger made deliveries all over Platte County and beyond, and he recognized the faces from loading dock to loading dock, but the men rarely appeared to remember him, and their conversations on the dock seemed impenetrable.

When he was fourteen, the year Squeaky Fromme tried assassinating President Ford, Roger became painfully conscious of his shyness around certain girls—so shy, he was incapable of speaking, of meeting their eyes. What he felt was a sort of helpless paralysis. Silently, he made up dialogues, hours of conversations that would never take place. Once in awhile he caught himself mumbling, hidden thoughts accidentally seeping through his mouth, given a voice. He hated himself for this, and now he hated how he felt around these men at the loading dock, strangers he'd seen every week for the past two years.

On his break, in the Sam's Club parking lot, he thumbed through *Helter Skelter*, but all he could concentrate on were the smudged photos, and of those photos, only those of women who'd come to visit him in the night: Squeaky, Linda, Leslie, Patricia, and Susan.

After lunch, Mr. Delahanty called Roger into his office.

"Have a seat, Rog," he said.

The boss, who was at least twenty years older than Roger and bald except for the mouse gray fringe around his head, examined the surface of his desk, as if searching for flaws, then touched his nose gently with his forefinger and thumb. The office was tidy. Hanging on his walls were several framed photos, and in each one, Delahanty was either holding up a fish or planting his foot onto the side of a large, dead animal. He touched his nose again and said, "Someone told me you've been picking up hitchhikers."

"Just one," Roger said.

"Company policy." Delahanty shook his head. "Company policy prohibits a driver to pick up hitchhikers."

Roger nodded.

"You should know better."

"You're right," Roger said. "I'm sorry."

"Don't let it happen again."

"It won't," Roger said.

Delahanty sighed. "Look," he said. He pinched his nose, then rubbed his palm across his desk as though fanning a deck of cards. He said, "I'm going to ask you straight out. Are you feeling okay?"

"Sure."

"You've got vacation time coming if you need it."

"What?" Roger said. "Have I done something wrong?"

Delahanty squinted at Roger, rubbing a large, moist palm over his smooth head. He couldn't keep his hands still. It was as if they had brains of their own, each hand attempting to conduct a life separate from Delahanty.

"You called my house four o'clock this morning," he said. "You spoke to my wife."

Roger shook his head, but he knew it was true.

"Now *Roger* . . ."

"It wasn't me," Roger said. "Why would I call your wife? Sounds like a prank."

Delahanty said, "Hmmmm. A prank. That's odd. Who would call my house pretending to be you, then tell my wife that *your* wife is having an affair? Don't you think that's odd?"

"My wife *isn't* having an affair," Roger said, but hearing himself say out loud what he'd been silently suspecting nearly broke him down right there in Delahanty's office. All along he'd thought he was in control, but now, for the first time in his life, he felt as if anything, anything at all, were possible. "If she was having an affair," Roger said, "I would know."

"Okay. All right," Delahanty said. "But no more hitchhikers. I mean, Jesus Christ, what were you trying to do, get the company sued?"

"No, sir," Roger said. "I'm sorry. I love this job."

And though he meant what he said, he was sorry he'd said it. Delahanty smiled, then laughed. He pounded his desk a few times with his fist and said, "That's a good one, Rog. For a second, you had me fooled." He rubbed his palms together and said, "Know what? You're a funny man when you want to be."

Without asking for permission, Roger took the rest of the afternoon off. At home, he found Tracy lying across the couch, asleep. She was wearing a sweatshirt he'd never seen before. *Chicago Blackhawks*, it said. Roger sat down across from her, leaned forward, and stared at her. He stared for nearly an hour, until the image of the Blackhawk Indian faded into a fuzzy swirl of abstract black-and-red streaks.

"I didn't know you liked hockey," he finally said.

Tracy opened her eyes, and when she saw Roger, she took a quick breath. "You scared me. When did you get home? What time is it?"

"I didn't know you liked hockey."

"What are you talking about?"

Roger pulled at his hangnail. His thumb had become infected, the skin surrounding the sore inflamed, almost too tender to touch. He yanked on it again, hard, ripping it almost free, but not quite.

"Don't do that," Tracy said.

"Why not?"

"You're making it worse."

"You should talk," Roger said.

"What's that supposed to mean?"

Roger said, "I didn't know you liked hockey."

"Jesus Christ!" Tracy yelled. "What are you talking about?"

He pointed at her sweatshirt.

"*This?*" she said. "I bought it at the Salvation Army two days ago. So what? It's a sweatshirt. It keeps me warm. I *don't* like hockey. In fact, I *hate* hockey."

Roger glared at Tracy for a moment, then stood and left the house. Coatless, he headed for downtown, a two-mile walk. The temperature had dipped well below zero, and his ears were throbbing as though someone had popped him several times about the head with their palms.

At the side of the road, Roger looked up and pointed at a low-flying airplane. The plane was so low, its shadow overtook a school bus, two pedestrians, and a pet store. Briefly, Roger himself was caught in the shade, then a blast of sunlight hit him again, and it was at this moment that he noticed his arm and his finger, the fact that he was pointing. He looked around, but no one had noticed, or if they'd noticed, they didn't care.

Roger walked quickly to a bar called the Jack O'Lantern for a drink. It was early afternoon. Except for the bartender, Roger was alone. He kept nodding without meaning to, thinking about Tracy and nodding. When he saw himself in the mirror, he quit moving his head and tried erasing all of his thoughts, but his wife kept returning. She'd come to him wearing another man's sweatshirt, eyes dark from long, sleepless nights, her diaphragm sealed-up inside her. His chest began to hurt, a distinct pain, as though someone were actually chewing on his heart. She was killing him. It was that simple.

Roger watched the bartender dunk dirty glasses into soapy gray water, his sleeves rolled to his biceps. He let himself get lost in the rhythm of the dunk, the hypnotic movements of a bartender in the middle of a lazy, shadowy afternoon. His mind began to drift, and eventually Tracy floated away.

Six hours later, Roger was halfway across town, leaning against the bar at Papa's, drunk, a plastic cup half full of beer in his right hand. He kept squeezing too hard, creasing the cup. Papa's was packed with bikers and paraplegics, its usual potpourri of clientele. Whenever Roger got drunk, he was amazed at how his mind simply traveled—certain French words he'd learned in high school, long forgotten, mysteriously returning (*l'oiseau, une parapluie*); graffiti he'd once seen in a public restroom somewhere in Virginia (*I'll crank your head for fun*); October, the first cold snap, seeing Tracy's breath in the church parking lot after the wedding.

The floor in Papa's was sticky. Pickled eggs lay piled in a dusty jar next to the cash register. Pool balls rolled from its coin-operated trough to the cave at the end of the table. The world of the bar had become Roger's world. He returned, again and again, to a single phrase: *the most graphic moment of your indiscretion.* It was an image, a flash that caused his windpipe to contract, his throat to click.

A man playing pool leaned into Roger and said, "I used to play better pool before I got shot in the head."

Roger nodded, and the man sank four striped balls in quick succession.

People pushed against Roger, trying to flag down the bartender, momentarily crushing him. And then the crowd parted, as if the bar itself were yawning, a gulf starting at the center of Papa's to where Roger stood, and beyond. At the center of that gulf was a midget, too drunk to climb onto his barstool, and a man in a wheelchair. The man in the wheelchair gripped his armrests and began pushing himself up, attempting to stand. Once on his feet, balanced, he let go of the chair. He took two careful steps toward the midget, placed his hands beneath the midget's pudgy arms, then, grunting, lifted him onto the barstool. Everyone had become silent, watching, mesmerized. And Roger was certain in that instant that God was trying to talk to him, that a man rising from his wheelchair to lift a midget onto a barstool was a message, a clue, and Roger started crying right there, in the middle of Papa's, because he couldn't fathom what the message meant, but he knew if he could interpret it, he would understand why all of this was happening to him, and then maybe, just maybe, Tracy would stop having an affair and everything would return to normal.

"Roger," Tracy said. She nudged him. "Roger."

"What?"

"Are you okay?"

"I'm fine," he said.

"You were talking in your sleep."

"Was I?" He yawned and said, "I've been having strange dreams."

"Like what?" Tracy said.

"You could call them religious, I suppose."

"How so?"

"The Second Coming of Christ," Roger said. "He comes to Death Valley, and they crucify him."

There was a moment of silence. Then Tracy said, "I've been having odd dreams, too."

"Oh yeah?" Roger said. "Odd how?"

"They're about you."

"Me?" Roger said. "What's so odd about that?"

"You're following me around town. You're trying to kill me."

"Really." Roger wanted to comfort her, but he couldn't think of anything comforting to say.

Tracy was smiling. Her dark mood had lifted. It was, as they say, an odd turn of events. But Roger had gone out of his way today, planning every move, hoping for just such a turn.

"This *is* romantic," Tracy said, "but why won't you tell me where we're going?"

"Because," Roger said. "I told you already. It's a surprise." He tried smiling, too, but Tracy was looking out the passenger-side window now, watching the scenery flick by.

"How much longer?"

"Not much," Roger said. "Half an hour. Maybe less."

They'd been driving for three hours. Roger had come home from work early, called the baby-sitter, then ordered Chinese. He washed last night's dishes. He clipped his toenails. After dinner, he asked Tracy to help him dress his thumb. While Roger applied the Neosporin, Tracy prepared the sterile gauze and surgical tape. She kissed his bandaged wound and said, "I think we should see a marriage counselor."

"Sure," Roger said. "That's a good idea." But Roger knew the truth: they would never go to a marriage counselor. It was over between them.

That night, when they pulled into Athens, Ohio, Tracy said, "What time is it? The baby-sitter's going to kill us, don't you think? What time did you tell her we'd be back?"

Roger ignored her. He followed the directions he'd been given over the phone. He was good at that sort of thing. It was his job, after all—finding places he'd never before been, locating them in a timely manner. They parked and walked across campus to a movie theater in the student union. Roger had spent two weeks placing phone calls to theaters, and when nothing panned out, he called the distributor and found the closest showing. Ohio University. It was Phi Beta Kappa's Cult Movie Night, and they were screening *Valley of the Dolls*. One night only.

"Hmmmmm," Tracy said. "*Valley of the Dolls*. Isn't this supposed to be a terrible movie?"

"The worst," Roger said. He pointed at the movie poster and said, "Look, though. Sharon Tate." Then he led her into the dark theater.

He knew he couldn't explain it to her, none of it. There was no place to begin, so all he could do was hold her hand, maybe squeeze it for reassurance; and as the lights dimmed even more, and as the first reel of the movie began to play, Roger whispered into Tracy's ear, "I'm sorry."

The movie, as promised, was awful. The acting, the script, the soundtrack—all of it. Though buried under the film's surface was Sharon Tate's future. And Roger Wood knew what Sharon Tate didn't: that soon she would be pregnant. That she would carry the child for eight and three-quarters months. That one night, for no good reason except random bad luck, she would be stabbed sixteen times. In the heart, the lungs, the liver. That a woman named Susan Atkins would taste Sharon's blood, just out of curiosity.

"Are you okay?" Roger asked.

"Shhhhhh," Tracy said. "Watch the movie."

Roger shut his eyes. He saw himself as he had been in the dream, holding Squeaky's hand, a chain of five women and one man, all of them skipping like children. They were going to see Charlie. And Charlie would welcome them, welcome Roger, probably hug him and offer food. After supper they would smoke a joint and drop acid; and sooner or later, the women would move closer to Roger, ruffle his hair, and tell him to loosen up. And all of this sounded good, the days and nights slipping pleasantly by, months, maybe years. But Roger knew this sort of freedom—the freedom to do whatever you please—came with a price; and as he stepped into Manson's arms, accepting his grasp, he let go of Tracy's hand. It was a compromise. But that's how it was, wasn't it? There would always be compromises. And the price of such freedom, Roger knew, was darkness.

Smoke

Mom said she needed to talk to me—"this minute," she said—that it was really important and couldn't wait, but I said, "Not now." I opened the sliding glass door, walked outside, and found Tex, my dog, who'd spent the better part of these past two weeks digging up the backyard. He held a bone lengthwise in his mouth, his fourth one today. He dropped it onto a small, neat pile next to the gas grill. He licked my hand, and I pointed at his nose and said, *Sit! Give me a paw!* but he just tilted his head, then ran away.

We found Tex two years ago, a pup smack in the middle of a downpour, a wet dog the size and color of a meatloaf. He was lumbering across the expressway, his dark head hung low, too depressed by the rain and lightning to care about the cars and trucks speeding toward him. Dad pulled over and Mom opened her door, and together we lured him into our car and into our lives with the promise of a good home and table food.

"He *smells* like a dog," my father had said. He snickered and called him a dog's dog—a joke I didn't get then and still didn't two years later, though I liked how it sounded.

"Tex!" I yelled, but Tex was busy in the backyard, digging where I couldn't see him. Our house was small, our front lawn tiny, but the backyard stretched away forever—one of the few in the city that did so, but only because if you kept walking, you'd run into a fence, and beyond that fence was an industrial park that nobody wanted to live near.

I sat on the crooked chaise lounge, just outside the rim of the buglight's light, and I watched and listened to the moths and June bugs and what-have-you touch down on the bulb, then flap crazily to get away from it. In the mornings, I liked to walk outside barefoot and check the yellow bulb, see the wings glued to the glass, touch what's left of those bugs who wanted too much of a good thing.

I was beginning to focus too intensely on the bulb, a dim yellow hole burning into my field of vision, when I caught Kelly, my sister, glaring at me from the kitchen. She was three years older than me and looked perfect under the outrageously bright kitchen lights. *Slinky*, I thought—a word I liked to say alone, in bed at night, before I drifted to sleep. She slid open the glass door, glared some more, and said, "Hank, is that you?"

"No," I said. "It's Ted Bundy, serial killer!"

Kelly stared blankly in my direction. She never laughed at my jokes, never thought what I said was funny. Dad called her a literalist. A dog's dog, I thought. She stepped outside, leaving Mom alone at the kitchen table, and shut the door behind her.

"Where's Dad?" I asked.

"Vamoose," she said.

"Bowling?"

"Yeah, right," she said, as if she knew things about Dad that I didn't, but I decided not to press. Kelly walked over to where I was sitting, and without looking at me, she said, "I'm depressed."

"Me, too," I said, smiling.

"No you're not," she said. "*I'm* depressed." From her back pocket, she pulled a folded, soggy sheet of paper. She handed it to me and said, "I'm manic-depressive."

What she'd given me was a photocopy of a page from the dictionary, the definition for *manic-depressive*, only she'd enlarged it eight or nine times, and the letters hung on the page like fuzzy caterpillars artfully shaped into words.

"Wow," I said, impressed by the size of the words, the jumbo letters blurry on the paper.

"It's chemical," she said.

"So," I said. "You're a depressed maniac."

"A manic-depressive, you clod."

"Who knows," I said. "Maybe I'm a manic-depressive, too."

She rolled her eyes and said, "I don't think so."

"How would you know?"

She sighed and took back her definition. She folded it carefully and stuck it into her back pocket. "A manic-depressive can always spot another manic-depressive," she said. "And you're *not* a manic-depressive."

"Maybe not," I said. "But I'm double-jointed." I showed her my knuckles and began popping one in and out of place.

She groaned and said, "Goodbye," though it had come to mean something far more than *goodbye*—a word so weighted, it was meant to send me off somewhere far away from her.

"My slinky sister," I whispered, and Tex, collector of bones, walked into the semicircle of light, another one clamped in his jaws, his eyes glowing red like the sole demon from a bad family snapshot.

Ralph hopped a fence he could've just opened, walked over to the chaise, and nudged me with his foot. Ralph had failed both the third and the seventh grades, making him the oldest eighth grader I'd ever seen. He had wispy sideburns and the shadow of a weak mustache. He spoke a language I knew and didn't know at the same time. Today he was wearing a skintight lime green T-shirt that said SOUTHSIDE IRISH, though technically we lived on the south*west* side of Chicago and Ralph was Lithuanian.

"Ralph," I said. "The fence has a latch."

"Latch snatch," he said and walked over to the sliding glass door to peek in on my mother who was staring at the table. Whenever she did this, she reminded me of Superman boring holes through steel with his eyes.

"What's wrong with *her?*" Ralph asked, serious now, backing slowly away from the house.

"I don't know," I said. "She's probably a manic-depressive or something."

Ralph nodded as though he'd heard of such things before. He shut his eyes and let the full impact of my mother's life soak into him like a hot breeze. Then he pulled a fluffer-nutter sandwich wrapped in cellophane from his back pocket, peeled back the plastic, and stuffed half of it into his mouth.

"My *sister* is a manic-depressive," I said. "Do you believe that?"

Ralph's jaw went slack, and in the dark hollow of his mouth, I saw swirls of marshmallow fluff and peanut butter and long strings of spit connected like cobwebs from his tongue to his teeth.

"Unless she's pulling my leg," I added.

"Oh," Ralph said and shut his mouth, as if amazement and disappointment were the pulleys working his jaw. "You want to know something?" he said. "I wouldn't mind boning your sister."

Ralph was always talking about boning my sister—this was old news—so I said, "What's the game plan tonight, Ralph?"

"Well," Ralph said, "my aunt and uncle and their idiot kid are on vacation, and they asked me to feed their dog."

"They asked *you?*"

He stuffed the last of his sandwich into his mouth, wiped his palms onto his jeans, and said, "Yeah. They asked *me*. What're you sayin'?" He pushed me hard with both palms.

"Nothing," I said.

"What's wrong with somebody askin' *me* to take care of their ugly, mangy, flea-infested pet, huh?" He pushed me again.

"Cut it out, Ralph."

Ralph smiled now and winked at me. He was like that. He'd beat you up one minute, buy you an ice-cream cone the next.

"Let's go," he said.

It was nine o'clock and dark, the last splotch of light disappearing even as we spoke. Ralph and I headed down Menard, walking fast as always, hands jammed deep into our pockets.

"Know what I heard?" Ralph said. "I heard Janet likes you. I heard she wants to get you in the sack." He winked at me and in a low growl said, "Janet."

"The Planet?" I asked, then caught myself. Janet the Planet was twice my size, but that no longer mattered. I would no longer play favorites, I had decided. Each name of each girl in the eighth grade had begun giving my heart an equal surge, a jolt in the dark of night. I promised myself right then and there never to call Janet "the Planet" again.

"Know what else I heard?" Ralph said.

"What?"

"All fat chicks give head."

"Where'd you hear that?" I asked.

"It's a fact," Ralph said. "Don't tell me you never heard that before."

"Never."

Ralph punched my arm too hard and said, "Check into it, my friend."

We walked to the part of town where people left junk all over their yards and porches—washers and dryers, Big Wheels with broken handlebars or cracked seats, roofing shingles piled against houses—a part of town where things were either missing or broken.

Ralph bent over and picked up two rusty nuts and a screw. He gave me one of the nuts, and I began rubbing it between my palms.

"You know Veronica?" he said. "Know what I heard about Veronica?"

"She likes me?"

"No. Get this. You know Lucky's?"

"Lucky's Tavern?"

"Yeah. You know the alley?"

"Behind Lucky's?"

"Yeah. You know what Veronica does behind that alley?"

"What?"

"She smokes guys."

I stopped rubbing the nut between my palms. I wanted to ask Ralph to say what he'd just said, to say it again so I could listen to how he said it, figure out what he meant. He was speaking in code.

"She smokes guys," I said.

"Five bucks a smoke," he said.

"When?" I asked.

"Every night," he said.

"School nights?"

"My cousin told me."

"Russell?"

"No. My cousin Kenny. You know Kenny."

"Yeah," I said, and I did. Last year Kenny got sent to jail for stalking his ex-wife and beating up her new boyfriend. Ralph had taken me to Kenny's twice, and both times Kenny had offered me a cold beer and told me about his job at the Tootsie Roll factory, and about the trouble with marrying a woman you couldn't trust as far as you could throw; but he treated me like we were old buddies and I had just stopped over to shoot the bull, which made me like him, despite my better judgment.

"Veronica smoke Kenny?" I asked.

"Shhhhhhh," Ralph said. "Watch this."

A small boy was approaching on a rusty Schwinn Continental, his legs barely long enough to reach the pedals. When he got close enough, Ralph stepped in front of him and raised his palm up, the way a traffic cop would. Then he took hold of the kid's handlebars and said, "Hey. Where'd you get this bike?"

The boy said, "It's my brother's."

"Uh-uh," Ralph said, shaking his head. "It's *mine*, and I think it's time you give it back." Ralph walked behind the boy, looped his arms under the boy's armpits, his palms pressed firmly against the boy's neck, then yanked him off the bike. It was a smooth move, and though I didn't think Ralph should have done it, it was as impressive as anything I'd seen lately on Sunday afternoon wrestling.

Ralph sat on the bike, squeezed the brakes twice, and said, "Hey, Hank. Watch this." He pedaled hard up and down the street, yelling, "Look. I'm Evel Knievel." He popped a wheelie, rode it high for a long time, then fell completely backwards, off the bike, cracking his head against the asphalt. The Schwinn wobbled a ways before smashing into a parked car.

"I think I've got a concussion," Ralph said. He stood and brushed himself off. His hair was matted to the back of his head. Silently, without any warning, he started waking away.

The boy was still on the ground, sobbing. I looked at him and shrugged.

Ralph scratched his head several times where a dark stain had begun to grow. I kept up with him, in case he died. Ten blocks later, I said, "You shouldn't have done that."

"Done what?"

"Scared that kid."

"What kid?" Ralph asked. "I don't remember any kid."

"No one likes a bully," I said.

Ralph said, "Are you still talking about that kid?"

We slowed down to a shuffle, stopping at a tree. Ralph touched his head lightly and said, "Want to go watch Veronica?"

"Why?" I asked. "You want to put her in a half nelson?"

"Maybe," Ralph said. "But I thought we could watch her smoke a guy first."

I shrugged. I tried shrugging off the whole night, but the truth was, I wanted to check out this smoking business. And I wanted to go to Lucky's. "I guess so," I said. "If you want to."

Lucky's Tavern was on the far edge of town—"a *dive*," my mother called it, "a dive where nothing but a bunch of ignorant rednecks go." Whenever Mom said this, Dad just laughed at her. The word *redneck* apparently cracked him up. But every time we drove by, I tried seeing inside through the dark-tinted windows, beyond the beer advertisements, to see, exactly, what a bunch of ignorant rednecks looked like. On hot nights, the door was propped open, and each time we drove by, the scene looked the same, like one of those dull moments frozen behind glass at the Field Museum downtown: two old men sitting at opposite ends of the bar, the bartender perched on a wooden stool next to the cash register, his head tilting back to watch the TV suspended above him.

When we got there, though, the alley was empty.

"No smoking tonight," I said.

"Take a load off," Ralph said, and he sat next to the Dumpster, hiding behind a stack of flattened boxes and a large wire rack of some sort, a magazine rack, probably.

Ralph said, "Tell me everything you know about your sister. We're practically the same age, you know." Ralph shifted on the gravel, stretching his legs, trying to get comfortable. When it came to Kelly, Ralph believed anything I told him, and normally I told him the truth. Today, however, I decided to make things up, saying whatever came to mind.

"She's only got one kidney," I said.

"No shit."

"She wet her bed until my mother bought her a rubber blanket."

Ralph said nothing, savoring the thought.

"She sleeps on her back and snores like a pig."

"I like that," Ralph said. "I wouldn't mind listening to that sometime, if you can arrange it."

I said, "She's really only my half-sister. We've got different fathers. Mom married some other guy first. Then she fooled around with my dad, and *whammo*, she got knocked up."

Ralph said, "So whatever happened to Kelly's dad?"

I shrugged. "Who knows. He was a drifter."

Ralph said, "Hm. Your mother and some drifter freak. I can see it."

"Yep."

"Jesus," Ralph said. "You're more twisted than I am."

And then I couldn't go on. I couldn't keep the lie inside, smothered where it belonged. So I told Ralph, smiling as I did, and when I finished, he reached over and grabbed me by the throat. He choked me harder than I expected, pushing his thumb into my windpipe, blocking the passage of air. When he let go, he said, "You shouldn't lie about your mom." And that was all he said.

We waited another hour at Ralph's insistence, but nothing happened. My throat kept throbbing, phantom fingers squeezing my neck between heartbeats, giving me the creeps. Then, at long last, the back door creaked open, though all that appeared at first were four fingertips clutching the door's edge.

"I should go over there and bite them," Ralph whispered. He bared his teeth like a werewolf and moved toward my forehead.

I yelled, and the man stepped around the door, a beer bottle dangling next to his leg from the tips of his fingers, a cigarette bent upward from his lips, the way FDR smoked. It was my dad. He just stood there in the light, squinting at us, until he recognized us and smiled.

"Hey, guys," he said. "What's going on?"

"Hi Dad," I said.

Ralph said, "Hey, Mr. Boyd."

Dad didn't seem a bit surprised to see us there, all the way across town, half underneath a Dumpster. He said, "How're you boys doin'?"

Ralph said, "Just hanging out. Watching people *smoke*."

Dad chuckled, but I doubt he knew what Ralph meant. No one ever seemed to know what Ralph meant.

Dad shook his head and flicked away his cigarette butt—a long, high arc, soaring like a bug on fire, landing in somebody's backyard. Whenever Dad did this, I was afraid he was going to set the whole city on fire, the way Mrs. O'Leary's cow had set the city on fire a hundred years ago. Dad said, "Son of a bitch pulled a straight out of nowhere. Do you believe that? Out of *nowhere*. And to think, I *dealt* it to him."

"Snake eyes!" Ralph yelled. "The doctor! Bingo!"

"A straight!" my father said, wagging his head.

"Yowza!" Ralph said. He raised his palm into the air, as if to high-five, and said, "My main most man!"

My father pointed his forefinger at Ralph and fired it like a gun. Then he looked at me and said, "Are you gonna be home later tonight?"

It was a stupid question: I'd never *not* come home for the night. But I nodded and said, "Yeah. Sure."

"We need to talk, son," he said. He raised his arm to wave goodbye and said, "We'll talk tonight," then stepped back into the bar, the heavy door slamming hard behind him.

"Jesus," I said. "Everyone wants to talk to me."

"You're like Ann Landers or something," Ralph said.

"I don't think so," I said. "I don't think they want my advice."

We took alleys to get to the house, and when we reached it, we approached from behind. At the back door, Ralph tried the door-knob, then jerked a screwdriver from his pants.

"What's that for?"

"They forgot to give me a key," Ralph said. He jammed the screwdriver between the doorframe and the door, and started prying.

"Hey," I said. "Don't do that. You'll bust up the woodwork."

"Listen, Einstein," he said. "What do you think they'll be more upset about—a broken door or a dead dog? Huh?" Ralph continued wiggling the screwdriver back and forth, pushing with all his weight, until the door finally popped open. He stepped inside and said, "*Voilà!*"

Ralph switched on a light and began searching the house. I stood in the kitchen, looking around for the dogfood bowls, the dogfood, and the dog. I checked the kitchen countertop for a note, directions on dog maintenance, but couldn't find one. I went to the living room and said, "Here, pooch. Here, poochy pooch."

The house looked exactly like all of my Italian friends' houses—furniture covered in see-through plastic, bisque figurines decorating the end tables, a three-dimensional Last Supper hanging above a humongous TV console.

"You sure we're in the right house?" I yelled. "Nothing personal, Ralph, but this doesn't look like the sort of place where one of your relatives would live. It's too clean."

I stepped into the bedroom to keep giving Ralph a hard time, but he wasn't listening: he was rifling through drawers, pulling everything out, and throwing it over his shoulder. He stood up and said, "What a dump."

"*You're* the one messing it up," I said.

Ralph walked back into the living room, picked up a figurine of an old man wearing a straw hat and holding a fishing rod, and said,

"Look at this crap. A house full of junk. And how much does this TV weigh? A gazillion pounds, probably. At *least* a gazillion."

"I can't find the dog," I said. "What kind of dog is it?"

Ralph pulled a newspaper clipping from his pocket, uncrumpled it, and said, "Hey. Go out front and tell me what the address is. We might be in the wrong house."

"You're *kidding*," I said. My heart began pounding.

"Hank," he said, looking at me for the first time since we'd entered the house. "You see anything that looks good?"

"What do you mean?"

"Computer, VCR, CD player?"

"No," I said. "Why?"

Ralph said, "Go check the address, okay?"

"Ralph," I said. "Where's the dog?"

"What dog?" Ralph asked.

I pointed to the newspaper clipping and said, "What's this?"

He handed it to me and said, "Here. I'm gonna look around some more. Now, go outside and see if *this* address matches the address outside. Is that too hard or *what*? Jeesh."

Ralph walked away, and I smoothed out the clipping. It was an obituary.

LORENZ—Nadine, 81, 7403 S. Luna, died Wednesday.
Services: noon, Saturday. St. Fabians, 8200 State Rd.
Visitation: 5 p.m. to 10 p.m., Friday,
Hamlin and Sons Funeral Home, 8032 S. Central.

If the clock on the wall could be trusted, visitation hours were in full swing this very second.

When Ralph returned, he said, "So what's the verdict?"

I waved the clipping at him. "This is *her* house?"

Ralph said, "Not anymore."

"Ralph," I said. "Let's just go, okay?"

He let out a long, disappointed sigh, the kind of sigh my father liked to make, and said, "You're right. There's nothing here but a bunch of old lady crap." On his way out, he picked up a waffle iron and said, "How much you think these things go for?" He lifted it high into the air, over his head, and said, "This would make a great weapon. Someone fucks with you, you pull this baby out and say, 'Hey. You want a waffle?' Then *boom*. You smash the dork in the face with it."

We stepped into the fresh air, and Ralph shut the door.

"She was *dead*," I said. "Jesus, Ralph. You broke into a *dead* woman's house. That's the lowest thing I ever heard of."

The waffle iron dangled beside Ralph's leg, and every so often, he chuckled, but I didn't feel much like talking anymore. Each time he chuckled, I had a gut feeling Ralph wasn't long for this world, and that I would have to make a decision over the weekend: keep hanging out with Ralph or cut my losses. There were pluses to both sides. *With* Ralph, no one would mess with me; they'd know better. *Without* Ralph, I might stay alive longer, and my chances of doing any serious jail time would be kept to a minimum. These were the benefits, short- and long-term, and though it should have been an easy decision, I knew it wasn't going to be. I liked Ralph. That was the sad part.

Ralph stopped in the middle of the street, as though he'd read my mind, sensing his own mortality, and he touched his hair, sticky now from the blood where he'd fallen off the Schwinn. He said, "I got hit on the head once with a sledgehammer."

"Really," I said. "Did it hurt?"

"Nuh-uh."

When we got to Ralph's house, he opened the gate and shut it without offering to let me come inside. I'd never been any closer than where I stood today, and I'd never seen his mother, though I always suspected she was in there, peeking out from between the thick crushed velvet curtains, watching our every move. He lived in a small house with gray, pebbly shingles covering the sides, and black shingles on the roof. The lawn was mostly dirt.

Ralph said, "You know why it didn't hurt?"

"Why?"

"It knocked me out cold," he said. "You know that tunnel of light everyone talks about? Let me tell you, pal, it's true. I saw it. I kept walking deeper and deeper into this bright light, and then I started getting pulled back, away from it, and the next thing I knew, I was awake and in bed. It changed my life, Hank. No shit. From that point on, I decided to be a different person."

"What kind of person was that?"

He grinned and said, "A mean one."

Ralph walked away, and as he reached for the screen door, I said, "How old were you, Ralph?"

"Eight," he said. He waved at me with the waffle iron, then disappeared into his house.

I wasn't feeling so good anymore. I held my gut and walked quickly along the dark streets. I was back in a part of town that made me queasy, an area my mother always told me to stay away from. When I was in the first grade, a high school boy was killed on this very street, clubbed to death with a baseball bat by one of his own classmates, a bully named Karl Elmazi. But the scary part of the story wasn't that a guy had gotten beaten to death with a Louisville Slugger. It was that the bully had ten of his buddies with him, and none of them, not a single one, tried to stop the beating.

For my mother, this was a powerful story with a good moral. "Pick your friends carefully," she liked to say, especially after one of Ralph's visits.

The dome light was on inside Dad's car when I got home, and Kelly was slouched in the driver's seat, her palm cupped over the mirror on the door. I crept up on her, hoping to scare her, but I didn't. In fact, she moved only her eyes, as if my being there constituted only the barest of movements.

"You still depressed?" I asked.

"After looking at you," she said, "I've become suicidal."

"What're you so depressed about, anyway?"

She reached over to the ashtray and picked up a lit cigarette I hadn't noticed. She said, "Everything and nothing. But I don't expect you to understand that."

I nodded; I *didn't* understand. It didn't seem possible.

I pointed at her cigarette and said, "You don't smoke," and when I heard what I'd said, I reached into the car and placed my palm on top of my sister's head, just to feel it. I'd heard that ninety percent of a person's body heat escapes out the top of their head, and this was what I felt: searing heat rising like a ghost from Kelly's scalp.

"Who says I don't smoke?" Kelly said, ignoring my hand. Then she snuffed out the cigarette in the ashtray.

I took my hand away and said, "What're you doing out here?"

"Waiting for Mom," she said, and this time I *did* understand. It was nearly midnight; Dad had been home only a short while. I could tell because the car's engine was still ticking. "We're going for a ride," Kelly said. "She says she wants to talk to me about something important." She rolled her eyes.

"Good luck," I said and made my way around the house, to the backyard. From a safe distance, I watched Mom and Dad through the sliding glass door. As usual, they were arguing. Tex came up behind me, his paws crunching the grass with each step. He was lugging a long, bent bone in his mouth, thin at one end, thick at the other.

"Tex," I said. "Holy smoke. What's *that?*"

Tex dropped the bone and jogged away, the way he'd been doing all week. I picked it up and held it close to my face to get a good view. It looked like a leg.

I walked over to the pile of bones next to the gas grill, crouched, and spread them out before me.

"Tex," I said, but I was whispering. I was too close to the house, too close to the buglight, the swarm of bugs, too close, it seemed, to everything. I made my way across the backyard, looking for Tex, listening. The yard was too large at night, though, and I couldn't see him or hear him. No doubt he was flat in the high grass, resting, listening to crickets, distant dogs, and to the power lines sizzling high above us before going back to work.

My parents were still arguing, but they looked so small out here, this far away, that it was impossible to take them seriously. If only they could've seen themselves, they might actually have laughed. Instead, Dad pointed at Mom, and it looked as if he were saying, *Sit! Give me a paw!* and Mom, as though she'd read my mind, or sensed what I had sensed, lifted her purse off the floor and left the house. A moment later, the car started. Dad stood alone in the kitchen while Mom revved the engine too hard, gunning it, trying to blow it up. When she finally let up on the gas, she backed out of the driveway, headlights spraying across our house as she aimed her car down the road that would eventually take her away from us for good.

"Tex," I said. But Tex wouldn't answer.

Dad opened the sliding glass door and walked outside, and I took a step back. He was staring right at me, but he couldn't see me. He pulled a pack of cigarettes from his shirt pocket and smacked the pack against his palm. I'd seen him do this thousands of times before, but only now did it register that here was a man smacking a pack of cigarettes into his palm, and I had no idea why.

Dad stood on the back porch, exhausted, lighting a cigarette, the weight of everyone's life crushing his head, this man I knew and didn't know—a dad's dad, I thought and tried snickering, but I'd never snickered before and couldn't do it now. Dad looked deeper into the backyard, searching for the sound he just heard, my half snicker. He tried to see but couldn't and gave up. He looked down. Leaning forward, he rested his hand on the gas grill for support. At first I thought he was fainting, collapsing from stress. A heart attack, I thought. A stroke. I was about to run toward him, to help him, then realized he wasn't dying at all—not yet, at least—but looking down at the bones Tex had found. Carefully, he lowered himself to his knees and began playing with them, arranging them like so, like a puzzle. Then he leaned back and studied what he'd done. I couldn't see it, not really, but I knew that he was crying. There was something about his posture, and about the way he touched the bones and simply stared.

He said something I couldn't hear, and I stepped back further into darkness. I sensed Tex close by, behind me, and I stepped back again, but I fell this time, my leg suddenly deep inside of a hole.

Tex nudged my arm with his cold nose, his gesture of need. I pulled my leg from the hole and reached into the ground.

"Dad," I whispered, but Dad couldn't hear me.

Dad was sitting now, resting against the grill, moving his hand through the air. He was petting the ghost of a dog he'd once known, and all the way across the yard I was touching that same dog's skull, still lodged in the earth. I tried to imagine the sorts of things firing inside Dad's head, and so I looked at Tex, concentrating on the bones beyond his fur and skin, beyond the Tex I knew—the dog *beneath* the dog—but I couldn't imagine anything at all. There *was* no dog beneath the dog. There was only Tex.

When Dad finally looked up from the bones, he peered out into the dark of the backyard and called my name. "Hank? Is that you out there?" he asked. "Hank. What are you doing?"

I didn't say anything. I was already filling in the hole, clawing frantically, trying to cover the skull.

"You okay?" he asked. "You hurt or something?"

I flattened out, placing my head against the ground, trying to keep as still as possible.

"They're all against me, Hank," he said, more to himself than to me. "Not you, too." He took a long drag off his cigarette, and while smoke escaped his nose and mouth, momentarily blanketing his face, he shook his head, then stepped back into the nervous quiet of our house.

The
First
of Your
Last
Chances

My girlfriend, Patrice, points at a cloud and says it looks like a cow. Another day, it's the profile of a lumberjack. Occasionally, the image gets more complicated: a fat man walking his poodle, or the head of a famous statesman, Winston Churchill or Henry Kissinger, hovering 10,000 feet above us.

"Look," she'll say. "Mousy Tongue."

"What?" And then I'll remember: it's a nickname, a pun in her vast repertoire of puns. "Ah, *yes,*" I'll say. "Got it! Mao Tse-tung. Of course, of course."

"See him?"

"Nope."

Two days ago, she saw my mother holding a spatula.

"Do you see her?" she had asked. "Right there—see that dark streak? That's her bottom lip. You know that look she gets? That's it to a tee, Michael. It's amazing."

But I couldn't see it. Patrice's clouds are not my clouds. It's been four weeks since we've had sex, and what I see each time I look up is raw carnality: clouds humping clouds, or long cumulus erections floating overhead, ominous as zeppelins, swallowing us with their shade.

"I'm sorry," I said, "but I don't see my mother up there."

"Really?"

"Really."

At work, Darren tells me he's recorded a voice-mail ad for himself in the personals. He's just a kid, turned nineteen last month—a tall, skinny, hollow-eyed college dropout. His cigarette is jammed in the corner of his mouth, and each time he speaks, he fills the cab of the truck with thick, blue gray smoke.

"They've got these different categories," he says. "*Looking for Love, Unusual Appetites, Three's Company.*"

I crank down the window, suck in a lungful of fresh air.

"So I recorded one under *All Tied Up*," Darren says. "For laughs, you understand."

"*All Tied Up*," I say. "And what was your message?"

"Oh, Christ, I don't know. 'Looking for a woman who can tame this beast.' Something like that." He's smiling and laughing, but there is genuine fear in his eyes. The reason he's telling me this is because he wants reassurance that what he's done is okay, but I won't give him any. When he realizes this, he says, "I've got my first date. Saturday afternoon." He says this quietly, almost as an afterthought.

"Hey, hey!" I say. "Congratulations."

Darren is hunched at the wheel, so I clap him on the back. My burst of enthusiasm perks him right up. "Her name's Tova," he says. "Get this—she asked if I was a dom or a sub."

"And?"

"I said, sometimes a dom, sometimes a sub. Depends on my mood."

"Good answer."

He squints through smoke and says, "You think?"

"Absolutely," I say. "When in doubt, straddle the fence."

Darren snuffs out his cigarette, and in a rare moment of self-confidence, he grins at me and says, "That ain't all I'll be straddling, pal."

After it gets dark, I carry a coatrack up from my truck to my apartment. I'm head of University Surplus—our job is to lug away whatever the departments don't want and offer it once a week to the public at a reasonable price—and every night for the past five years I've taken a little something home for myself, a bonus for making it through another day. Yesterday it was a file folder from the Department of Mortuary Science and Funeral Service. Today it's a coatrack from a dean's office. Tomorrow we're removing every last item from the old Student Health building, which is scheduled for demolition, and I've got my eye on a magazine rack from the waiting room. What I'd *really* like is a water fountain—we have three of them—but I haven't yet figured out the logistics for hooking one up inside my apartment.

After dinner, I go to Patrice's. She lives across the street from Wrigley Field on the top floor of a brownstone. Clearly, I have done something wrong—I have erred in any of a thousand ways—but Patrice won't tell me what I've done. Whatever it was, though, it happened a month ago, and this is why the sex has been cut off. Any minute now I expect Patrice to give me an ultimatum. She has a pun for this, too. *Ultimatum* becomes *old tomatoes*, as in, "They've been living together for five years, so Marcy finally gave Jack the old tomatoes: marry her or move out." Like Mousy Tongue, the old tomatoes is part of another language, a language with a past I can't quite wrap my brain around. It's another Patrice from another time in her life talking to people I've never met. Nonetheless, I see the old tomatoes coming, and I'm prepared to duck.

Outside Patrice's window is a gorgeous view of Wrigley Field. I'm in the middle of moping, staring mindlessly at the empty ballpark below, when Patrice walks over and starts mussing my hair, what's left of it. She pushes it around until the top of the fringe that surrounds my head curls up onto the bald spot like a pair of horns trying to sprout. I read this as a sign of forgiveness, but when I try to return the touch, a brush of thumb against her breast, she grabs my wrists and leans back, surveying her work. Patrice is a classics major at Northwestern, and what she's doing is fashioning me into a famous Roman.

"So," I say. "Who am I?"

"What do you mean?"

"I mean, which Roman am I?"

Patrice opens her mouth, but the first vibrations of an approaching train stop her from speaking. It's the Evanston Express roaring up from the Belmont stop south of us. Patrice's apartment is so close to the tracks, I could lean out her window, if I felt like it, and knock on the passing train's windows. Every time a train goes by, it's an event around here. First, pots and pans rattle. Then the leaded glass of Patrice's bay window starts to shiver in its sockets, thrumming harder and harder. Then the beast itself appears—whistle blowing, metal grinding against metal, showers of sparks thrown at us from the hot rails. Eventually, the last car blasts past us, and the train snakes around another apartment building, disappearing from view. This happens several times an hour, all day long and most of the night.

"Wow," I say when it's over. "It's like friggin' Cape Canaveral around here. How do you stand it?"

"Stand it?" she asks. "How do I stand *what*?"

"Living here," I say.

Patrice lets go of my wrists and glares at me. I'm in trouble again, so I try steering us back on course. "Hey!" I say. "You never told me who I am. I'm a Roman, right? Come on, Patrice. Tell me. Who am I?"

"Nobody," she says. "You're nobody." Then she heads for the kitchen.

"We talked dirty on the phone last night," Darren says. Darren speaks out of the corner of his mouth, the corner without his cigarette, but the cigarette still bobs up and down with each syllable.

"Watch where you're walking," I say. "Keep your mind on work." We're carrying a gynecological examination table out of Student Health. It's the fifth one we've moved this morning, and I am now acutely aware of all the never-before-used muscles in my body, muscles that feel prodded with sharp instruments one second, then set ablaze the next. There are fifty-two rooms in Student Health—four of which are large waiting rooms—and we need every last thing cleared out of here by Monday morning before the wrecking ball strikes the east wing.

Darren says, "I've never talked dirty before. I mean *really* dirty."

"Why do you think I'm interested," I say. "Why?"

"She asked me if I've ever done a woman in the, you know, in the *butt*."

I get a better grip on the table by looping each of my arms underneath a stirrup. I grunt, heave the table higher.

Darren wiggles his end of the table through a doorframe. "Do you and Patrice ever talk dirty?"

"Patrice does. But that's just how she is. She talks dirty to everyone."

Darren and I stop when we reach Betty. Betty is the better of our two dump trucks—reliable, most days; Veronica, on the other hand, is sluggish, unpredictable, sometimes hard to start. My other two workers are loading Veronica full of cabinets with sliding glass doors, each cabinet as heavy as a pool table.

"I bet Betty here talks dirty," I say, lowering her lift. "Don't you, honey?" We scoot the exam table onto the lift, then I hit the lever so we can ride up with it. The back half of the truck is already cram-packed full of shit—waiting room furniture, upright scales, even the rubber torso of a woman, apparently for teaching breast self-examination techniques.

Darren flips the butt of his cigarette out the back of the truck, and without warning, he breaks into his impression of Tova: "*I want you to take that nice big throbbing cock of yours,*" he says, "*and I want you to stick it as far up my hairy ass as you can get it.*"

Two undergraduate girls appear just then from between Betty and Veronica. They are on their way to class, taking a shortcut across campus, thick books clutched to their chests. They glance quickly into the dark cavern of the truck, and when they see the two men inside—one hollow-eyed and talking dirty, the other sweaty and out of breath—they turn away quickly and pick up their pace.

Darren chuckles sheepishly. He fiddles with the stirrups, then stops what he's doing and says, "Just what the hell are these things for anyway? I've never seen them on any examination table *I've* been on." He wiggles the stirrups again, pushing them in and out of the table, the way a bored child would.

I reach over, take hold of Darren's chin, and playfully wag it back and forth. "You're in over your head, my friend," I say. "*Way* over."

After work, I sit in the darkened office and read through the printouts of our stock. We always have more discarded items than we have room to store—too many dormitory desks, too many chairs, too many outmoded computers and achingly slow dot-matrix printers. This is the hour when I decide what I'm going to take home. Will it be an oscillator today or will it be a set of free weights? Pyrex beakers or a swing-arm lamp? *This* or *that*? I'm never at a loss for things to choose from. The fact is, enough junk passes through here in a year's time to furnish a small country.

I settle on one of the small jewels of Surplus: a Bell and Howell sixteen-millimeter projector. The mere sound of its chugging sprockets and clicking shutters is enough to lull me back to grade school, all those long mornings spent slouching in webs of light while grainy films about photosynthesis, Stranger Danger, and reproduction danced and jerked before our eyes.

I carry the projector out to my truck, then return to Surplus. After some digging, I find a box of empty reels, two new projector lamps, and a stack of biology films about a fictional guy named Joe.

When I arrive at Patrice's apartment, she buzzes me in, but by the time I climb the stairs up to the third floor, she's already in the shower. I turn the Cubs game on and wait. The game on TV is the exact same game being played right outside Patrice's window at Wrigley Field. I hate baseball, actually, but I decide to do an experiment. I try to see if I can detect the millisecond delay in the broadcast. When the crowd outside the window roars over a nicely executed play, the crowd on TV roars as well. So here I sit: ear toward the TV, thumb on the remote control's volume, hoping to catch a moment so small it boggles the mind.

This is the sad way I occupy my time these days instead of having sex. Patrice is in the shower, and just a month ago I'd have been in there with her . . . *Patrice's back mashed up against the tub surround, her right leg raised and jutting out, the ball of her foot pressing down onto the tub's edge to give her some leverage while I move in and out of her, in and out.* This is how things used to be around here: *panties, still warm in the crotch, resting on the floor,* a sight that rarely fails to get me hard. But not anymore. Nope. I am reduced to watching a sport I hate and acting like a child. Another month, and I'll be outside plucking apart grasshoppers and poking sticks mindlessly into sinkholes of mud.

"Hey," I yell. "Is everything okay in there? You turned into a prune yet or what?"

No reply. Half an hour has come and gone, and Patrice is still in the shower. Then Jose Hernandez hits a home run for the Cubs, and the crowd roars loader than ever. There is no difference, I decide, between real time and TV time, so I give up my project. I turn to the picture window, hoping to see the ball as it soars out of the park and onto Waveland Avenue, but as soon as I lean closer, the window's glass explodes into the apartment, causing me to duck and fall out of my chair. For a second I think it's Jose Hernandez's ball that has smashed the window, but when I regain my balance, I see that it's a rock the size of a golfball. I poke my head out the broken window and catch a glimpse of the culprit, a grown man. He's running down the street, looking every so often over his shoulder, making sure no one's on his heels. I'm about to yell, but he turns a corner and disappears from my sight.

Patrice steps from the bathroom wearing a robe I've never seen, an extra-fluffy salmon-colored towel wrapped swami-style around her head. She doesn't seem to notice the shattered glass all over her living room. All she notices is *me*. She stares a bit, then yawns and says, "Oh. You're still here. Well, I need to paint my toenails," she says. "So if you'll excuse me." And then she is gone again, locked in the bathroom, leaving me once more to my own devices.

I sweep up the glass, seal the rock up inside of a Ziplock baggie, and set it on the kitchen table with a note (EXHIBIT A, it reads). Then I take the A/B train home.

Saturday morning, Patrice and I take a stroll through Lincoln Park while two men we don't know fix her window.

"They'll steal your CDs," I say.

Patrice shrugs.

"They'll take your TV," I say.

She shrugs again.

"Okay," I say. "It's your junk, not mine. Want to go to the zoo? The monkeys are always worth the price of admission."

"Monkey shmonkey," Patrice says.

"Not in the mood to visit the relatives today? So be it," I say.

We plop down onto a park bench, deciding our next move. Patrice leans her head back, and I figure she's soaking in the sun when she says, "That big cloud? Right there?" She points.

"What is it?" I ask.

"Hairy ass," she says.

"Really!" I say. At long last, I think. Abstinence has finally taken its toll on Patrice. We are riding the same wave. We are both seeing sex where there is no sex.

Patrice squints, shades her eyes, and says, "Hairy Ass Truman."

"Ah," I say. "Of course." First, Mousy Tongue; now, Hairy Ass.

"The cloud next to it?"

"Yes?" I say, but I am tired of her antics, tired of funny names and pointless cloud gazing.

Patrice turns to me and says, "It looks like *you*." She says this like an accusation.

I look up, and for once I see what she sees. The cloud *does* look like me. But it also looks like I'm wearing a fedora, and it would appear that I have a hard-on that's roughly twice as long as I am tall.

"And look," Patrice says. "Gerald Ford's over there. Sort of hovering behind you."

But now I'm lost again, unable to see anything other than myself.

"Gerald Ford," I say. "Now, *there's* a fascinating man, if you ask me. Here's a guy who forgave Nixon for his crimes. Nixon! Of all people! Ford found it in his heart to forgive this awful, evil man." I say all of this without any pretense of subtlety. The man who broke Patrice's window, I've decided, is her new lover, and what I need from Patrice is forgiveness, even if it means forgiveness for crimes I can't remember committing.

"It's called a pardon," Patrice says. "Ford *pardoned* Nixon, and I'm sure it was agreed upon before Nixon resigned. Part of the deal, I imagine."

I stand from the bench. I pace back and forth, then stop in front of Patrice. "I know what this is about. The old tomatoes, right? Don't tell me it's not. You're going to give me the old tomatoes. Am I right?"

I am saying all of this louder than I mean to, and people are watching us. They are watching *me*.

"Okay," I say. "Okay, okay. What did I do? I can't take this anymore. Tell me, would you? Tell me what I did so you can pardon me and we can move on."

"Why should I tell you if you can't remember?"

"Why?" I say. "*Why?*" Her question is a preposterous follow-up to my question, but I store it away as evidence—*concrete evidence*—of the difference not just between Patrice and myself, but between *all* men and women, from Adam and Eve to every last couple, fat and thin, young and old, here with us today in Lincoln Park.

I soften my voice and ask one last time: "Why?"

Patrice narrows her eyes. She says, "Does the word *fudge* mean anything to you?"

"Fudge? Are you saying I *lied* to you about something? Is that it? I *fudged* the truth?"

Patrice lets out a deep, hoarse sigh. It is a sigh of disgust, a sigh of finality. She stands and gathers her belongings. "Look," she says without looking at me. "I need to get going. My paper on the Triumvirate is due on Monday."

Patrice walks away, and I yell to her back, "I have *never* lied to you. Do you hear me? Never!"

Only after Patrice is gone and I have made a public spectacle of myself do I understand the fudge she means. My apartment is across the street from a shop called the Fudge Pot—they specialize in expensive fudge and chocolate—and a month ago Patrice gave me a twenty-dollar bill to buy her a brick of Turtle Deluxe. Two days later I found that same twenty-dollar bill crumpled in the front pocket of my jeans, and I had thought, *A windfall . . . too good to be true!* Here was twenty dollars I couldn't remember—a miracle, it had seemed, since I had less than ten bucks left to my name and payday was still a week away.

"Jesus Christ," I say. "*Fudge!*"

But it's not the fudge that's gotten to her. I realize that now. Fudge was merely a clue, a fingerprint attached to the larger issue at stake, and the only reason Patrice even brought it up was so that I might figure everything out for myself.

On the day that Patrice had given me the money to buy fudge, she had also broached the subject of me moving in with her. "It just makes sense," she'd said, and she started to tell me how much money I'd save in rent, but I cut her off: "Tell you what. Let's talk about this when I bring your fudge over. We'll sit right here and gorge ourselves on the most expensive chocolate in the city and hash out this moving-in-together thing once and for all. Whaddaya say?" "Deal," she said, and I said, "Deal." And then I never brought the fudge.

I had forgotten about the fudge, truly, or else I wouldn't have been so surprised at finding the twenty bucks two days later. It's possible that I subconsciously pushed the fudge aside, and this may be so. This was *not* the first time Patrice had suggested that I move in with her; it *was*, however, the first time I had agreed to talk about it. We had struck a deal! We may have even shook on it. But once the fudge was out of my mind, so was the deal. Until today.

"Ah, shit," I say. "Shit."

Parents move their children along. Couples look anywhere but at me.

"Shit, shit, shit," I say and throw my hands up and sigh.

There is a message on my answering machine from Darren when I get home. His afternoon date with Tova is over, and he's calling me from the emergency room at Rush-Presbyterian.

His voice, trembling, whispers from my machine: *I need a ride. And bring a soft pillow, would you?*

I am there in less than twenty minutes, watching the poor bastard limp toward my truck.

"Darren," I say, offering my hand, pulling him up into the cab.

"Ow, ow, *easy.*"

"What happened?" I ask.

"I need a drink," he says. "I need a drink to help the Darvocet go down."

"You really shouldn't mix—" I start to say, but Darren raises his hand.

We go to a bar called Smoky Joe's, and Darren sits quietly, wincing when he shifts from one haunch to the other. He shivers periodically and shakes his head as if trying to empty it—trying, I suspect, to shake off what must surely have been the horror show of his life, his date with Tova.

After an hour of silence and three shots of rail whiskey, Darren says, "It started out in good fun. I mean, hell, when she started talking dirty to me face to face, I couldn't *wait* for her to tie me to the bed. You'd have felt the same way."

"Of course," I say.

"I had one of those gags in my mouth. You know, the kind with the red ball. So I can't talk, right? And she says, 'I'm going to give you three chances to bail. I'll ask you three different times what you want me to do, and if you want me to stop, just wiggle the little toe on your right foot.' Simple enough, right? So she gives me my first chance right then and there, but since she hasn't done anything to me yet, I don't wiggle jack-shit. Then she does all sorts of, you know, *good* things to me, mostly with her tongue, so when she asks me the second time, I don't do anything again. Why would I? Hell, I was having a real bang-up time. Then she brings out the heavy artillery, and I start screaming my head off.

Hot wax, whips, dildoes—you name it. She even burnt me with my own cigarette." Darren opens his palm to show me, but I can't see much more than a blemish. He says, "She never asked me a third time. She never gave me my last chance."

"You're lucky she didn't kill you," I say.

"You're telling *me*," he says. "Swear to God, I thought it was check-out time."

We order more beer, more shots. Darren starts to light a cigarette, but once the lighter is in his hand, he thinks better of it, meticulously returning the cig to its pack and dropping the lighter back into his droopy shirt pocket.

"Jesus," I say. "This whole Tova experience, something like this'll probably sour you for good on dating."

"You'd think so, wouldn't you?" Darren says. "But I'm not so sure about that. I know you're not going to believe this, but it's opened my eyes. I was sitting in the emergency room and I started thinking, there's so much out there, so much shit I've never even *heard* about. It's weird, I know, but this whole experience brought that home for me. It made me realize that I haven't even scratched the surface yet. I don't know how to say this—I mean, Tova wasn't the right woman for me, but she unlocked this massive door of possibilities. *Infinite* possibilities, man."

"You're drunk," I say.

"No, no, I mean it," Darren says.

"I shouldn't have let you mix the booze and pills," I say. "Listen to yourself. A woman just rammed you with a dildo, and you're waxing philosophic on me."

"Okay," Darren says. "Whatever. But I don't see what's so goddamn exciting in *your* life that you think you can criticize *mine*." He lifts his drink and starts to lean back quickly in his chair, his cue to me that the conversation is over, but a sharp pain rockets through his ass, and Darren lets out a yelp that causes half the patrons to turn and look at us.

I'm pissed, but I don't say so. I stew instead. I can settle into silence like no one else I know. Part of why I'm pissed, though, is because Darren has unwittingly stumbled upon a few sad truths. What *is* so goddamn exciting in my life? Why *do* I think I'm in a position to criticize him?

"Excuse me," I say. On my way to the men's room, I stop at the pay phone and call Patrice. I get her answering machine, so I leave a message, telling her to meet me at my apartment at midnight, that we need to talk tonight, we need to hammer out, one way or the other, what's left of our future together. "The old tomatoes," I say and hang up.

Back at the table, I ask Darren if he can give me a hand. "I need to move a few things from Surplus to my apartment."

Darren lets out a loud stage laugh. "Are you kidding?" he asks. With much more caution this time, he leans back in his chair. Then he proceeds to wag his head at me and snort and look around the bar at the other patrons, all for dramatic effect. "Haven't you heard anything I've been saying?" he says. "I mean, look at me. I'm in pain. I can barely *walk*."

I remove four fifty-dollar bills from my wallet and slap them down in front of him.

"Okay," Darren says. "All right. What the hell."

Darren and I haul the last heavy item up to my apartment by nine o'clock. After Darren leaves, I shower and shave, and by the time Patrice knocks at the door just shy of midnight, everything is in perfect order, so I yell for her to come in.

"What's all this?" she asks. "What's going on here?"

I'm standing behind the check-in partition, hands clasped on the counter. I'm wearing a long, white examination coat and a stethoscope around my neck. From the *Highlights for Children* scattered about the room to the Norman Rockwell artwork on the wall, my apartment has been converted into a doctor's office, courtesy of Surplus and the old Student Health building.

Patrice reaches across the check-in counter, lifts the stethoscope, and holds it to her mouth. "*You*," she says, "are a man with a loose screw. You realize that, don't you?"

"Do you have an appointment?" I ask.

She drops the stethoscope. She huffs and shakes her head. "Yeah, sure, why not?"

"Well then," I say. "Please have a seat." When she doesn't move, I point to the waiting room.

"This is too much," she says, but she does as she's told. She sits in the middle of a row of connected chairs. When she realizes that I'm not going to say anything right away, she crosses her legs and picks up a magazine, flipping through it once, quickly, then tossing it aside. She taps her fingers impatiently on the chrome of the chair's armrests. I open and close filing cabinet drawers, making a show of it, before flipping off the lights. "Hey!" Patrice yells, but I shush her. The old Bell and Howell sixteen-millimeter projector starts to chug, and a funnel of light shoots across the room. The shadow of Patrice's head floats on the screen behind her.

"Scoot down," I say.

Patrice looks over her shoulder, sees the eerie silhouette of her own head, then slides down onto the floor. The movie is a classic: *Joe's Heart*. It is one in a series of movies about Joe's various organs. I sit next to Patrice. I press my mouth against her ear and ask, "Are you here to see a physician?"

"I guess so," she says, playing along, seeming to get into the spirit of the night.

I loop a lock of Patrice's hair behind her ear, and while Joe's heart pounds around us, I lean in and kiss her cheek. "What do you think about Joe?" I ask softly. "He seems in pretty good shape."

Between kisses, Patrice says, "He should probably avoid strenuous activity. Too much stress on his heart—" we kiss "—might kill him."

"You think?" I ask.

"Absolutely," Patrice says.

"Here," I say. "I want you to follow me."

She hesitates. "I don't know," she says. "I don't think we should go to the bedroom."

"The bedroom!" I say. "Ha! What kind of a doctor do you think I am? That's the *examination room*. And I need to *examine* you. So *please*. Please do as I say. Let's not put up a fight."

Amazingly, she doesn't. She stands, and with one finger hooked into my collar, she tags along behind me.

"Wow," she says when I open the door. "Look at this."

The room has an examination table, pale green cabinets, and three shiny canisters labeled for gauze, cotton, and tongue depressors. I say, "Please remove your clothes and slip into this." I hold out a thin, pale green gown with ties in the back.

The room's only window is open, the curtains are parted, and it is cooler here than in the rest of the house. Antiseptic. The lights are off, but there is moonlight to see by, moonlight and the play of light and shadow from the movie in the other room. Joe's heart thumps on, gently vibrating the floor. My own heart pounds away, beating, I realize, much harder and faster than Joe's.

"You'll feel better," I say, "once you've put this on."

Patrice takes the gown. She shrugs out of her sweater, then un-latches her bra. She uses the ball of one foot to remove the shoe of the other, then she wriggles free of her jeans. She is standing in front of me in nothing but panties and socks, and when she peels down the panties—silky fabric rubbing against thick ring-lets of pubic hair—the friction creates static electricity, and blue sparks flicker and crackle between Patrice's legs. The hair on my arms lifts. In an instant, the air in the room has become danger-ously alive.

"May I leave my socks on?" she asks. She is wearing white tube socks scrunched down to her ankles.

"You may not," I say. "The socks must come off as well."

She removes them using only her feet. "Okay. I'm sockless now," she says.

"Sockless indeed," I say. "Now up on the table." I pat the sani-tary sheet that covers the exam table. "Upsy-daisy," I say. She tries being as gentle as possible, but the paper sheet still crunches beneath her. "Lean back," I say. "Relax. There you go. Now, put your feet in the stirrups." Patrice takes a deep breath. "Good, good," I say once her feet are in place. "Now, scooch forward. That's right. Scooch right up to the edge of the table."

Joe's heart suddenly quits beating. The last of the film runs through the sprocket, and a blast of hot white light illuminates the living room, brightening our room as well. Patrice's gown is wadded up around her waist. Between her legs, she is wet and thick, as open and raw as a fresh wound, and I am about to touch her, to put a finger inside of her, but then I stop. "Mousy Tongue," I say. I reach over to a box of powdered rubber gloves and pull four out. I take the first one, wrap it around her left ankle and the stirrup, and tie it in a knot. A second glove keeps her right ankle from moving. I tie her wrists to the insulated pipes above and be-hind her head.

"You're going to torture me," she says.

"Nope," I say. "I'm going to *cure* you." I wheel over a table of surgical instruments, on which sets a pair of scissors. Starting from the bottom hem, working my way up to her neckline, I snip away the gown. "Patrice, Patrice," I say. Patrice is completely naked now and goose-pimpled in the chilly room.

"Do something to me," she says.

"I will," I say, and I lift the lid off the top of the tin canister labeled GAUZE. I reach in and pull out the first of what I owe her.

"What's that?" she asks.

"Turtle Deluxe," I say. "See these canisters? They're full of fudge. All three of them. Sixty dollars' worth of fudge, to be precise. Interest on your twenty bucks," I say. I hold the fudge near her mouth, but not close enough for her to reach it. Patrice lifts her head off the table, opens her mouth. "C'mon," I say. "Have some." Patrice tries touching the fudge with her tongue, but she fails. When I finally give her a bite, I stand back and watch her savor it. The noises she makes—deep groans of satisfaction—are the same noises she makes when I am inside her and moving slowly. She swallows the bite, licks her lips.

"We had a deal," she finally says.

"The fudge has arrived," I say. "The deal's back on."

"I want to make something perfectly clear," she says. "I'm going to give you one more chance, but there is a finite limit to how many chances I can give." She is shivering as she speaks. The veins beneath her skin are visible, and there is evidence in every soft tissue of her body that the blood inside those veins is pumping hard and fast. "Understood?" she asks.

"It seems to me," I say, "that you're the one tied up. I'm not sure that you're in the best position to negotiate."

"Well, look at you," she says. "If it isn't my little Caligula."

She shifts her focus to the fudge again and parts her lips. She strains to reach my hand, arching her back and stretching the rubber gloves. I let her take a huge bite this time, a bite nearly too large for her mouth.

"Is that enough?" I ask.

"No," she manages to say.

I give her yet another bite, though there is barely room for any more in her mouth. "Mmmmm," she says, and while she chews and swallows, dribbles of juice running down her chin, I slip out of my clothes. I ask her if she wants more, and she nods. I am standing between her legs. I lean forward and place the last of the fudge in my hand onto her tongue. Outside it is dark, the hoots and jeers of nighttime carousers drift up to the open window, and the clouds passing the moon look like clouds.

The
Politics of
Correctness

At first Nick thought it was his heart—arrhythmia, palpitations, something stress related—but as the thrumming grew louder and the windows began to vibrate, he realized it wasn't his heart at all: it was rap music blasting from an approaching car. Nick shut his eyes, the monotonous beat consuming his life. It was as though the house itself had become a heart, and Nick were inside, lost in a chamber, dizzily trying to escape while the world swirled around him. Blood pulsed through his eyelids, and when he tilted his head up toward the ceiling light, he actually saw red. The car, apparently, had stopped.

Nick and Karen had been pulling up carpet tacks, finding hundreds more than they'd anticipated. He stood now, walked to the front door, and cupped his palms against the diamond-shaped window, peering out into the dark. "It's *him* again," he yelled to Karen. For the past three weeks, since they'd moved into their new house, a gold Malibu with dark, smoky windows had begun to park in front of their mailbox. The driver always played music full volume until someone else drove up to talk, parking driver's window to driver's window, the way cops park and talk to one another.

Nick returned to the bedroom, where Karen sat cross-legged, her palms red and puffy from pulling up the tacks. He said, "Why us? What the hell does he have against *us*?" But even as he spoke, Nick knew the answer to that one. Before they had bought their house, it had been on the market for a year, long enough for the local crackheads and dope pushers to appropriate it as their own. Now, in addition to suffering the brain-wrenching stress of financing a home, it was beginning to look as though Nick and Karen would have to reclaim their house from thugs as well.

Nick said, "I should call the police."

Without looking up, Karen said, "I wouldn't do that." She continued working the vise-grips, trying to loosen a nail, twisting it right and left. She had studied to be an interior decorator, but after they'd moved to town, over a year ago, she settled for a part-time job selling wallpaper at the Paint Depot. Now, these past three weeks, she'd slipped far too easily into the leisure of home repair. Nick knew that sooner or later he would have to broach the subject—they needed more money—but each time he considered putting it on the table for discussion, he hesitated, then let it go altogether, fearing a blowup. Their last blowup had sent Karen running to the Starlite Motel for the night. The Starlite was a notorious location for various rendezvous of indiscretion (TWO HOUR NAP SPECIAL, the marquee advertised), and Nick couldn't bear the thought of Karen spending another night there.

"I wouldn't call the police," Karen said. "The guy in the Malibu might retaliate. Why don't we just wait and see what happens? Maybe he'll find someplace else to go."

"All right," Nick said. "Okay. Sure. Let's wait." And when he sat down, he took a hammer and pounded in two nails he couldn't release.

In the men's room, in the privacy of a stall, Nick tried composing himself before having to go teach. For two weeks now he'd been promising to hand back his students' essays, but each night after dinner he would sit on the couch and stare at the stack piled on the coffee table, falling into a deep trance and unable to move until Karen came along and nudged him.

Nick was what the English Department called "part-time," though he taught four classes each semester, and of those four, three were freshman-level writing courses. He had made the grave error of thinking it was going to be easier than this. When he was nineteen, an English major at Southern Illinois, he would spend long hours at the library, piling stacks of journals in his cubicle, rubbing his fingers across the words, feeling the letterpress. There was something about the smell of the books themselves, as if they'd been tucked away in somebody's attic, that made him drowsy; and while he drifted off, he'd try to imagine an older version of himself, this older Nick wandering through some wooded campus, a leather-bound copy of *Omoo* tucked securely into the pit of his arm, on his way to meet with students who'd sought him out for an independent study. There were other fantasies, too. Sabbaticals: sitting in his own private library at home, feet propped up, a volume of the OED like a concrete block in his lap, a snifter of port within reach—all of this he'd imagined while the fluorescent lights of Morris Library hummed overhead, a steady buzz like a thousand winged insects getting ready to descend upon him, lift him out of his chair, and carry him away.

Now, at thirty-five, his student loans totaled more than $72,000. Each day he plodded across a quad littered with abstract art of the 1970s—steel beams, for the most part, welded together by M.F.A. students. Out of the corner of one's eye, the campus could easily have been mistaken for an abandoned construction site. What little free time Nick had these days was spent reading carelessly typed essays about "The Big Football Game!" or "The Big Summer Vacation!" or "The Big Car Accident!" Every three weeks he picked up a new batch, and each time he did this, he wanted to kill himself. The stack of ungraded papers was like a dead horse strapped to his back.

Last spring, at a department meeting, a senior faculty member asked Nick how he was getting along, and Nick remarked off-handedly that a four/four courseload was draining.

"You know what I mean?" he said. "I just feel *drained* all the time."

He'd expected a few sympathetic nods—nothing more, really—but to his horror, the tenured faculty began examining at length the metaphorical implications of the word *draining*.

Joy Lampert, director of composition, took the lead. She had a genius for turning everything into a political issue. Not the politics of government, but the more elusive kind: the politics of speech, the politics of sex, the politics of race. For her, every topic, every word and gesture, had a political implication.

"It's so *medical*," Joy Lampert said. "It's as though we're living in medieval times, and what we do here is strap our faculty down for a bloodletting. I don't know. *Draining*. It's not a healthy way to look at teaching. We need to be more positive. If *we're* not positive, how can we expect our students to be?"

Which led Joy to the next issue at hand: changing the name of the writing lab.

"There it is again!" she said. "That *medical* metaphor. Why would our students want to come to a *lab* for help? They probably assume we're going to take a blood sample!"

Oh, for Christ's sake, Nick wanted to say, *you've GOT to be kidding*. But he couldn't say a word. At the end of each semester, he was dispensable. And there was the new house to think of, along with the weight of everything the new house meant: his marriage, in particular.

Now, sitting in the restroom, Nick racked his brain for an excuse, something his students might actually buy, when someone knocked on the wall between the two stalls.

"Excuse me," a voice said, "but who am I sitting next to?"

Nick didn't say anything.

"Who's there?" the voice said.

Nick looked for a screw hole in the wall, making sure no one was peeking in on him. He despised public restrooms and had always feared the wandering eyes of perverts. When all appeared to be safe, he said, "Nick."

"Nick *who*?"

"Henderson," Nick said.

"Are you feeling well, friend?"

"Why?"

"You were mumbling."

"Really? Hm." He cleared his throat. "Well, who're you?"

"Quentin Brock."

Nick had seen his office—Quentin Brock, Professor Emeritus—but he'd never seen anyone entering or leaving, and no one had ever mentioned him.

Quentin said, "Be careful. This job can push you over the brink. I've seen it happen too many times, my poor colleagues locked up at Riverdale, reciting Polonius's famous speech to Laertes over and over to the doctors and nurses. 'To thine own self be true.' You know the speech, I'm sure. It's a sad thing to see, my friend. Terribly sad."

There was silence. Then Nick said, "I need to go. I think I'm late."

Quentin said, "Be very careful. This is a dangerous place."

"I'll try," Nick said.

Leaving the mailroom, Nick nearly knocked Joy Lampert to the ground. He reached out to make sure she was okay, but she took a step back, away from his hand, as though he had reached toward her not to help but to feel her up.

"Nick," she said, catching her breath. Then she forced a smile and motioned with a nod toward the stack of junk mail he was holding. "I certainly hope that you and your partner can make it to the party this year."

"Me and *who*?" he said. "Oh-oh, my *wife*, you mean."

Normally, Nick tossed his departmental mail into the recycling bin without so much as even a cursory look, but at the mention of Joy's party, he looked down and found her invitation to the annual costume party. It had been photocopied onto blue-and-white marble paper, the words painstakingly written in calligraphy. A dialogue balloon spewed from Shakespeare's mouth: OPEN BAR(D)!

Joy said, "I hear you and Karen have bought a house. I hope I'm not prying, but is it true?"

"Fourth and Temple," Nick said. "What do they call that area? T-Town?"

"Oh really," Joy said. She lowered her voice and said, "That's exciting, isn't it? It's a very *multicultural* area."

"Yeah, well," Nick said. "Sure. You could call it that, I suppose. Thing is, the house was in our price range. You know—*cheap.* About the only thing in town we could afford, to be honest."

Joy said, "I only wish it were more—I don't know—*diverse* where I live."

Nick had been to Joy's house before: cupolas, vaulted ceilings, a library. "Tell you what," Nick said. "I'll trade you." He winked at her and smiled, hoping to keep things light, but Joy had already pursed her lips. It was a gesture she made whenever someone said something she didn't want to hear. She did it so often, though, that lines had begun to radiate from her mouth, giving the impression of a permanent pucker.

She checked her watch and said, "I better go," and walked away.

Surely she knew the truth about T-Town. Surely she understood Nick's reservations. All she had to do was open the newspaper. Murders, rapes, burglaries—all of it was happening in T-Town. Where Joy lived, they piped *Frank Sinatra's Greatest Hits* over a PA system during the long winter holidays. They placed candles in bags and set them along the sidewalks on Christmas Eve. In T-Town, if you weren't careful, they burned your house down for you, no charge.

———

Nick lifted the first freshman comp essay off the top of the stack.

GRADUATION

THE BIG DAY WAS FINALLY HERE!!!

Nick got up and poured himself a gin and tonic, stirring it with his finger. He stumbled upon Karen in the bathroom, where she stood wearing goggles and rubbing a putty knife up and down the window frame. For the past three days she'd been stripping away layers of paint, and for the first time since she'd begun, she could see wood.

Nick picked up the can of paint stripper, read the label, and said, "What do you think? If I drank this, would it kill me?" He leaned toward Karen and flicked a paint chip off her goggles. Karen dipped her paintbrush into the coffee can of stripper, then slathered more goop onto the window frame. Instantly, old paint bubbled.

Karen was certain they could restore the entire house—it had been rental property before they bought it—and each day she found signs of promise: hidden under the green shag carpet were oak floors; beneath chipped paint, brass doorknobs and ornate plates with holes for skeleton keys. But all of this struck Nick as the height of futility. Often at night, while drifting to sleep, he pictured them restoring not a house but a sinking ship—the *Titanic* at the very moment of impact—and while he searched desperately for the life jackets and rafts, Karen was busy unrolling the new linoleum.

Nick sat on the toilet seat, the fumes making him weak and lightheaded. He watched his hands shake. Before he could say anything, his feet began to tingle, and for a split second, he thought he was experiencing brain damage. The warning on the can, after all, had been put there for a reason, and he was beginning to berate himself for not taking it seriously. But the tingle in his feet became stronger, followed by rattling windows and vibrating walls and the distinct pounding of rap music louder than it had ever been before.

Nick stomped into the living room. He pressed his face against the diamond-shaped window, which buzzed against his forehead.

"Karen," he yelled. "He's on our lawn!"

The Malibu was parked on the stretch of lawn between the sidewalk and the street. Its front bumper touched the post of his mailbox. The passenger-side window crept part way down, and a gloved hand emerged, tossing four bottles onto Nick's property. The car suddenly lurched forward, pushing the post of the mailbox so that it jutted from the ground at an angle. The Malibu backed up, digging up the lawn with a rear tire, then pulled onto the street and squealed away.

Nick opened the front door and walked outside. He picked up one of the bottles—a 40-ounce Colt 45. He tried yanking the mailbox back into place, but the post only wiggled in the ground, its door hanging open like a giant postmodern tongue sticking out at him.

At the annual textbook meeting, Joy held up a thick anthology and said, "Take this one, for instance. It *claims* to be multicultural, but I'm not so sure." She pursed her lips.

Irene, a Ph.D. grad student—self-appointed pack leader of women's studies—rifled angrily through the first anthology. "Hmmph. Just another Dead-White-Male-centered textbook." She dropped it onto the floor for emphasis, startling everyone in the room. "Why do we even *need* a textbook?" she asked. "I say, empower the students! Let's use *their* essays as the text for the course!"

"That is certainly an option," Joy said.

Nick shifted his weight in the tight confines of his student desk. He checked his watch. He thumped its face a few times with his forefinger, fearing it had stopped. Then Joy singled out a grad student Nick had never seen before, a woman whose chair hadn't been pulled tightly into the circle. Joy said, "Lauri. I see you've brought along a book. Would you like to *share* it with us?"

Lauri said, "Not really. It's just a grammar handbook. It wasn't on the list of approved texts, so I guess I need you to sign this sheet." She leaned forward, extending her arm with the piece of paper. When Joy didn't reach for it, Lauri said, "The secretary told me I need your approval." She pointed to the exact line where Joy's signature was required.

"Now *Lauri*," Joy said, wagging her head. "Really. Don't you think they *know* all of that already?"

"What? You're kidding, right?"

Joy said, "It's just that grammar handbooks are so . . . oh, I don't know . . . *patriarchal.*"

Lauri said, "Patriarchal? What are you talking about?" Her pen slipped from her hand, rolling to the center of the circle, and though everyone watched it roll away, no one budged to retrieve it.

Joy said, "You know how I feel about handbooks, Lauri. They're so intimidating. So structured. It's important that we don't *silence* anyone."

Lauri stuffed the handbook into a backpack, stood, and worked her way toward the door. She said, "So the answer's *no*?"

"I'm sorry," Joy said, and when Lauri stepped out into the hall, the door slamming shut behind her, Joy shut her eyes.

Irene huffed and said, "She doesn't get it, does she? And look at all that makeup she was wearing. Talk about male-identified!"

Quentin Brock knocked once and said, "Is that you, Nick?"

"Yeah, it's me."

"Are you a Renaissance man, Nick?"

"Nineteenth century," Nick said.

"Don't ask me why, but I took you for a Renaissance man. No offense."

"None taken."

"Nineteenth century, you say? British? American?"

"American," Nick said.

"I prefer the Russians myself. Tolstoy. Dostoyevsky. Chekhov."

Nick was rubbing his fingertips across primitive drawings of genitalia, over the gouged religious verses and the gay-bashing death threats written in Magic Marker. It was the universal discourse of restroom stalls, perhaps the only time his students actually took freewriting seriously.

Quentin said, "Friend, you should be careful. You're not a Renaissance man, but surely you've read Marlowe. Remember what they did to Edward the Second?"

Nick dimly recalled a hot poker. Was he thinking of the right play? "Oh, come on," he said. "They're not *that* bad."

"Don't kid yourself," Quentin said.

The bathroom floor was covered with canvas tarps. Using the flat edge of a screwdriver, Karen pried off the paint can's lid. Carefully, she poured thick white paint into a tray. "Maybe you're reading this Joy character all wrong," Karen said. "Maybe she's got a point."

"A *point*?" Nick said.

"Sure," Karen said. "I mean, I *hated* grammar lessons in school. I *loathed* them. I *still* don't know what a dangling participle is. And you know what? I don't care. What good's it ever going to do me?"

"Listen," Nick said. "The point is this: she humiliated that poor girl in front of her own colleagues. Joy was trying to teach her a lesson. This doesn't have anything to do with a goddamn comma splice. Jesus, Karen, whose side are you on, anyway?" He waited a moment for an answer, then gave up and walked to the kitchen to fix himself a drink. While standing in the kitchen, he found himself slowly engulfed by a crescendoing brightness. Then a spotlight bloomed across the kitchen cabinets. He opened the side door. He didn't expect to see the Malibu—no music was playing—yet there it sat, high beams on, parked in his driveway. His first impulse was to shut and lock the door. But the initial wave of fear soon passed, eclipsed by rage, and Nick found himself drawn toward the car, fueled by adrenaline.

Before he could think through what he would say or do, he knocked on the Malibu's window, but nothing came of it. He knocked again, and this time, as his fist met the window, Nick felt as though he were hovering above the scene, watching himself knock on this stranger's car. He knew he should compose himself, turn, and walk back into his house to call the police, but the driver's window crept open about an inch, enough for Nick to see the top of someone's head.

Nick said, "This is private property."

Someone inside the car laughed.

Nick said, "I want you to move this car right now."

More laughter floated his way.

Nick cleared his throat. "I could just as easily call the police."

At that, the door swung open, stopping shy of Nick's knees, and a tall black man with a badly pocked face stepped from the car. The man's eyes, though glazed over, were serious and unblinking. He wore leather gloves and a thick player's jacket, the kind of jacket gang members killed one another for.

The man said, "I *dare* you to call the po-lice. I'll kick your sorry *ass*. I *dare* you to call the mother-fuckin' po-lice, man."

"Look," Nick said. "I don't think I'm being unreasonable." He tried draining his voice of anger, hoping to prove that he could construct a rational and sound argument. He said, "I own this house, you're in my driveway, and I'm asking you to move. It's that simple."

"You gonna call the po-lice, huh?" the man said. He stepped around the car door, walking toward Nick. "You the *man*, huh? That it? You the *man*?"

Nick shuffled backwards, his thoughts heading in various logical but polar directions. He reprimanded himself for not thinking this through; searched his memory for the nearest makeshift weapon; made a list of everything Karen had done to the house, along with everything she'd planned yet to do.

Nick said, "This is private property." Having said so, he turned quickly and broke for the door. He barely made it inside and pushed shut the door when the man began twisting the knob. The twisting stopped, and Nick thought, *Thank God, it's over*, but when he pushed aside the thin curtain and looked out, a gloved fist smashed through the window. Nick backed up, glass shards resting on the tips of his shoes. Once the door began to buckle with each kick, the gravity of the situation became instantly clear to Nick: this man, this *stranger*, was going to break into their house and kill them.

"*Karen!*" Nick yelled. "*Karen, call the police!*" But even as he yelled, he knew Karen couldn't hear him. The bathroom fan was running.

Nick fumbled with the portable phone, punching buttons, but his fingers kept pushing too many of the wrong numbers. He switched the phone off, then back on. Calmly, he pressed 9-1-1, but he moved around the house in a state of panic, searching for protection, though nothing he and Karen owned looked capable of inflicting bodily harm. A woman on the line tried asking Nick questions while he clawed through a drawer, searching for knives. He was talking over the woman, jumbling his words, one thought leapfrogging another. Back in the kitchen, where he was most likely to find a weapon of some kind—an ice pick, a skillet, a corkscrew—he noticed that the man was heading back to his car. Nick crept up to the busted window and peeked out, hoping to catch a license plate number, but the plate was covered with a sheet of smoky plastic. Soon after, the car backed up and disappeared behind a scrim of dust. Nick stepped from his house and stood in his driveway, clutching the portable phone to his head while his neighbors stood on their porches or lawns and looked on. "They're getting a big kick out of this," Nick was saying into the phone. "They're loving every goddamn minute of it." And while Karen stood behind him, a paint roller in her hand, asking, "What happened to the window? Who are you talking to?" a muffled voice in his ear was telling him to please calm down and start from the beginning.

Mitch Crowley, clad in camouflage and an orange hunter's cap, introduced himself as the sole owner of Target Used Guns.

"You want protection?" he said and reached into the display case, pulling out a snub-nosed .38 for Nick to examine. "This one here will do the trick. We got it from a police force, and despite what you might think, the police don't use their guns all that much. It's not one of ours, though. It's from the Korean police force, but it's not a chink gun, no sir. It's a genuine Smith and Wesson, and it'll do the job. Of course, that's if a .38's what you want. I've got .22s, too. Hell, I've got .22s coming out of my *ass*. But some guys won't touch a .22. They say it's only good for girls or faggots, but let me tell you, it won't make a goddamn difference if you shoot someone in the heart with a .38 or a .22— either one will put the perp down and out of commission."

Nick took the gun from Mitch and held it. On the wall, behind the owner, hung a poster of Hitler. It said, NEXT TIME I COME BACK, NO MORE MISTER NICE GUY.

At that moment, Nick felt a hundred thousand miles away from the bulletin boards outside the English Department, where posters called for papers on "Queer Theory," "Pedagogy of the Oppressed," and "Postcolonialism." Yet here he was, only ten blocks away, where the world of the English Department—

what they did and what they talked about—meant absolutely nothing.

"How much?" Nick asked, twisting the gun back and forth.

"That one there's two hundred. Not a bad price."

"I like it," Nick said. "I like how it feels. Only thing is, I need to talk it over with my wife."

"Absolutely," Mitch said. "Bring the little lady by. See how it fits her hand. We can change the grip, but maybe it's too heavy. You wouldn't think of buying her shoes without knowing her size, would you? Hell no!"

Mitch took the gun from Nick, his forefinger on the trigger, and said, "So what's your line of work?"

"Teacher. I teach English."

"Really? I shouldn't say this, but I hate English. I hate writing, and I hate reading. Always have."

"That's funny," Nick said, "because I hate teaching it."

That night, on their way to the costume party at Joy's house, Nick told Karen that he'd priced a few guns. "Something to think about," he said.

They drove several miles, coasting from the decrepit houses of T-Town, past Sherlock Holmes's Mobile Homes, and through the downtown campus. Then came the bungalows built before the Second World War, followed by a castle divided into luxury apartments, and, finally, the neighborhood of Victorians. Before Nick turned off for Canterbury Avenue, where Joy's house could be found shrouded in soft party light, Karen said, "I don't want a gun in the house."

"Okay. Whatever." Nick parked the car so fast he hit the car in front of him. "Ooops," he said. He got out and slammed the door. He stayed a few paces ahead of Karen until they reached Joy's house. Then he jerked open the door and said, "After you."

Inside, they bumped into the likes of Gertrude Stein, Shylock, Andrea Dworkin, Phillis Wheatley, and Oscar Wilde. Joy had hired a professional bartender, a man Nick recognized from Barrymore's, and leaning against the bar was the chairman of the department, Bart Gerard, looking as he always did—tweed jacket with arm patches, wool slacks, scuffed wingtip shoes—except for one new touch: a Charlie Brown mask held tightly against his face with a rubber band. His gray curly hair loomed above Charlie Brown's bald head.

Bart spotted Nick, raised his drink high into the air, as if to toast, and said, louder than necessary, "Good Grief!" Then he inserted the straw into the slit of Charlie Brown's plastic lips and drained his drink.

Nick ordered a mixed drink for himself and a wine cooler for Karen. As he stood waiting, Gertrude Stein—director of women's studies—walked up to him, poked her finger into his solar plexus, and said, "Good costume, Henderson. You're the only Walt Whitman here."

Nick reached up and checked his beard and mustache. Only an hour ago he'd applied it to his face with spirit gum. He'd bought the suit at a Salvation Army, something that might pass for nineteenth-century garb.

"I hate to disappoint you," he said, "but I'm not Walt Whitman. I'm Herman Melville. And Karen here, she's Zelda Fitzgerald."

Karen, dressed like a flapper, held a copy of *The Great Gatsby* in her free hand.

Stein eyed both of them suspiciously, then wandered away. In the distance, Nick could hear Bart Gerard greeting the new arrivals. "Good Grief!" the man kept yelling.

Nick finished his drink and ordered another. He thought of his students' ungraded essays at home and of the next batch he would be picking up on Monday, and he finished three more drinks in rapid succession.

"So," Nick said. "What do you think?"

Karen looked above her, surveying the rim of the ceiling. "This house is *beautiful*. I mean, my God, look at all the work they put into it."

"Yeah, well," Nick said. "I'm sure they hired it out."

Karen said, "Look in that room over there. Is that the bedroom? Look at the wainscoting. And look at the leaded glass. I bet that's original." Then she gasped. "The wallpaper!" she said. "Do you see that? It's called Modern Pastiche. We sell it at the Depot. Guess how much."

Nick shrugged. "Couldn't tell you."

"One hundred and ten dollars," Karen said, "per double roll. And I'd say this took, oh, let's see . . ." She looked around. "Fifteen double rolls? Twenty, maybe?"

"TWO THOUSAND DOLLARS FOR WALLPAPER!" Nick yelled. He walked to a wall for closer inspection, scratching at it with a fingernail. Then he leaned in close and sniffed it.

"It's beautiful, isn't it?" Karen whispered behind him.

"Jesus Christ," Nick said, shaking his head. "Well, if you want to meet the hosts, they're right over there. That one's Joy," he said, pointing. "And the guy next to her. That's Ted, her *partner*."

"They're not wearing costumes," Karen said. "Don't you think that's odd?"

"Sure they're wearing costumes," Nick said. "Just read their name tags. *She's* Ann Berthoff, and *he's* Peter Elbow. Very clever, these people. *Very clever*."

Karen looked at Nick, confused, her eyes narrowing.

Nick gasped and covered his mouth, feigning surprise. "Don't tell me you never *heard* of Berthoff or Elbow. Why, they're famous composition theorists." He waved his arm, a game-show gesture. He slammed his drink and said, "An oxymoron, of course, my dear."

"You're drunk already, aren't you?"

"Hey. Did I tell you? I saw the strangest thing this morning. A poster of Hitler. You want to hear what it said?"

"Please don't embarrass me tonight," Karen said.

Nick leaned toward her, and through clenched teeth he said, "I want to kill that son of a bitch in the Malibu. I want to see him go down." He turned and ordered another drink.

Soon, with a pitcher of rum and Coke, Nick led Karen to a card table where they sat alone. The party was in full swing, a rotation of jazz standards in the CD player. Gertrude Stein was slow-dancing with Oscar Wilde, while Andrea Dworkin whispered something into Shylock's ear. Charlie Brown stood at the door, passing out name tags and raising his drink high into the air. Grad students wandered off to the bathroom, heads down, trying, no doubt, to remain inconspicuous but returning flushed and smiling, obviously stoned. While Nick poured one rum and Coke after another, Karen sat beside him and read *The Great Gatsby*.

Then Joy and her husband, Peter Elbow, came over, and Joy said, "Are these seats taken?"

Nick motioned with his hand to sit down.

Joy said, "You make a *very* convincing Walt Whitman, Nick."

"Really?" Nick said. "That's odd, because I'm *not* Walt Whitman. I'm Herman Melville. And this is my wife, Zelda Fitzgerald."

"Why, yes, of course," she said. "*Zelda.*" She smiled and nodded vigorously, pleased with the politics of Karen's costume. "What a wonderful choice. Zelda Fitzgerald." She cleared her throat and said, "Did you know that Zelda would write short stories and that F. Scott would publish them under *his* name? A crime. Literary *rape*, I call it."

"Is that a fact," Peter Elbow said. "*He* would publish *her* stories under *his* name? Hmmph." He shook his head.

Nick jiggled his pitcher. Ice rattled at the bottom. "Excuse me," he said, "but I need to fill this baby back up."

At the bar, Nick stood next to a grad student whose name tag said Allen Ginsberg. Nick smiled and said, "Where's your costume, pal?"

The student, a thin boy with a wiry goatee, said, "It's in my shirt pocket."

"I don't get it."

"A one-hitter, dude. Wanna get high?"

Nick joined the student outside, between two healthy shrubs, and smoked a solidly packed one-hitter until he accidentally sucked the burning tip through the brass core. "Shit," he said. "I burned my tongue." He wandered back to the house, locked himself in the bathroom upstairs, and stared in the mirror at his tongue. A small black dot was on the tip, surrounded by a dark red circle. He let go of his tongue and stepped out of the bathroom and into the hall, thinking he'd heard someone whispering to him, but all he found were the ghosts of dead family members staring at him from sepia photos on the wall, and as he walked to the stairwell, they followed him with their translucent eyes.

Downstairs at the bar, Nick found his pitcher of rum and Coke replenished. Carefully, he carried it to the table and plopped down in his chair. He kept pinching his tongue and pouring rum and Coke in his lap.

"Here, honey," Karen said. "Why don't you put that down?"

"I'm thirsty," Nick said and smiled at Joy. Then, for lack of anything better to do, he leaned forward and began telling Joy and her husband about the man in the Malibu and what had happened to him yesterday.

"So this is the fourteenth, fifteenth time since we moved in that this little prick has disturbed my peace, right? But this time—*this time*—he's parked in my driveway. *My* driveway. No music. He's just parked on my property with the high beams shining into *my* house. So I go out there and knock on his fucking window. BAM, BAM, BAM. Nothing. I wait and knock again. Then the guy gets out, and he's this tall black bastard with a really bad complexion. Scary. You know what I'm talking about, right? Pockmarks. Shit like that and—what?" The mood, he sensed, had shifted. "What did I say?"

Joy looked away from him, her lips tightening.

"Don't tell me," Nick said. "Acne. That's it, isn't it? You had bad acne once, and I just put my foot in my mouth."

Joy cut her eyes back at him, her jaw muscles bulging from clenched teeth. "Tell me," she said, her voice dangerously steady. "Why is it important for you to identify the man as an African-American?"

"What do you mean?"

"What *difference* does it make if he's an African-American?"

"He just was," Nick said. "It's a fact."

"You're missing my point," Joy said. "It may, indeed, be a fact, but what difference does the man's race make?"

"Look," Nick said. "All I'm saying is, I'm white and he's black. It makes a difference. It puts the story in context."

"It's *not* just a matter of context. You were implying something by indicating the man's race, and I'd like to know what you were implying."

"All I'm saying is, in T-Town race makes a big difference."

Joy said, "Well, maybe you haven't considered the socioeconomic differences. Maybe he has a *reason* to be angry at you."

Nick slammed down his pitcher and said, "Look. It's not like I spend two thousand dollars on wallpaper. You know what I'm saying?"

Joy looked at her husband, who shrugged.

"That's what you said, wasn't it, honey?" Nick said. He reached for Karen, but Karen leaned away from him. "Two thousand bucks, right?"

Karen said, "We should leave now."

"No, wait," he said. He walked to the bar and found a curved knife with a narrow blade for slicing fruit. He took the knife and said, "I want to see something."

"Nick," Karen said. "*Please.*"

Nick rubbed his hand along the wallpaper until he found a seam. Then he took the fruit knife and slid it between the seam, carefully separating the wallpaper from the wall. "Look. Just as I suspected. It's paper," he announced. "Two thousand dollars for this, and it's only fucking *paper*!" When he turned to smile at Karen, he neglected to remove the knife and made a long horizontal slice through the wallpaper. "Whoops," he said. He tried pressing the wallpaper back to the wall, but it wouldn't stick, and when he turned around for help, he realized that everyone had stopped what they were doing to watch him.

"I think you should go now," Joy said. Her voice was the only sound in the room.

"Sure," Nick said, and he walked to the bar to return the knife. Before the bartender could deliver his final order, a shot of whiskey, Karen came up to him. She was out of breath, her right palm clutching her chest as though she were on the brink of reciting the Pledge of Allegiance.

"I'm leaving," she said.

"Oh, hell, Karen, it's no big deal. I was just trying to prove a point."

"You've embarrassed me," she said. "I'm staying at a motel tonight."

"Christ, Karen. You're overreacting."

"And I don't want a gun in my house. I don't trust you. You've got a temper."

She pushed her way through the crowd, and before Nick could decide what to do—wait for his drink or chase after her—she was gone.

In the bathroom, Nick lowered himself to his knees and rested his chin on the cool rim of the toilet. He flushed once, and as the water sprinkled his face, he puked until nothing else would come up. When he finished, he stood, wobbled, and opened the door. Downstairs, he swayed through the crowd, pushing the oppressed out of his way. Before he could escape, the department chair stopped him, his arm held out as though he were a bouncer. Through his mask, he told Nick that they would need to talk: Monday, eight sharp.

"I'm sorry if I offended anyone," Nick said.

But Nick could see only the faintest slickness of eyes beyond the pinpoint holes of the chair's mask, and what he saw was dark and not at all promising.

———

On his way home in the cab, Nick stared out the window, watching as the Victorian houses quickly whisked past and the rental property of T-Town materialized: the sagging porches, the piecemeal houses with naked lawns, cheap toys littering the neighborhood. And when they pulled up to Nick's house—the only house on the entire block worth the investment—Nick sensed for the first time why his neighbors resented him. Of *course* they would resent him. Why hadn't he seen this before? It was foolish for him to think that he and Karen would ever fit in. It was presumptuous and naive, and the thought of everything Karen had done to improve the house nearly broke him down right there, in the backseat of the taxicab. But what could they do? Move?

Sitting on his porch, Nick worked hard at bringing back his drunk. He clutched a flask of Southern Comfort and kept a fifth of Jim Beam near his feet. There was a slight breeze, and every so often, his beard blew sideways. Hunched forward, he pulled his thriftshop suit jacket together, and when he shut his eyes, the entire porch seemed to sway with the motion of a ship.

Maybe Joy *was* right. Maybe it *was* a socioeconomic issue. He'd grant her that much. But the real problem—the problem Joy would never admit—was that they'd both been duped. Joy's vision of the downtrodden was no more grounded in reality than Nick's absurd fantasies of life in academia. One was merely the flip side of the other. Abstractions: this is what they'd bought into. And yet Joy had made a cushy life for herself, capitalizing on her abstractions of the oppressed, while Nick had sunk himself irretrievably into debt. He'd fallen prey to a sentimental notion—the same fault of soul that plagued his students, causing them to fail nearly every time they set pen to paper—and the fact that he'd allowed himself to believe in such a ridiculous fabrication was enough to make him want to claw his face and run howling down the street.

Nick heard footsteps now—he'd hoped it was Karen—but when he opened his eyes, he saw emerging from the fog a woman he recognized but whose name he couldn't remember. She stepped close enough to trigger the sensor light on his porch, and Nick yelled, "Hey!"

The woman glanced back at him, then picked up her pace.

"Lauri!" he yelled, alcohol giving him that sudden and unexpected clarity, unlocking the minutiae of his life.

She stopped. She looked back at him over her shoulder.

"Lauri, right?" he said. "I teach in the English Department."

She squinted, and when she moved closer, Nick could see that she, too, was drunk. It was one-thirty in the morning; the bars downtown had closed half an hour ago.

"You look familiar," she said.

"A Dead White Male," he said.

She smiled and said, "Melville. You're Herman Melville."

Nick touched his beard. "I'm wearing a costume."

"Henderson," she said. "Right?"

"I was in that meeting the other day," he said. "The textbook meeting. You want a drink?"

Lauri joined Nick on the porch and sat down in the lawn chair next to him. "That meeting," she said. "I wanted to *strangle* that woman. I wanted to reach over, grab her by the throat, and *choke* her to death." She looked down at Nick's feet and said, "Hey, what's all this shit?"

Nick picked up a crowbar and a can of pepper spray. He handed the spray to Lauri and said, "You need to be careful around here."

"Where am I?" she said.

"T-Town."

"You're kidding," she said. "I was looking for a party and got lost." She took a swig of Southern and said, "I wanted to rip off all her jewelry and *feed* it to her."

Nick smiled, nodded. He was grateful Lauri had stumbled upon him. This was what he'd been needing all along. A compatriot. A soul mate. And at least from here on out, when they saw each other in Burnett Hall, they could share between them the semiotics of their discontent: rolling their eyes at the sight of Joy, feigning heart trouble during department meetings, cringing together at such skin-crawling rhetoric as *negotiating identities*, *blurring the lines*, and *making meaning*.

"Charlie Brown was at the party," Nick said. "So was Oscar Wilde. Do you know Quentin Brock by any chance?"

"Quentin Brock? I thought he was dead. But maybe I'm thinking of someone else. Hey, does this stuff work?" Lauri sprayed a blast of hot pepper into the night air. A faint breeze blew it right back at them, and they both started coughing for their lives.

Nick said, "Jesus." His eyes teared up. His lungs seemed to be collapsing. He took a few swigs from his flask. When their coughing finally subsided, Nick said, "You should have been there. I ripped her wallpaper. I burned my tongue. My wife left me." He tried remembering more of the night, but already it was fading. "It hurts like hell," he said, and he stuck his tongue out to show her the burn.

"I never felt so humiliated in my life," Lauri said. "I mean, just who the hell does she think she is anyway? Gandhi? Martin Luther King?"

"I don't know," Nick said, "but her husband's Peter Elbow."

"Oh *really*," she said, as if this revelation explained everything. She yawned and said, "Well, whoop-dee-do."

Then neither said anything more. They passed the flask of Southern back and forth until it was empty, then worked on the fifth of Jim Beam. Nick held the crowbar, Lauri the pepper spray, and together they sat on his porch, hoping, just hoping, for someone to come up and try something. Tonight they would teach the poor son of a bitch a lesson in politics.

The
Grand
Illusion

I graduated from eighth grade the summer Cheap Trick introduced America to Budokan. That was 1979, and at my graduation I leaned forward and whispered into Lucy Bruno's ear, "I want YOU to want ME."

Lucy spun around and said, "Not if I live to be a hundred. Not if I'm old and blind as a bat and smell like potted meat."

My friend Ralph, keeping his eyes on Lucy, leaned into me and said, "I love potted meat. I eat two cans a day."

Lucy Bruno shivered, then turned away from us.

Ralph had failed both the third and the seventh grades, making him the oldest person ever to graduate from Jacqueline Bouvier

Kennedy Grade School, an honor he hoped the principal would note during his commencement address. He sat next to me during the ceremony, a cowlick rising up off the top of his head like a giant question mark, while the first wiry beginnings of what he insisted upon calling "porkchop sideburns" sprouted on either side of his face.

I looked above and beyond Lucy's nest of hair, at Gina Morales, our valedictorian, standing on stage and smiling into the day's last great blast of sunlight, her braces winking each time she moved her brainy head. I'm not sure what came over me, but every girl that day made my heart lurch. I wanted to lean forward and whisper into the delicate whorls of each girl's ear what I had whispered into the delicate but unforgiving ear of Lucy Bruno: I want YOU to want ME.

Two days after graduation, plans of monumental proportions were well under way. Styx, it was rumored, was going to perform a surprise concert in our city's reservoir. The reservoir was bone dry, used these days only for drainage, the perfect spot for a full-blown rock concert. Members of Styx had grown up on Chicago's South Side, and the word on the street was that they just wanted to pay back a little something to their hometown fans. The only mystery now was the concert's date. Every night a procession of cars crept slowly around the reservoir, watching for the arrival of Styx's road crew. Our classmate Wes Papadakis had vowed to camp out until Styx arrived, and some nights you could hear the faint reverberations of "Come Sail Away" or "Lady" floating up from the very bottom of the reservoir's concrete basin where Wes, clutching his boombox, lay like a castaway atop his bicentennial inflatable mattress, waiting.

I went over to Ralph's house to see what he knew about all of this, but when I got there, he was on top of his mother's garage, peering through a magnifying glass. I made my way around to the alley, found the ladder, then climbed to the top of the garage. "Ralph," I said, tiptoeing across the lumpy tar, afraid of falling through. "What are you doing?"

He pointed at Mr. Gonzales, his next-door neighbor, and said, "I'm trying to set that son of a bitch on fire." Mr. Gonzales was sitting in a chaise lounge and drinking a beer, naked except for a pair of Bermuda shorts. He was unemployed that year and was almost always outside, as naked as you could get without actually being naked. Crushed beer cans decorated his lawn, glinting in the sunlight, while a tiny speck of light from Ralph's magnifying glass seared into the man's bare shoulder blade.

"Why?"

"Shhhhh," Ralph said. "Watch this. Here it comes."

Mr. Gonzales twitched a few times, then reached up over his shoulder and swatted the dagger of light, a phantom mosquito.

"Jesus," I said. "How long have you been doing this?"

"Two weeks," Ralph said. "I put in at least an hour a day. Some days, two. Every once in a while I think I see smoke."

"But *why*?"

"Why what?"

"Why do you want to set him on fire?"

Ralph reached into a grocery sack and pulled out three Big Chief notebooks, a thick rubber band holding the batch together.

"What's this?" I asked.

"It's my revenge list," he said. "It's a list of everyone I'm going to get even with."

"Really," I said. I removed the rubber band, eager to read the list, expecting to find our teachers' names sprinkled among Ralph's schoolwork and doodles, but what I found was a much more frightening and detailed accounting. On each page were twenty names—I saw Lucy Bruno's in there, Gina Morales's name not far from it—and each notebook, according to its cover, contained a hundred pages.

"Ralph," I said. "There must be *six hundred* names here."

Ralph jammed his magnifying glass into his back pocket. He said, "Look. I've met a lot of people since the third grade, okay?"

The pages were filled with everyone I knew, including my parents—everyone, as far as I could tell, except for me and my sister, Kelly.

"Geez, Ralph. Who's *not* on this list?"

Ralph shrugged. "Are you done reading that yet?" he asked.

He snatched the notebooks away and stuffed them deep inside his grocery sack.

I liked Ralph, but danger always lurked close behind him. Sooner or later he was bound to drag me along with him into the swamp of low-life crime, and I'd been meaning all year to break off my friendship with him, only I couldn't figure out how to do it without repercussion. His revenge list now confirmed what I'd feared all along, that Ralph wasn't going to make it easy for me.

"Styx," he said after we had climbed down from the roof and I had told him why I'd stopped by. "You want front-row tickets to the reservoir concert? I'll talk to my cousins, see what I can scare up."

"Great," I said. "I appreciate it."

My sister, Kelly, had her first real boyfriend that summer, a skinny bucktoothed kid named Unger. Unger was not at all the sort of future in-law I had ever imagined. The only way I ever pictured him in our family tree was dangling from a rope tied to one of its limbs. And I suppose I made my feelings clear to him by pulling out my Mortimer Snerd ventriloquist doll each time he came over, settling the doll onto my right knee, and yanking the string that opened his mouth, out of which came, "Hi, my name's Unger," or "Boy, my girlfriend, Kelly, is one hot babe. I can't imagine what she sees in me," or "What's an orthodontist?!"

For her part, Kelly quit speaking to me, except to insult me. "*Your* problem," she liked to begin, "is that you're a sexually confused boy whose only friend is a hoodlum."

Sadly, she was more or less right on both points. Ralph *was* a hoodlum, and sex *did* confuse me, especially the particulars, even though Ralph had once smuggled onto school property a color photo of a naked man holding a naked woman upside-down.

Ralph slipped the photo to me one day during history and whispered, "This is what it's going to be like day and night once we get out of school."

The activity in the photo looked like some new kind of calisthenic, something Mr. Mica, our PE teacher, might have forced us to do before a savage game of Bombardment, the main differences being that we'd have been wearing our regulation gym clothes and there would not have been an exotic parrot in the background watching us. The photo, nonetheless, raised more questions than it answered. Was this what Kelly and Unger did together when I wasn't around to abuse Unger with my Mortimer Snerd doll? Was this what my parents did at night while I was upstairs trying to fall asleep?

As for Ralph, I was still determined to break things off with him, but the next day he called to say that he had a surprise for me, and when I showed up at his house, he appeared on his front stoop, grinning, a giant tie dangling from his neck. He met me at the gate and said, "Here," pressing into my hands another neck-tie, equally as large. "Put it on."

"What?"

"Put it on. I know where Dennis DeYoung is having dinner tonight."

Dennis DeYoung, Styx's lead singer, was the man who gave meaning to our otherwise useless summer. "You're kidding," I said. "*The* Dennis DeYoung?"

"No," Ralph said. "Dennis DeYoung the child molester."

"How do you know he'll be there?" I asked.

"Sources," Ralph said. Ralph's sources were his cousins, all employees of the Tootsie Roll factory on Cicero Avenue. In addition to working the assembly line, they doubled as music insiders, privy to the secrets of the world's most successful rock stars. Robert Plant, for instance, couldn't hold a note if not for the electronic vocal augmenter installed in each of his microphones and controlled by a man working a soundboard. Gene Simmons had had a cow tongue surgically attached to his own tongue. After *Frampton Comes Alive* became the best-selling album of all time, Peter Frampton ballooned up to four hundred pounds and moved to Iceland, too fat to play his guitar anymore; his new albums, all flops, were written and performed by his identical twin brother, Larry Frampton.

Though I was wearing a yellow T-shirt with an iron-on decal of a gargantuan falcon, our school's mascot, I slipped the tie over my head and tightened the knot. We walked nearly two miles to

Ford City, the area's first indoor shopping mall, then over to Ford City Bowling and Billiards, home to a few dozen pool-hustling hooligans who liked to pick fights with adults and flick lit cigarettes at kids. Next door was a Mexican restaurant: El Matador.

"You sure this is where Dennis DeYoung's supposed to be?" I asked. "It's sort of *rough* around here."

Ralph adjusted his tie's knot. "This is the place. From what I hear, he loves Mexican."

We stepped into the crushed-velvet dining room, decorated with sombreros and strings of dried red peppers. A fancy acoustic guitar hung on the wall next to our table.

"You think he'll play a song while he's here?" I asked, pointing to the guitar.

"Maybe," Ralph said. "I wouldn't mind hearing a little 'Grand Illusion' tonight. A cappella," he added.

"No kidding," I said. I started humming "Lorelei" when I noticed that Ralph's thoughts were elsewhere. He looked as though he were staring beyond El Matador's walls and into some blurry vision of his own past. Years ago, Ralph had admitted to me that he wanted to do something that would make our classmates remember him, and for a fleeting moment, while playing the bongos in Mr. Mudjra's music class, hammering out his own solo to Led Zeppelin's "Moby Dick," Ralph had succeeded in winning the hearts of twenty-one seventh graders, one of whom was me. We watched, awestruck, as one of our own moved his hands in expert chaos, keeping up with the music in such a way that we were not quite sure *what* we were watching. Veronica Slomski and Isabel Messina, sitting in the front row, wept after Ralph had finished.

I had a feeling Ralph was rolling those ten minutes over in his head right now, and so I asked him if he was okay, but he just cut his eyes toward me and said, "Of course I'm okay. What the hell's *your* problem?"

"Nothing," I said.

When the waitress arrived, we ordered drinks and several appetizers, along with our main courses and dessert—everything at once. I had never ordered my own food at a restaurant (my mom or dad always took care of it) and so I was unprepared when the food began arriving in droves, plate after plate, way too much for a single table. Even so, Ralph and I scarfed it all down, until our bellies poked out and we could no longer sit up straight in our booth.

I groaned, and Ralph did the same, only louder. I spotted Lucy Bruno and her parents on the other side of the restaurant. All three were staring at us, so I lifted my glass of pop, a toast, while Ralph carefully peeled back his eyelids and stuck his tongue out at them. Lucy shrieked and looked away.

Ralph said, "I can't get that potted meat wisecrack out of my mind. I friggin' *love* that stuff."

"When do you think Dennis DeYoung's gonna get here?" I asked. "I'm not feeling too good."

"Maybe he's not coming tonight," Ralph said. "Maybe he ate Chinese tonight. I hear he likes Chinese, too."

When the check came, Ralph said, "It's on me." He pulled a bent pen from his back pocket, flipped the check over, and wrote, *IOU a lot of money. Thanks.*

"Good one," I said. "We can hide the money under an ashtray. Give her a heart attack until she finds it."

Ralph stood from the table, stretched, then started walking away. I had to grip the edge of the table and brace myself to stand. For the first time in my life, I felt like a fat person. "Hey, Ralph," I said. "Don't forget to leave the money."

Ralph turned quickly and shot me a look that said, *Shut up.*

I didn't have any money, so I had no choice but to follow. My heart felt swollen, pounding so hard it hurt: food and fear, a lethal combo. Outside, beyond the Ford City parking lot, I asked Ralph what exactly had just happened.

"We didn't pay for our food," he said.

"Why not?" I asked, my stomach starting to gurgle more dangerously.

"Listen," he said. "Restaurants work on the good faith system. They give you a check, and you're supposed to put the money inside. You wave to the waitress on the way out, and she waves back. 'Have a nice day,' she says, and you say, 'Will do.' Well, they got stiffed this time. The way I see it, I'm teaching the whole industry a lesson."

"What lesson's that?"

Ralph grinned. He said, "Not everyone's honest."

"Oh. I see," I said, but I didn't.

After the restaurant incident, I avoided Ralph, afraid he was going to land me in jail, where I would grow old and rot. A few days later, while concocting hair-raising scenarios in which the cops come roaring up to my parents' front door looking for me, I walked into my bedroom and found Unger holding my Mortimer Snerd ventriloquist doll.

"What the hell are *you* doing in here?" I asked.

He pulled the string at the back of Mortimer Snerd's head, and Snerd's mouth opened. Unger messed with the string some more until Snerd's teeth chattered. Then, in a high-pitched voice, and without moving his lips, Unger repeated what I had said: "*What the hell are YOU doing here?*"

"Hey," I said. "That's pretty good. You can throw your voice."

Mortimer Snerd turned his head first left, then right. "*Hey,*" Snerd said. "*That's pretty good. You can throw your voice.*"

I felt silly now for all those times I'd used Snerd to insult Unger, not so much because I'd insulted him, but because I had made no bones that it was *me* doing all the talking. I had never bothered to change my voice, and I had always moved my lips. Unger, on the other hand, reacted to everything the dummy said. He asked it questions, treating it as a creature beyond his control, which is what drew me into his show. For their finale, Unger drank a tall glass of water while Snerd sang "You Light Up My Life."

When he finished, setting Snerd aside, I stood up and applauded. "Jesus," I said. "You should go on *The Gong Show.*"

"I've thought about it," Unger said.

"Seriously," I said. "You've got talent."

Unger blushed. I don't think I'd ever actually seen another boy blush before, so I quit complimenting him. "What are you doing here, anyway?" I asked. "Where's Kelly?"

"Oh, she's still at pompom practice," he said.

"Pompom practice," I said. "What the hell's that? I didn't know Kelly did anything at school."

Unger smiled and said, "There's a *lot* you don't know about Kelly." He tried to look mischievous when he said it, but then he blushed again, and I had to look away. It embarrassed me too much to watch.

"Listen," I said. "I don't want to hear about you and Kelly. If I want to watch a horror movie, I'll stay up and watch *Creature Features*, okay?"

Two days later, I found Unger in my bedroom again. "What the hell?" I said.

Unger blushed, but Mortimer Snerd said, "*I hope you don't mind. We were just practicing.*" And then Snerd laughed: "*Uh-huck, uh-huck.*"

"Hey," I said. "That sounds just like him, Unger. Seriously."

Unger set Snerd aside. "I found some of my dad's old Charlie McCarthy records. I worked on it all weekend."

I stared at Unger; I didn't know what to say. I didn't know anyone my age who spent all weekend working on *anything*.

Unger said, "I came over to tell you about this great idea," and then he told me about how he and a few of his friends were going to start a band, an *air* band, and how they needed a drummer.

"I can't play the drums," I said.

"It's an air band," Unger said. "All you do is *pretend* to play. We'll put together a tape with a bunch of songs, and we'll play those at parties."

"Whose parties?" I asked.

"Anybody's parties," he said. "This is the best idea we ever thought of. People will pay us to come over and play. They'll think we're a hoot."

Hoot was a word only my grandparents used, but I tried to ignore it. Maybe he'd picked it up over the weekend, listening to Charlie McCarthy. "People will actually *pay* us?" I asked. "Are you out of your mind?"

"There's nothing out there like this," he said, "and that's what you need these days, a gimmick."

He seemed so sure of our success, I couldn't help getting a little excited myself. "What'll we play? You think we could play some Styx?"

Unger frowned. "Maybe," he said. "I don't know, though. I'd

have to talk to the other guys. We were thinking about some cutting edge stuff, like Roxy Music or Elvis Costello or the Knack." He looked at his shoes and said, "The thing is, we need a place to practice. Do you think we can use your basement?"

I laughed. "Are you kidding? My parents would never let a band practice in their basement." Unger stared at me patiently, waiting for my brain to catch up to the conversation. "So what you're saying," I said slowly, "is that *no one* would actually be playing any instruments?"

"Right."

"Would I need a drum set?"

"Nothing," Unger said. "All we need is a boombox, and Jimmy Cook has that."

"And you want *me* to be the drummer," I said.

"You'd be perfect," he said.

"Okay," I said. "Sure. I'll do it. Why not?"

After I joined the air band, Kelly quit talking to me for good. She thought the whole thing had been my idea, a ploy to keep her and Unger from seeing each other. The rehearsals, as it turned out, were pretty grueling—two hours each night, five nights a week.

"We have to practice," Unger told her, a whine creeping into his voice. "How are we going to get any good if we don't practice?"

I felt totally ridiculous at first, the five of us pretending to play instruments that weren't even in the room: Joe Matecki tickling the ivory, Howlin' Jimmy Cook belting out the lead vocals, Bob Jesinowski sawing away on the electric guitar, Unger dutifully plucking the bass, while I went nuts on the drums. But after a few weeks, an odd thing happened: I started getting into it. The more I picked up on the quirks of different drummers, the more I would lose myself to the music. And when I shut my eyes, an amphitheater would roll out before me, thousands of crazed girls screaming, crying, throwing themselves against the stage, their arms in the air, stretching and arching toward me. It was as if I were holding a gigantic magnet, and the girls—weighted down with silver bracelets, pewter rings, and stainless steel watches—couldn't help themselves from being pulled into my circle of energy.

Once, in the midst of such a vision, my arms flailing wildly to the Who's "Won't Get Fooled Again," I opened my eyes and saw Ralph standing at the foot of the basement stairs. My mother must have let him in and told him to go on downstairs. The other four guys in the band were lost in their own private worlds, twitching or swaying or, as with Unger, bouncing up and down, eyes squeezed shut.

"Ralph!" I yelled over the music. My voice startled the other band members. They looked up, saw Ralph, and stopped playing. Someone reached over and turned down the boombox. No one knew quite what to do with their hands now that their instruments had vanished. Jimmy violently scratched his head, using the tips of all his fingers. Joe rubbed his palms so hard against his jeans, I thought he was going to spontaneously combust in front of us.

"Hey," I said to Ralph. "The porkchop sideburns are looking good. They're really coming in." Ralph didn't say anything. He looked from one musician to the next, squinting, sizing us up. "Ralph plays the bongos," I said, hoping to snap Ralph out of whatever trance he appeared to be falling into. "I've never seen anyone play the bongos like him, either," I added. "You should've seen him last year in Mr. Mudjra's class. *Man.* You guys would've dropped dead." I smiled at Ralph, shook my head. "Listen. I got an idea. Why don't you play the bongos in our band? That'd be okay, wouldn't it guys?"

Unger said, "I don't know. We'd have to talk about it. I mean, we've been rehearsing and everything. Our first gig's next week."

"Well," I said, "he can sit in, though, can't he?"

"Sure," Unger said. "You want to sit in with us, Ralph?"

"C'mon, Ralph. Sit in with us."

Ralph's focus seemed to widen now to include all of us at once. Then, without so much as a word, he placed a business card of some kind onto my dad's toolbox, turned, and walked back upstairs, disappearing into the light above.

"Okay," Unger said. "Back to work."

After everyone had left, I walked over to my father's toolbox. What Ralph had left behind was not a business card. It was a ticket for the Styx concert. The ticket was made of blue construction paper with black ink that had bled until each letter looked sort of hairy. It said, STYX: LIVE AT THE RESERVOIR. NO CAMERAS. NO RECORDING DEVICES. RAIN OR SHINE. There was no date on the ticket. No time, either. No seat number, no address. I kept it with me, though, tucked in my back pocket, ready at a moment's notice to be there, to be a part of history.

Bored, I went upstairs to my room and made a few dozen crank phone calls to Lucy Bruno, asking her if it was true that she liked Hugh G. Rection. After the fourth call, Lucy fell headfirst into the teeth of my trap. Angry, she blurted out what sounded like, "Whose huge erection?" and I yelled back, "Mine!"

This game went on for a few hours until her parents picked up another phone and announced that the line was tapped, and that the police would be at my house in short order. I didn't believe them, of course. After all, I had deepened my voice and put a couple of tube socks over the mouthpiece, but their threats caused me to question what I was doing. Why was I making prank phone calls in the first place? What sort of person was I turning into?

On the night of our first gig, the five of us showed up early. We were to play in the rec room of a new condo on the far edge of town, and from the looks of it, everyone at the party was at least five years older than Unger, who was sixteen.

"Who set this gig up?" I asked.

"Jimmy did. These are his brother's friends."

A man wearing a powder blue tuxedo came over and introduced himself as Chad. "Bad Chad," he said and laughed. "What do you guys call yourselves? The Air Band? Is that what your brother told me, Jimmy?"

"Yeah, that's right."

"What sort of shit do you play?"

"Anything," Unger said. "You name it."

"Disco?" Chad asked.

"You bet," Unger said. "We play disco all the time."

Chad was one of those rare white guys who tried, but failed, to pull off an Afro. From a distance, it appeared that a small toxic cloud—a vapor—had attached itself to the top of his head. He'd also jammed a jumbo pitchfork of a comb into the 'do to give it that final touch, but each time Chad nodded, the comb wiggled wildly.

Chad said, "You can set your equipment up over there."

"Cool," Unger said.

While Joe set up the boombox, the rest of us took our positions. We had made several specialty tapes: Hard Rock, Disco, Punk, even Country. I knew from all our weeks of practice what to do and when to do it, so I shut my eyes for dramatic effect. "Play That Funky Music" was the first song on our disco tape, opening with the electric guitar and followed by vocals. Then came the drums, a simple but seductive beat.

Moving my head in and out, finding the groove, I played well over a minute before looking up and into the audience. No one was dancing. No one was singing along. They stood in groups of two or three, watching us. The only people getting into the song were the other guys in the band, who were clearly as lost in the music as I had been. Chad—*Bad Chad*—ran the tips of his fingers along his suit's lapels. Our eyes met, and I stopped playing.

Somewhere along the way there had been a misunderstanding, and the very thought now of the gap between their expectations and what we were actually doing made me instantly queasy. They had expected a real band; we hadn't even brought instruments. The gap couldn't have been any wider.

Chad motioned with his head, so I reached over and turned off the boombox. I might as well have been a hypnotist clapping my hands: Joe, Jimmy, Bob, and Unger suddenly came to, shaking their heads and looking around, bewildered. As simple as that, I had snapped them back to the here and now.

Chad took two steps forward and opened his mouth, as if to scold us, but nothing came out. He shut his eyes and shook his head, then stopped and looked at us again—crazed, this time—before throwing his arms into the air, turning around, and stomping toward the keg at the back of the room.

Summer was winding down, and I hadn't seen Ralph in over a month. Kelly and Unger had broken up, but Unger still came over to practice throwing his voice. Meanwhile, our air band was put indefinitely on hold.

One night at the beginning of August, with a tornado watch in progress, Unger and I sat in my room, and I watched him put on a show with my Mortimer Snerd doll. I had to admit, his new act was pure genius. Using his boombox, he played Rolling Stones songs, and while Mortimer Snerd lip-synched the lead vocals, Unger actually sang backup. It was dizzying to watch. I couldn't even begin to imagine how much time he'd spent at home figuring out the logistics of it all.

Every few minutes my father would bang on my bedroom door to upgrade us on the status of the approaching storm. "The watch is on until ten o'clock," he said the first time. "That's for *all* of Cook County"; then, an hour later, "It's been upgraded to a warning now, guys. Eighty mile an hour winds. Hold on to your hats."

At first, all we heard was the soft patter of rain, though not much later, our lights started flickering while fists of hail pounded the side of our house. Somewhere upstairs, a window shattered.

"Wow," I said.

"Sympathy for the Devil" was playing now, and Unger kept singing the Oooooo Ooooooo's until an explosion nearby caused us both to jump.

"One of those giant transformers must have blown up," I said, though before I finished saying it, our lights shut off for good. "Great," I said. Unger didn't say anything. His battery-operated boombox chugged on, and Mick Jagger continued singing. It was my favorite part of the song, the part where Mick asks who killed the Kennedys, and so I closed my eyes. While Mick's words rumbled through me, I felt a hand touch my knee, then Unger's breath against my face, then his mouth against my mouth. Before I understood what was happening, his tongue swiped across my lips.

When he leaned back, I screamed. When he put his hand against my mouth to quiet me, I bit down, sinking my teeth into his knuckles, then *he* screamed. My father bolted into the room with a high-powered flashlight, yelling, "What's wrong? You guys all right? What happened?"

"We're all right," I said. "Nothing happened."

My father swung the flashlight toward Unger. "Cut your hand?" he asked.

"Nah," he said. "I'm okay."

"Jesus Christ," Dad said. "The two of you'd better quit screwing around then. This house is under *siege*. The basement's flooding and two windows are smashed out. I sure as hell don't need any extra horseshit on top of it."

"No problem," I said.

Much to my horror, my mother insisted that Unger spend the night. She put him up in my bedroom, so I took the couch in the living room and wrapped myself in a quilt. I don't know what time it was when I finally fell asleep, but I woke up the next morning to my father nudging me with his foot.

"Don't you know this kid?" he asked. He pointed his big toe at the TV.

I was so tired I could barely make sense of where I was or what was going on, but when I finally did, I saw my father in his La-Z-Boy, holding a bowl of cereal, still nudging me with his foot; my mother and sister, side-by-side, staring at the TV screen; and Unger, who blushed when I looked at him.

"I remember him from back when you were in Cub Scouts," Dad said. "Isn't that the same kid?"

On TV was Wes Papadakis, and he was being interviewed by Walter Jacobson of Channel 2 news. The interview had been conducted late last night, and it was the hottest story on all the stations. Later I would hear the whole thing, how Wes had been sound asleep at the bottom of the reservoir when the storm hit, and how he had been there—as he had been there every night— waiting for the arrival of Styx. Apparently, he'd fallen asleep listening to *Pieces of Eight* when the first ball of hail cracked him on the head. Not much later, he noticed water pouring over the sides, filling the reservoir. The sides proved too muddy for climbing out, leaving him, as he saw it, with only one option: to ride the storm out. And that's exactly what he did. Clutching his bicentennial inflatable mattress, and with all the city's flooded streets draining toward him, Wes floated twenty, thirty, forty feet, until he reached the upper lip of the reservoir and, swept along by a heavy current, rode his raft down Rutherford Avenue, all the way home.

"It's a miracle," my mother said, "that he's alive."

Kelly, tears in her eyes, turned and asked if I had his phone number.

"*No*, I don't have his phone number," I said. Until last night, Wes had been a mere shadow on the playground, a bit player at recess. Could his life really have changed that quickly?

"They should give that kid a medal," my father said.

"A medal?" I asked.

My father cocked his ear and turned his head slowly, pointing his chin at me. *And what have you done lately?* was what this look meant. Disgusted, my father finally turned away. "Hell," he said. "They should at least give him a key to the city."

My mother agreed. "That's the *least* they could do," she said.

I didn't see Unger anymore until I started high school. For those last few weeks of summer, I couldn't shake the thought of Unger's mouth against my mouth, his tongue swiping my lips. Panicked, I called Lucy Bruno three times in three days, finally convincing her to go to Haunted Trails Miniature Golf Range with me, where, much to my own amazement, I chipped a fluorescent green golf ball off Frankenstein's head. The manager promptly asked us to leave, I walked Lucy home, and we never spoke again. Whatever Lucy Bruno had thought of me before our date was now confirmed in spades by my recklessness with a golf club, by the threat I posed to society, and by the fact that I was far more amused by what I had done than anyone else at the golf range.

The day before the first day of high school, I stuck my Mortimer Snerd ventriloquist doll and a hacksaw into a grocery sack with the general plan of sawing off Mortimer's head, and I walked to the reservoir where I intended to perform this act. Carefully, I made my way down the slope. I had never been down there before, but now, after everything that had happened with Wes, I wanted to see it.

Styx, of course, never showed up that summer, and now that I was down here, I couldn't imagine how it was going to happen anyway. There were no electrical outlets, the sides were too steep for people to sit, and the acoustics were awful. What had Wes been thinking? What had *any* of us been thinking?

"HELLO," I yelled for fun. "HOW ARE YOU?" I listened to my voice hit the wall and come back toward me. It bounced off another wall, then came back again. This continued for a while, my voice bouncing and creeping up behind me, to the side of me, or head-on, fainter and fainter, until it became a bunch of half words and grunts, then nothing at all.

"HELLO," I yelled again. Just then, someone from above yelled, "HELLO," and together our voices surrounded me, one voice answering the other, overlapping, mocking one another. I looked up. A cop was peering down at me. With his billy club, he motioned for me to climb out of the reservoir. After struggling up to him, he said, "What's in the bag?"

"A ventriloquist doll and a hacksaw," I said.

He nodded. "You see this sign?" He tapped it with his club. NO TRESPASSING, it said.

"No," I said. "I've never seen it before."

"It's there for a reason," he said. "Kid almost drowned a few weeks ago."

"Wes Papadakis," I said.

The cop looked at me, as if what I'd said made absolutely no sense to him. He said, "Got to start teaching you kids the meaning of laws. Got to start somewhere."

I guess I thought he was simply talking out loud because I was smiling when he read my rights to me, then pulled out his handcuffs. He asked me to set my bag down, and he cuffed my hands behind my back. I was still smiling, but I was starting to get the chills, too.

"What's so funny?" the cop asked.

"Nothing," I said.

"Well," the cop said, "I wouldn't be smiling if I were you."

"I'm cold."

"It's August," he said. "You can't be cold. It's ninety degrees."

"I'm freezing."

With his hand on top of my head, the cop guided me into the backseat of his cruiser. "You know what? All you kids are nuts." He shut the door. After settling himself into the driver's seat, he set my bag down beside him and said, "That kid who almost drowned? He was nuts, too. Kept saying he was down there waiting for *sticks*, whatever the hell *that's* supposed to mean. *Now* look at him. A goddamn hero. You ask me, this whole city's nuts."

At the police station, the cop uncuffed me and returned my bag before pawning me off to a woman cop who sat at a desk, smoking a long, thin cigarette. "Identification?" she said.

"I don't have any."

"How old are you, honey?"

"Thirteen."

"Boy," she said, "they get younger every day." She stood up and said, "Hold your horses, okay?"

I passed the time looking over some mug shots, until another cop, a bald one, lugged Ralph in, shoving him hard into a chair. Like me, Ralph was holding a grocery sack. The cop said, "Don't do anything that would require us to shoot you. You got that?"

Ralph shrugged.

"I wouldn't hesitate to use force," the cop said, leaving the two of us alone.

"Hey, Ralph," I said. Ralph looked over, and I smiled at him. "They got me, too," I said. I expected him to get up and come over, but he didn't. Instead, he narrowed his eyes at me, as if I were the witness called in to point him out in a lineup.

"I'm under arrest," I said and laughed. "Do you believe that?" I shook my head, unable to believe it myself. "Hey! You shaved off your porkchop sideburns," I said. "Why'd you do that?"

Ralph touched his face, where one of the sideburns had been, as if he no longer remembered what had been there. "What's in the bag?" he finally asked.

"A ventriloquist doll and a hacksaw," I said. "What's in yours?"

"My revenge list."

"Oh yeah," I said. "That's right. I forgot about that." I knew, of course, that my name had been added to Ralph's revenge list—how could it not have been?—and the very thought of its being there gave me goosebumps. "So," I said, changing subjects. "What'd they get *you* for?"

"Skipped out on a restaurant without paying the bill."

My heart sped up. "El Matador?" I asked.

"Nuh-uh. They never caught us for that one." He grinned, pleased that we'd gotten away with it, and I relaxed. "*Last* week," he said, "they nailed my cousins for selling fake Styx tickets. Styx's management heard about what they were doing and they set up a sting operation." He shook his head and said, "Norm and Kenny. They're *screwed*."

Had Ralph forgotten he'd given one of the tickets to me? Had he known all along that it was a fake? I didn't tell Ralph, but I still had the ticket; I kept it on display in my bedroom, sealed under the glass top of my dresser, next to a stub for the only White Sox game I ever went to.

"What they nail you for?" Ralph asked.

"Trespassing," I said.

Ralph snorted.

"They caught me in the reservoir," I said, "you know, where Wes Papadakis almost drowned."

Ralph nodded, then turned away. He crumpled shut the top of his grocery sack and waited for his officer to return. We both seemed to know that this would be our last conversation, and Ralph must have seen no point in prolonging the end of it. I knew deep down that in a few years our classmates would not only *not* remember the day Ralph had played his bongos in Mr. Mudjra's class, but that they would have a hard time remembering Ralph at all. He was old enough to drop out of school now, which I'm sure he was planning to do, and then it would be only a matter of time before he moved through the town like a ghost, invisible even to those who had once known him.

Meanwhile, Wes Papadakis had become the South Side's very own Noah. His journey out of the reservoir would be passed along to children for generations, as powerful as any Bible story—*more* powerful, since he was one of our own. Whatever any of us had done before, whatever accomplishments we'd achieved, it all paled by comparison. No one would ever forget the morning they first saw Wes on TV, his raft blown up to look like the American flag, the previous night's lightning still snapping in the distance; and while rain pelted the umbrella above his head, Wes looked directly into the cameras and into our homes, and he told us his story.

The bald cop returned and said, "Looks like we'll have to put the two of you in a holding cell until we get your parents on the horn. Come along now. Both of you."

Ralph and I walked side by side down the police corridor, trailing the cop. Our grocery sacks rubbed together, and when we passed the police station exit, Ralph looked out the glass door and into the sunlight, as if considering making a break for it. And I had decided in that instant that if Ralph bolted for the door, I would bolt with him. I was hoping he'd do it, too. Nothing before had ever seemed so real to me as that moment, waiting for Ralph's decision. But Ralph suddenly faced ahead, setting his jaw in grim defeat, and I remained beside him, already sorry for knowing who between us would be the first one set free.

The
Greatest
Goddamn
Thing

———

"It's hotter than snatch in here," Billy G says, rolling down the car window. He reaches over and flips the heater from high to low. He squints at the sun, moans a bit, and says, "Jesus H Christ."

This is all Billy G's said since I picked him up, so I ask something just to keep the conversation rolling. "What's the H stand for anyway? Jesus *H* Christ?"

"It stands for Hard-Ass. How the hell am I supposed to know?"

"Sorry I asked."

"How the fuck would I know?"

"I don't know," I say. "It was just a question."

Billy G's my older brother. They sent him to the can after he stabbed a guy nobody liked. It probably wouldn't have been so bad—nobody liked the guy, after all—but there were complications on the operating table, and they're saying he may never breathe right again. The word is, he's near dead. So Mom and I, we've afforded Billy G a few days of freedom. We scraped up enough bail and got him out before he's sentenced.

"You getting along okay in the joint?" I ask.

"Shit," Billy says. He sighs and shakes his head.

I'd promised myself not to ask him about the joint, but I've gone ahead and done it anyway. When I was a kid, Billy G told me I had a crack in my head that made it hard for me to remember things.

"We'll have us a blast these next two days," I say.

"We *better*," he says, and he means it.

For half an hour we drive without saying a word, and the silence starts killing my ears. It's like wearing stereo headphones with the volume turned all the way up, but nothing's playing. So I begin swerving all over the road for diversion.

"What the fuck are you doing?" Billy asks.

The car starts to jackknife, and I yank the wheel to the right, maintaining perfect or near-perfect control.

"Nothing much," I say. "Breaking the tension, I guess."

"Well *quit* breaking the tension," Billy says. "It'll get us arrested."

"Sorry," I say. I grip the steering wheel tightly with both hands—the way they're teaching me to drive in driver's ed—and I ease the car back into the right lane.

"How old are you?" Billy asks.

"Sixteen. Sixteen and four-twelfths," I say. I concentrate for a moment, then reduce the fraction. "Sixteen and one-third."

"Pull over at Skid's, up here to the right."

Skid's is Billy G's favorite bar, and I do as I'm told. Besides, I've never been to Skid's. The building, though, looks like a dilapidated barn—something a cow might walk away from instead of into. And behind it are three old sky-blue mobile homes, which aren't so mobile anymore.

"Act like you're twenty-one," Billy says. "In case the place gets raided. Pigs, you know."

"Sure," I say. "Twenty-one."

Inside, Skid's doesn't look much better than outside: sawdust and dirt floors, wooden posts holding the place up, light bulbs dangling from wire as thin as dental floss. Next to the bar is a tall, skinny Christmas tree wrapped in strings of flashing red and blue lights. The second we walk in, people start yelling out to Billy.

"Billy G! What the fuck?"

"Billy, man. I heard you stabbed the bastard."

"Way to go," they say. "He had it comin'."

"If *you* didn't stab him," the bartender says, "*I* would've."

Billy G smiles and says, "I *wish* you would've."

Larry Furguson's the guy Billy G stabbed and who nobody likes. Billy G'd taken the day off work, and all he wanted was to catch a couple of ugly fish to fry up when he got home, but Larry Furguson showed up and started preaching. Billy G and Larry've had their differences in the past, so Billy hauled off and socked Larry to keep him shut, but Larry fought back, dirty as always. Billy G says he didn't mean to stab Larry, though. Not that hard, at least.

Everyone cracks Billy on the back now. They buy him drinks, dedicate songs on the jukebox to him, smile when he passes by. I'm guilty by association, so people hand me drinks and slap me on the back, too.

I finish dancing a really slow song with Melinda, the only girl in the bar, and we were dancing so close, she's given me a hard-on I could stir cement with. She's twenty-four or -five and wearing jeans ripped in the seat and a hot pink tube top I can't stop looking at.

After the dance, she says, "So you're Billy G's little brother."

"Yes ma'am," I say.

"Tell me," Melinda says, leaning closer. "What's the G stand for? You know: Billy *G*."

I hear Billy G across the way telling his story. "Heat lightning pops the lake," he says, "and I stab the bastard with my fishing knife. It was that simple."

"I'll tell you what the G stands for in Billy G," I say, "if you tell me what the H stands for in Jesus H Christ."

"Humdrum," she says. "Now what's the G stand for?"

"Godlike," I say.

She pats my knee and says, "Well, look at you—a real-life *comedian*."

"Knock knock."

"Who's there?" she asks.

"Banana," I say.

"Banana who?"

"Banana," I say.

"I know this joke," she says. "Let's dance again."

Banana, I think.

She narrows her eyes at me and says, "I wouldn't mind taking a chance on some jailbait tonight."

"Really!" I say, but all I can think of is a big greasy worm on a hook and Billy G biting into it, the bait that drew him in, the worm that led him to the can.

———

Larry Furguson's twenty-nine, same as Billy G, and on two occasions, Larry killed all our cats. The first time, before I was born, he shot them with a bow-and-arrow set he stole from the Catholic high school. The second time, he hung them from the weeping willow, and it was the first thing Mom and I saw when we opened the door that morning: six cats limp-necked and swaying in the wind. But that's not what finally got to Billy G. A few years back, Larry Furguson started passing out religious pamphlets at the filling station. He started preaching in the parking lot of the A&P. "I found the Lord," he'd yell, standing on the hood of his car, shaking a Bible. "I *found* the *Lord*!"

"I found the Lord, too," Billy G says now. "I found him hosing my girlfriend!" He snickers.

Billy G's sitting at an old upright piano, off to the side. It's the sort of chipped-wood piano our balding music teacher in grammar school played, except this piano has one of its rollers missing, and it tips towards me, though after I have enough to drink, the piano straightens up and everything else begins to tip.

Billy G fiddles with the keys, and I figure any moment he'll break into a riff; he can bring the house down if he wants, but all he does now is poke at the keys and say, "If you're gonna kill cats, kill cats. If you're gonna preach, preach. But don't kill cats, *then* preach. That's what I say."

Everyone is drunk. I'm drunk for the very first time, and I'm having a blast. *All* of us are having a blast. We're breaking mugs, pissing out of the designated window, flipping for the worm at the bottom of the tequila—though some of us suspect foul play with the bottle. Melinda claims she saw Jake Potter taking it with him to the window we've all pissed out of at least once tonight.

"It's the ceremonial pissing ground," Jake says. "And I wanted a swig while I whizzed. So what?"

"But maybe you missed and pissed in the bottle," someone says.

"Or maybe you pissed in the bottle on purpose," Melinda says, as if she knows something the rest of us don't.

"Give me that bottle," Jake says. "*I'll* drink it. A little piss won't kill me. In fact, a little piss is *good* for you every once in awhile. Who was it that said that?"

Jake Potter was in the army and discharged for reasons he won't say. No one tells him that no one ever said that, and Jake drinks what's left in the bottle, capturing the worm in his mouth, then wiggling it at us on the tip of his fat, ugly tongue before he swallows it.

"Worms aren't so bad for you, either," I say.

"You see," Jake says, "this kid knows, don't you?" He ruffles my hair, then looks like he wants to puke. But that passes, and he starts hooting like he's in the wild. Which he is.

One by one, we begin to realize that Jolene Furguson—Larry Furguson's sister—is standing in the doorway and watching us. Her hair looks like an upside-down bird's nest, and her shoulders are hunched as if she's been carrying someone on her back for a mile or two.

"Where's that lousy bastard?" she yells. "I know he's here."

She's looking around the way a person would if the lights had been turned off, though maybe she's drunk. *I'm* drunk, so it's hard to tell. She sways a little from side to side. At first I think she's pointing a garage door opener at us, but when the light catches her hand, I see it's a gun, and she's pointing it all over the place without even trying.

"Shit," I whisper.

The lights on the Christmas tree blink, and I shut my eyes, but everything starts spinning slowly to the left, so I open my eyes again.

"He's dead," she says. At first I think she means Billy G, that she wants to kill him.

"He died this morning," she adds, and now I know she means Larry, her brother. All eyes sneak over to Billy G, whose head is down and whose own eyes are clamped shut. When Jolene lifts the gun, Jake whispers, "Fuck it," and runs toward her, screaming like the madman he is. He tackles her to the ground and beats her arm into the floor until she lets go of the gun.

"Rope!" he says. "Get me some rope!"

The bartender messes around in the back room, then reappears with a coil of rope thick enough to hog-tie a mobile home.

"Great!" Jake says and lifts Jolene off the floor. Jolene's slapping Jake on the face harder than I can bear to watch, but my guess is Jake's used to getting slapped. He takes her to the post in the middle of the bar and quickly, expertly, ties her to it, the thick rope holding her snug. From his back pocket, Jake pulls a red-checkered bandanna and shakes it in front of him like a cheap magician. He blows his nose into the bandanna, then uses it to gag Jolene, tying it around her head.

"You're lucky," Jake says. "If you were a man, I would've shot you with your own gun. Through the noodle," he adds, and he places the tip of his forefinger against her forehead, slowly cocks his thumb, and says, "Boom."

A party has officially been declared for Billy G, though it's not a party celebrating who he is or what he did. It's a going-away party. "They'll nail me to the wall if I stay," Billy G keeps saying, so Jake Potter has given him the keys to his pickup, and every last one of us has vowed or sworn or crossed our hearts to hold onto Jolene until morning, giving Billy G at least a seven-hour head start. In the meantime, Billy G wants to have a good time, and he wants us to have one, too. "For *me*," he says. "Have a good time for *me*."

Billy G sits at the piano and hits one of the black keys again and again. Harry, the bartender, passes around trays of shots. "These are the vodkas," he says, pointing at one of the trays, "and these are the whiskeys. These are the schnapps, and these are the gins." I listen and nod, then reach for the shots like they're samples at a grocery store, making sure to try a little something from every tray.

Once we drink enough, six of us form a train and dance circles around the post Jolene's tied to. Melinda's in front of me, and I hold her hips, wrapping my arms all the way around her to let her know I'm still there. Jake Potter's our leader, and when he starts smacking his mouth with the palm of his hand like an Indian, the rest of us do the same, our knees bouncing high into the air, our heads tilting back, then forward.

Jake Potter stops and says, "We should build a fire around her. You know, douse her with gasoline, then throw a match at her."

Jake looks as serious as an owl, and I glance nervously around. Then I see he's joking. His back's to Jolene, and he's giving us the wink, letting us know he's just snowing her.

I try getting in on the joke. "Why don't we just shoot her," I say, but I can tell by everyone's reaction they think maybe I pushed the joke too far. Even Melinda thinks so, until I give everyone the wink, including Jolene.

I walk over to Billy G to see what he's up to, but he's telling his side of the story again. The same people are sitting next to him, people who've heard it a dozen times, but they keep nodding at Billy and smiling at all the right parts.

Billy leans back, cracks his knuckles. "So I tell him to get up," Billy says. "*Get up, shithead,* I say, but then I look at him close, and I see something different. It's his eyes. It's how he looked after he killed my cats. *The fuck you're born again!* I say. So get this. He reaches over and grabs a corkscrew I got sitting next to my cooler and starts jabbing me in the leg with it. So I get my fishing knife and I stab him back for the hell of it, but I swear to God, I didn't think I could really *stab* him with that thing. I thought I might *puncture* him a little, but I never thought I could *stab* him."

I slap Billy G on the back and say, "You did the right thing. Stab the motherfucker. He deserved it." Then I look over and catch Jolene Furguson glaring at me, and even though nobody liked Larry, I shouldn't have said what I said. He's dead now, and Billy's leaving town for good. "Jesus, I love this place," I say, changing the subject, looking around. "I *love* it!"

Billy G smiles, as does everyone else, but when I look at him, I get the chills. His smile is crooked, not quite right, the smile of a doomed man. I suddenly don't feel too good anymore. Dancing like an Indian shook up everything in my stomach, and I'm on the brink of getting sick.

Outside, I feel an arm around my shoulders; I keep my hands on my knees.

"You know," Jake Potter says, "I did this so much in the army, I started thinking it was my job. Watching over people while they yakked, that is. Making sure they didn't yak on themselves, shit like that. That was my specialty: spotting people across the bar before they lost it. A talent, for chrissake."

"Mmm," I say. The sweat on my face feels like gigantic ice cubes, and tears sting my eyes; I can't believe how much better I feel.

"You all right, pal?"

I nod.

"You know what?" he says. "You're okay. Just don't go around stabbing people the way your brother does, and you'll do fine."

I'm sitting alone at the back table, sipping a beer to make myself feel better. The night's dying down, and Jolene Furguson has fallen asleep tied to the post. Everyone's forgotten about her, as they should. Melinda sees me and walks over.

"Hey there," she says, sitting. "You feel better?"

"As good as better can feel," I say.

"I've been thinking," Melinda says. "You know Harry S Truman? Well, the S doesn't stand for anything. It stands for S. Maybe that's what the H stands for in Jesus H Christ." Melinda's eyes are droopy in a way I like. She's drunk, but she's been drunk before, so I suppose it doesn't really matter to her that she's drunk. For me, though, it's different.

"The G," I say, "in Billy G. It's the same thing. It stands for G."

Melinda smiles, leans over, and kisses me on the cheek. "I like you," she says. "You shoot straight from the hip, and I like that."

I picture myself with a holster and a pair of six-shooters. I look at Jolene, asleep at the post, and I feel like I'm in the Wild West. I lean over and kiss Melinda on the lips. I'm sixteen, drunk for the very first time, and kissing a woman eight years older than me. It feels pretty damn good.

"I live in trailer B out back," she says. "I'm not letting you drive home tonight, drinking what you've drunk."

I nod. I know I've drunk so much I'll probably just conk right out, but I'd be *happy* conking out next to Melinda; it'd be more than I've done so far in sixteen years.

Jake Potter suddenly crashes into our table, scaring the shit out of me, and flops into a chair. "Lovebirds!" he says. "Do you solemnly swear to tell the truth, the whole truth, and nothing but the truth?"

Melinda and I look at one another; under the table, we're holding hands.

"What I mean is," Jake says, "do you, Melinda, take this boy to be your lawfully wedded husband?"

"Sure," Melinda says, squeezing my fingers.

"Do *you*, Billy G's younger brother, take Melinda to be your— HEY," he yells, swinging around. "PIPE DOWN! I'M CONDUCTING A WEDDING OVER HERE!"

Billy G salutes us from afar.

"Anyways, anyways, *do you?*"

"You bet," I say.

"Good, good," Jake mutters, standing up, wavering. He saunters away, looking somewhat embarrassed now for bothering a couple of newlyweds.

What follows is an awkward moment between Melinda and me, now husband and wife. "The honeymoon," I begin, but Billy G saves us, climbing on top of the bar, wobbling back and forth.

"Shhhhhh," he says, his finger to his lips. He can't stop giggling. I don't ever remember seeing Billy G giggle, and I can't decide whether to giggle with him or not. "Shhhhhh. Quiet. Quiet," he says.

Melinda scoots next to me and whispers, "I love when he does this."

"Does *what*?" I ask.

"Don't worry," she says. "It won't hurt him." And without knowing why, I'm scared.

Billy G says, "Jesus, I wished it'd worked out better than this. But you guys are all right. Harry wants me to play one last time. Before I go." He looks my way and winks. "Harry, dim the lights!"

The lights start fading until everything looks like a photo taken without a flashbulb.

"The grain alcohol, Harry," Billy G says.

Harry hands Billy G a big bottle. Billy G takes it, hops down from the bar, and walks over to the old piano. "Jake? Care to do the honors?"

Jake's shape moves toward the piano, then he starts pouring grain alcohol all over Billy G's hands. I can't really see it, but I can hear the glug-glug of the bottle. "Ready?" Billy G whispers. "Lights out, Harry . . . Jake's ready."

The lights blink out. Melinda palms my knee and leans her head onto my shoulder. I put my arm around her, my hand on her bare stomach. Without thinking, I stick my pinkie into her belly button, but she doesn't say anything, so I keep it there.

Jake lights a match and sets Billy G's hands on fire.

"*Jesus,*" I say, but Melinda holds me back. Then Billy G starts playing a wild jazz tune, his flaming hands moving back and forth across the keyboard. His face glows from the flames, and for a moment I can tell he's looking my way, smiling. Everyone's hooting and yelling and chanting his name. It's the greatest goddamn thing I've ever seen. Jake splashes more grain alcohol onto Billy G's hands, and the flames shoot higher. Through all of the commotion, I hear Jolene Furguson scream. I seem to be the only one who's heard it, too. It's a muffled scream because of the gag, but she must've woken up, seen the fire, and figured Jake Potter wasn't joking about torching her after all. But no one pays attention to Jolene; it's Billy G they watch.

Melinda starts nibbling my earlobe, and suddenly—miraculously, really—I feel as if I might not be sleeping tonight after all.

I keep watching Billy G, and as the flames get smaller and Jake's bottle empties, Billy G starts playing slower and slower, like a toy piano that needs winding. When the flames burn all the way out, leaving us in the black of blacks, the room gets deadly quiet— the silence, I imagine, heard only before a firing squad. Car keys jingling, sneaking away, my brother whispers as he passes by, "Remember me."

Roger's New Life

Roger Wood had been living in town only a month when the neighbors began to watch him.

Every night, Roger saw their slightly parted curtains, the almost imperceptible shuffle of fabric; then, when the moon was full and white and passing between clouds, Roger'd catch a flash of skin or eye, then darkness again.

Tonight, Roger didn't look. He knew they were watching, so why look? Why give them the benefit? Roger stood under the dim and yellow bug light, moths swooping and flapping near his head. He held onto a long nylon leash, while his dog, Geronimo, pulled into the darkness.

"Attaboy, Geronimo," Roger said. "Good dog. Good boy."

Geronimo was a half-blind cocker spaniel, eighteen years old, the oldest dog Roger had ever seen.

"Easy does it," he said, and he began reeling the dog back up the steps.

In the living room, Tracy lay on the floor, sunning in the glow of the TV. The kids had gone to bed.

"There's a cool breeze out tonight," Roger said.

Tracy rolled onto her side and lifted her leg into the air, pointing her toes. Then she pulled her leg toward her until something popped. "Roger," she said. "What's that smell?"

Roger sniffed, though sniffing wasn't necessary. "It's the house," he said. "We'll adjust."

"I don't think it's the house," Tracy said.

"Then what?" Roger asked. "What is it?"

In the past month, since the move, Geronimo had become an embarrassment of age. His toenails, knobby and curling under his paws, clacked against the sidewalk. The fur was sparse. Fatty deposits clung to his back like insects. And then there was the smell.

Tracy's body kept changing, TV light and shadow massaging her legs, torso, and face.

Roger shut his eyes and said, "It's the house, Trace."

But the house smell was different. The house smell was dust, wet wood, and newspaper. The smell on Geronimo had the same weakening power of old meat left out too long in the sun.

Roger Wood worked at UPS, delivering packages. Tracy Wood had joined the PTA, hoping to establish herself in the community. In Laramie, the town they'd lived in before, Tracy had always considered herself a community person, helping with both the blood and food drives, organizing the town flea market, sometimes walking along her street with a giant plastic bag, picking up trash everyone else pretended not to notice.

Roger felt he should do more with his time, but most nights he came home from work exhausted and locked himself in the garage. He knew the neighbors watched, and he could imagine what they thought: *Perhaps he makes things in there. Handicrafts. Furniture.* But Roger didn't have the right tools, and if he did, he wouldn't have known how to use them. *Perhaps he keeps things hidden away in there. Pornographic magazines. Smut.* But Roger's own interest in pornography had ended fourteen years before, when he was twenty-one.

For an entire year, Roger had ordered and collected the most hard-core pornographic magazines legally available. He kept a secret P.O. Box, a place he'd go to only at night, alone, the key to the box gripped in his right hand long before stepping through the wheezing automatic doors of the post office. The magazines had become more expensive, more graphic, more fetish oriented, though the quality of the magazines often diminished. Some looked homemade, printed on cheap newsprint paper, words and photos smearing under Roger's thumbs. Roger suspected that some of the material he'd received, despite its availability, was actually illegal. It made him nervous. He was being watched, he thought. The post office kept an eye on people like him. Twice, Roger had gone so far as to send nude snapshots of himself to some of these magazines, photos taken from the waist down with a Polaroid, but none of these ever made it to print. That whole year, Roger felt a strong need for sex, and he felt it every day, every minute it seemed—that jumpy, anticipatory anxiety. Once, Roger experimented with acid, a drug he'd hoped would counteract his urges and soothe him, relax him, sweep him away. Instead, his body felt electric, his skin an inferior way to keep his skeleton, nerves, and organs inside. For five hours, he wanted to escape the shell of his body. He wanted *out.*

After a year, Roger tied all of his magazines into several large bundles and took them to the city dump. Fourteen years had passed, and only in the deepest of uneasy sleep did any of this ever come back: vague memories of bondage; high heels and cinnamon-flavored body lube; hermaphrodites. It had been an odd year, almost hazy in the bleary-eyed way Roger just sat and watched people, hardly ever speaking. And when he did speak, his voice had scared him. It had become a deep, scratchy whisper, the voice of someone he didn't know.

Tracy Wood finished making dinner, while Roger, Zach, and June sat around the table. Zach was in the sixth grade, June in eighth. Their new school was older and larger, vines choking its walls, suffocating the bricks.

Zach eased the fruit bowl toward him. Covertly, he removed an orange and started squeezing it. He exchanged the orange for a banana, piercing his fingernail through the peel—tiny half-moon cuts, each exactly the same.

"Zach," Roger said, nodding slowly, parentally, toward the fruit bowl.

Zach lifted the bowl and placed it on the counter behind him, as if he realized the temptation to vandalize fruit would be too great with the bowl still in front of him.

"How's school?" Roger asked.

June rolled her eyes; Zach shrugged and mumbled.

Tracy set the table: plates, silverware, pot holders, salt and pepper. She brought the food from the kitchen, pan after pan. When she finished, she said, "You guys eat. I've got to run or I'll be late."

"You can't eat?" Roger asked.

"Meeting starts at five," Tracy said.

Roger felt a rush of warm, sticky breath against his hand.

"Quit begging, Geronimo," Roger said. "Stop it."

"Don't make me feel guilty," Tracy said.

"What did I say?" Roger asked. "All I said was, can't you eat?"

"That's not how you said it," Tracy said. She put her purse onto the edge of the table.

"Oh boy," Roger said. Roger looked across the table at the kids, but their heads were lowered. Steam whirled from the pressure cooker, the giant bowl of corn, the pile of rolls. Roger began to sweat, then looked down at his plate, peering into his own blurred reflection. "I'm sorry," he said. "I didn't mean anything by it."

Tracy said, "Just don't make me feel guilty." She took a deep breath, holding it longer than necessary. She said, "This is our new life. Isn't it?"

Whenever she said this, Roger imagined that all of them had been killed in a car accident, violently dismembered, but somehow they'd been given a reprieve, so here they were, in their new life, and their punishment was to be happy in any given moment.

"Well?" Tracy asked. "Isn't it?"

"Yes," Roger said. "It's our new life."

Roger's UPS truck was huge and dark brown and solar heated, and sometimes when he drove by, the neighbors waved to him. Other times they simply watched the truck, mesmerized, staring as though it were an unexpected hearse come to take them away.

After work, Roger messed around with his new band saw. Tracy had picked it from a catalogue and ordered it for his birthday. "All that time you spend in the garage," she'd said when it arrived, "you might as well put it to good use." It was a gift, but Roger didn't know how to build anything. He'd sit in the cold garage at night, rubbing his hands together, and he'd think of things to do with the saw. It reminded him of the paper cutter from his grammar school art class, an industrial green device that remained on the ledge near the windows. Mrs. Boyle, their teacher, was the only person allowed to use it. "I knew a girl who chopped her arm off at the elbow," she'd say, hoping to ward off potential trouble. Then she'd point to one of the girls in class, a quiet girl, and say, "Come to think of it, she looked an awful lot like *you*." All day long, Mrs. Boyle chopped shreds of dull-colored construction paper—orange and black at Halloween; burnt oranges and browns at Thanksgiving; weak pinks for Valentine's Day. The paper was soft to touch, almost fuzzy, and they used it to make everything: Indian headdresses, chain links, Get Well cards for classmates laid up in the hospital.

Roger Wood lifted the band saw's arm and clamped a pencil into the vice. He lowered the arm and cut the pencil in two. He clamped a ruler, a cheap plastic one, into the vice, and sawed the ruler in two. The handle of his shovel was next. Then his baseball bat, a Louisville Slugger. He found some wooden shoes in a box, two pairs he and Tracy had bought in Holland, Michigan, after standing in front of a gigantic windmill. He cut each shoe into sections of four. Next, he removed his wedding ring, clamped it into the vice, and lowered the blade. Sparks nipped his hand; the motor moaned and the blade snapped. Roger jerked the cord from the wall socket. He loosened the vice and tried putting his ring back on, but the gold, still hot from the saw, burnt a small hole through the flesh of his knuckle.

It was early Saturday morning, after three, when Tracy finally walked in, reeking of smoke and booze. She hadn't told Roger she would be late, but when she came in, she explained that she'd gone out with the other parents. "After hours," she'd said, yawning, as if this were a sufficient explanation.

She slept on the sofa, on her side, her right arm slung up and over her forehead, reminding Roger of women in silent-film melodramas, the kind of movies he'd watched on his Super-8 projector before his marriage, before his obsession with pornography. Roger stayed awake, and for two hours he watched her. Tracy always snored after a long night drinking, and tonight her snoring was extraordinarily loud. From where he sat, across the room, he measured her head between his forefinger and thumb, and each time he did this, he convinced himself that her head was no more than two inches high. "Two. Two and a half," he mumbled. Then he woke the kids, and together, along with Geronimo, they sneaked out of the house.

Roger drove first to an out-of-town Quik Trip, where he bought two packs of cherry danishes and two six-packs of Coke. Outside the store sat a vending machine for bait, and for a dollar twenty-five in quarters, Roger bought a Styrofoam cup of worms.

"In case we fish," he said.

That night, sitting around the remains of campfire, Roger stared blankly at his wound, the burnt knuckle, all scab now. From time to time, he mindlessly rubbed at the sore. The air was dense with insecticide and the smell of burnt wood. He had sprayed Zach and June twice. For his own protection, he wore jeans and a long-sleeved shirt.

"Surely it's not *that* hard of a question, is it?" he asked Zach.

Geronimo lay on his side and scratched, beginning to whine. June massaged her arms and stared through the top of the flame, where everything looked wavy through the gas.

"Rats with big fangs," Zach finally said. "That's what would scare me."

"What about rats with no teeth, just gums?" Roger asked.

Zach considered this, then grinned. "Gums ain't scary," he said.

Roger squeezed the boy's thigh, then turned to June. "Well?" he asked, smiling. "What scares you?"

June was twelve. The night before, she'd cut her bangs too short. "Blood," she said. She hugged her knees.

"Your turn, Dad," Zach said. "What scares you?"

Roger rubbed his knuckle. He couldn't find any proof, nothing tangible, but he was sure Tracy was cheating on him. He had a feeling. He'd had a feeling once before, when they lived in Laramie, and he was right: Tracy had been seeing a man named Jack Toole, and he'd seen them driving together in a flatbed truck, Tracy leaning her head all the way back and blowing smoke above them. It was the way she had leaned her head back and blew smoke that first caught Roger's attention before they'd even met.

"Flesh," Roger said.

Zach said, "Sick."

"Shhhhh," June said, nudging her brother.

That night, Roger stayed in the cab of his pickup, while Zach, June, and Geronimo slept huddled together outside on the cool ground without covers. The dirt looked good, the coolness of the earth against them. Geronimo stayed awake all night, scratching. He scratched without hesitation, whimpering, sometimes licking a stray arm, hoping, one might think, for a reprieve, a moment without itch. The children began scratching, too. They turned over several times in the night, shifting for comfort, and in the hallucinatory hours of sleep, they itched.

The clinic was too crowded, the air thick. Roger thought he could taste illness in the room, a sour film on the roof of his mouth. Parents didn't watch their kids, and so they were everywhere, hovering everywhere like moths. Roger kept flexing; he tried to relax.

Later, in the examination room, a tired Asian man wearing a lab coat stood before the three of them. Since the man did not identify himself, Roger could only take wild stabs guessing his position: Was the man a pediatrician, a surgeon, a lab technician? He could have been anything.

The kids looked awful, their legs bloodied from scratching. They stood in underclothes, side by side, reminding Roger of abused children he'd seen on TV. Zach shivered and wouldn't stop crying from the urge to claw his skin.

"Sarcoptic mange," the man said. "I saw them in the microscope."

"Mange?" Roger asked.

"Tiny bugs," the man said. "Do you have a dog?"

Roger nodded.

"Geronimo," June said.

"Does he scratch?"

"Never stops," Roger said.

"Take him to the vet. Get him dipped. Wash all clothes. Vacuum the rug. Clean the couch, all your bedding. Here's a scrip for the kids." He scribbled, then peeled a sheet of paper from his pad. "Treat everyone at the same time: the kids, the dog. Very important. If one still has it, they just pass it back and forth, back and forth. The pharmacy's downstairs."

In the pharmacy, Roger stood next to a rack of brochures and read about angina. The kids crouched in the far aisle, almost in tears. Roger could hear the sound of fingernails moving up and down, up and down. The noise was ceaseless and rhythmic, like old windshield wipers.

"Wood," the pharmacist said. "Roger Wood."

The pharmacist smiled at the kids and handed each a heart-shaped sucker—one red, one purple. He leaned close to Roger, over the counter, and said, "Be careful with this medicine. Don't leave it on them for more than twelve hours."

"Why?" Roger asked.

"It might cause seizures."

Roger stayed in the garage for most of the next three weeks. At night he covered his head with a pillow, fastening it close to his ear with the crook of his elbow.

The mites, as the doctor had warned, were hard to kill.

"We can't sleep, Mom," Zach had said after the first treatment. "I hurt all over. I can't take it." He fell to the floor and began crying. He rubbed his face against the shag carpet. He ran his nails up and down his legs. Roger crouched to feel the carpet. The shag was wiry, its thick bristles wrapped tightly together.

"Get up," Tracy said to Zach. "Cut it out."

"He can't help it," June said. "We're going crazy scratching. We can't stop."

"*Please,*" Tracy begged. "*Please stop.*"

"I'm on fire!" Zach yelled.

"A zillion bugs," June said, "eating us."

That night, Roger climbed the stairs to say goodnight, to tuck his kids into bed, but he stopped midway when he heard their muffled voices in the bathroom. A strip of light glowed from under the door.

"Higher," June said. Then, "No, no. Higher."

Roger crouched, holding the bannister. He was conscious of his breath, the hidden wheeze catching in his throat.

June said, "That's enough."

They dimmed the bathroom light to amber, as they always did, and stepped into the hall, totally naked but shiny and metallic now from the medicine, glimmering in the half-light. Roger remained crouched, watching as though Zach and June had arrived from another world, skin pieced together with shards of silver. That night, in bed, Roger had itch dreams. He dreamed of gouging Zach and June with rakes and knives and sandpaper, anything to stop the itch. He used a nail file on Zach. On June, he tried dousing her with witch hazel and rubbing her skin with sheets of Velcro. Nothing worked.

The nights finally cooled off, the mites died, and the children's legs scarred over. In the process, scratching day and night, scratching endlessly, Geronimo lost his fur. Zach said he looked like a walking hunk of clay. But Roger thought the worst: that Geronimo had been turned inside out, his fur now growing inward. No one wanted to pet the dog anymore, except Roger, who often reached over and ran his hand across Geronimo's back. The skin felt silky and hot, though it was hard to look at the dog, and the smell got noticeably worse. The kids often tied him outside for five or six hours at a time.

In the garage, Roger sat in a lawn chair and stared at the band saw. He'd bought three two-by-fours and a box of assorted nails, but all of this stayed near a tricycle in the corner. When the band saw was running, Roger just kicked back and listened to it purr. He wasn't sure anymore what his wife was up to. He knew she was having an affair; he figured it was Phil Lubbock, the school principal, the man who ran the PTA. She'd mentioned his name twice before in passing, and the name had stuck: Phil Lubbock. *It's the name of a city,* he thought. *Lubbock. Lubbock, Texas.* He said it over and over, aloud, until it sounded like a man drowning, gasping for air: *lubbock, lubbock.*

Roger got up and began sawing. Before midnight, he'd sawed old board games in two, stacks of newspapers, hammer handles, a football. He sawed whatever he could find and whatever he thought he could saw.

On Sunday, everyone wanted to go to the church carnival.

"For the kids," Tracy had said; but Roger could tell how much she'd wanted to go, too. It was part of their new life, doing what other people did, being in public.

At the carnival, Roger held out two crumpled ten-dollar bills, one for each child. "Let's meet back at eleven sharp," Roger said. Zach and June snatched the money and took off running.

The Octopus Ride swiveled close by, and Roger sensed that the gates keeping people back had been set up wrong. The twirling black cars looked as if they might swoop too close and hit someone in the head. The Salt-and-Pepper Shaker rose and fell, rose again slowly, halted, then fell. A tiny girl in a bumper car rode in endless backwards circles. The floor of the Spinning Wall dropped, and everyone screamed.

An older man and woman walked over to Roger and Tracy, and the man extended his arm. "Well, hello there. I don't think we've really met."

They were Roger's neighbors, and Roger nodded a few times

and said, "No, we haven't. We've been so busy." Roger gripped the man's hand, shook it, and said, "Roger Wood. And this is Tracy."

"Roger, Tracy," the man said. "I'm Waldo. And this is my wife, Kay. Kay's got laryngitis. Hurts like hell to talk."

Kay pointed to her throat and smiled.

"Waldo?" Roger asked. "What the hell sort of name is that?"

"Roger," Tracy whispered.

"His name's *Waldo* for Christ's sake."

Tracy stepped forward and carried the conversation. "Laryngitis," she began. "That's *awful*."

Roger refused to listen. He nodded, but he watched the blurred faces on the Octopus instead of paying attention. He concentrated all of his focus in one area and let the faces stretch by. Maybe his kids were on there; maybe not. Soon, all he saw were indistinguishable patches of flesh. Flesh and darkness.

"You shouldn't have been so rude," Tracy said.

Roger looked around. Waldo and Kay were gone.

"They're Peeping Toms, Trace. I don't want them near us."

"What?"

"Watch out," Roger said. "Careful where you walk. One of these rides might hit you."

"What are you talking about?" Tracy asked.

"They come so close," Roger said. "They've got the gates all set up wrong. Carnies," he said. "They're all the same."

"Roger," Tracy said. "I don't know what you're talking about, but you're scaring me."

"Sometimes," Roger said, "they forget to put the screws in or bolt something down. They're a pack of careless, ignorant sons of bitches."

"Roger!" Tracy said.

Roger said, "I know about you. I know all about you and Phil Lubbock."

Roger tied Geronimo to a pole in the backyard. Every night, for the past week, Geronimo pulled toward the light of a loading dock—the back entrance of a tape factory, which was two blocks away. Geronimo never whined or moaned or barked; he just pulled. Somewhere in his blindness and eye fog, Geronimo saw something he wanted.

In the garage, Roger carefully changed the blade of the saw. He'd moved small items from the house and into the garage, sawing them in half or sections of four. There was no logic to what he took, no pattern, no sense to it. He took what he thought the band saw could handle.

Tracy had denied it all, but what could she say? *Yes. I'm screwing the principal. I fuck him at night, while you're at home. I fuck him and I think about the kids, how good they are, how much I love them.* Could she honestly have told him this? What had he expected?

For the next two weeks during work, Roger drove his UPS truck through the parking lot of the grammar school, circling the tiny lot with a truck driver's precision, circling and watching. Someone had taped old, faded construction-paper turkeys and cornucopias in the windows. In one of the rooms, Roger thought he could see his old art teacher, Mrs. Boyle. Logically, he knew this couldn't be so: why would she be living here, three hundred miles away from the small Illinois town where Roger had attended her class? Unless, of course, she'd been following him all of these years, keeping track of where he lived and what he was doing. But the longer Roger looked, the more he was convinced that what he saw in the window was a stationary shadow. The shadow of an overused coatrack, perhaps. Or the shadow of a giant chicken-wire and papier-mâché statue. At recess, Roger watched a tall, thin-haired boy push Zach onto the blacktop; June stood alone, near the monkey bars, pulling her own hair.

At home, Geronimo remained outdoors, tied to the post, pulling every night toward the distant loading dock. Tracy had begun saying short, repetitive prayers before dinner, bowing her head, thanking God.

"Let us be thankful for this food," she said. "And for this home. And for our health. And for our new life."

"Lubbock," Roger said one night. It was no longer a person's name. To him, it had become a simple sound effect, a last ditch effort for a man under water to be heard: *lubbock, lubbock.*

The kids snickered.

Roger continued: "lubbock—*HELP!*—lubbock, lubbock. Bloop, Bloop, Bloop. Bloop, Bloop."

Tracy got up and walked to the bedroom, locking herself inside.

"She fucks him," Roger said, "and thinks about you kids, how good you are, how much she loves you. But she still fucks him."

"Dad," June said, starting to cry. Zach merely looked around, as if he'd suddenly found himself in another's home, eating with people he'd never before seen.

That night, while everyone slept or pretended to sleep, Roger quietly disassembled the kitchen table. Piece by piece, he took it into the garage. He carefully reassembled the table, taking his time, making sure it didn't wobble. Then he turned it upside down, balanced it on the body of the band saw, and tried cutting it in two. The blade wasn't long enough, so he had to saw the corners off first. Forming a vague system, a pattern, he did this for hours, until daylight, until the table lay in forty-two pieces piled in the corner of the garage.

That morning, Roger explained the problem to Tracy, that he'd taken the kitchen table into the garage, that he intended to fix what was wrong with it.

"The table," he said. "It wobbles."

Tracy stared at him.

"What am I supposed to do?" Roger asked. "It wobbles."

———

Tracy Wood was at the PTA meeting; Roger sat on the front steps of his house and stared into the sky. The moon was enormous, and Roger couldn't help thinking he'd been transported to another planet. It was a game he'd played as a child—staring in the distance, staring intently until everything became fuzzy and grainy, then pretending to be somewhere else, another country, another planet. Roger stared at the moon so hard now, it seemed to move toward him in waves.

"The moon is coming," Roger whispered. "Here it comes."

The front door of the house opened slowly. "Daddy," June said.

"What's wrong?" Roger asked.

June's face was red, and she was sniffling.

Together, they walked around the side of the house, through

the gate, and into the backyard. Zach was on his knees, leaning over Geronimo.

"Oh God," Roger said and crouched next to Zach.

Geronimo lay stretched on his side, silent. Roger lowered himself and stared into the dog's left eye, but all he could see was the reflected pinpoint light of the back porch, and darkness. Roger unhooked Geronimo's leash.

"Dad," Zach said.

"It's okay," Roger said. "You kids spend time with him. He had a good life. He lived a long time."

That night, the kids in bed, Roger hauled the rest of the furniture into the garage: two end tables, a love seat, a recliner, a bookcase. He sawed everything in half.

At two in the morning, Roger waited for Tracy. He sat on the front porch, arms crossed, the moon coming at him in waves. By four-thirty, a small foreign car pulled to the curb, and the passenger-side door swung open. There was laughter, the high-pitched, free laughter of a reckless night. Tracy stumbled out of the car and said, "Whoa!" She laughed. The man who drove the car mumbled something; Tracy looked back at Roger, then turned to the car. They whispered together some more, and the door shut. The car idled away — the automobile equivalent, Roger suspected, of a man on tiptoe.

Tracy walked toward Roger, carefully, self-consciously. "I fucked him," she said. "I got it over, out of the way." She waved her right arm, as if she were a magician. "It's what you wanted, and now it's through." She smiled and leaned her head back, the way she would had she been smoking. "I hope you're happy," she said.

"I am," he said.

Tracy's eyelids lowered. She yawned. Then she shook her head and moved past Roger, into the house.

Roger walked to the side of the garage and picked up a heavy-duty plastic garbage bag. Inside was Geronimo. He was heavier than Roger expected, much heavier than the times Roger had simply lifted and carried him down the stairs. He'd always been a fat dog for his size, but in the stiffness of death, his weight seemed to triple.

Roger started down the middle of the street. He knew the neighbors were watching. He could see the parted curtain of the living room. They were probably getting a kick out of him at this very moment. *Roger and his garbage bag. Look at him. Where do you think he's going?* But Roger kept walking. The sky had begun to lighten some, deep-deep blue now instead of black. Somewhere, Roger would buy a shovel and bury Geronimo. But not anywhere near here. In the country, perhaps.

The pavement seemed to move through his shoes, past the flesh, connecting, finally, with the bone of his feet. Bone and pavement. Bone and pavement. Roger created an internal rhythm for himself to listen to, and this kept him going: *bone and pavement, bone and pavement.* After an hour, Roger hit a fork in the road. Without hesitation, he followed the road to the left, because that's how his body leaned. That's where the weight of Geronimo pulled him.

Torture

Mr. Polaski sat cross-legged on the sloped roof of his house and yelled, "Goddamn you, Ruth. Just put the ladder back where I had it. *Now!* Do you hear me?"

Mrs. Polaski had gone inside, shut all the windows, and turned on the central air, drowning out her husband's pleas. Mom and I thought we could see the flickering of a television set, too, though maybe what we saw was only refracted sunlight, a prism of colors shifting across the windowpane.

"Jack," Mom whispered. "Do you think they can see us?"

We were standing on the back porch, a screened-in addition to our house, perfect for spying in broad daylight. I'd just returned home from my first year away at college, my car barely unloaded, but already I was back in the mix of things—*things* meaning our neighbors and what little intrigue they brought into our lives.

"I don't *think* they can see us," I said. "What happened, anyway?"

"I don't know," Mom said. "They were fighting this morning, then she took the ladder away. He's been up there since nine o'clock. She's teaching him a lesson, I guess."

"Hmmmph," I said. Mom was sucking on a cough lozenge and smoking a cigarette. "You got a cold?" I asked.

"No. Why?"

"You're carrying a bag of cough drops with you," I said.

She opened the bag and said, "Want one?"

"Not really."

"I'm addicted," she said. "When I'm not taking them, I start coughing. It's all in my head, though. What do they call that?"

"Psychosomatic," I said.

"That's right," she said. She unwrapped another lozenge, popped it into her mouth, and returned to the kitchen. Periodically, between chopping onions or smashing bread crumbs into a bowl of meat, she would join me on the porch to see how things were progressing.

"Still there?" she'd ask.

"Still there."

I kept watching, as absorbed as I'd once been years ago with bugs. It was a scientific, detached sort of fascination, as though Mr. Polaski were not a man on a roof, but a grasshopper trapped in a spider's web, or a ladybug crawling into the volcanic opening of an anthill. I wanted to see what would happen next, but there was no emotional investment in it for me. I might as well have been staring at him through a telescope; I felt that removed from the man's life.

Our family had learned it the hard way, that neighbors were nothing but trouble. Most of my life we had lived in apartment buildings on Chicago's South Side, and for a short while some of the neighbors had been our friends. Eventually, though, we began to notice patterns—how, for instance, they allowed their kids to run amuck whenever they came over to our apartment for a visit. Boys and girls, ranging in age from three to ten, would hop up and down on our furniture, scuffing the coffee table with their shoes, before strolling into my bedroom and systematically breaking one toy after another. They were a malicious lot: snapping off the handlebars from my Evel Knievel motorcycle; dragging the phonograph needle across my Elton John *Captain Fantastic* album; pulling out my stamp collection, licking the backs of my mint-condition NASA stamps, and sticking them to each others' faces. Once, while serving lemonade to my guests, I opened the door to my bedroom and saw a moon buggy affixed to a girl's forehead. I screamed, dropped all three glasses, and ran to the bathroom, where I locked the door and pulled my hair. Meanwhile, their parents remained at the kitchen table, strangely oblivious, bumming one Lucky Strike after another, managing, between gulps of coffee or quick, jumpy drags of cigarette, to wax philosophic about Tupperware or Jell-O-and-fruit recipes. And yet these same parents (on those rare occasions when we would beat them to the punch and stop by *their* apartment) would make damn sure that I sat quietly on their plastic-covered sofas and used coasters for the lukewarm tap water they served, while their kids flaunted new, expensive toys—wise enough, at least, to keep a safe distance from me since they knew (or sensed) that I was an Old Testament sort of kid (*An eye for an eye*, I believed) and given the chance, I would seize such a moment to smash everything of theirs that I could get my hands on.

When I was in the fifth grade, our family moved to a condominium with the hope that if people owned the place they lived in, they would treat each other differently. And they *did*. They wanted to control you more; they wanted to spend your money on things you didn't need. Each family paid a monthly fee that went into a fund, and the money in that fund could be used for whatever we had unanimously agreed upon. Each building had a president, elected by the tenants, and in our third year in the condominium we discovered that Mr. West, *our* president—a life insurance salesman who lived on the second floor—had been embezzling the fund money and producing phony receipts for services we'd neither voted on nor seen the results of. There were twelve units in the building, and six of us sued the president. For whatever reason, five families remained loyal to the man, refusing to impeach him, so we felt compelled to sue them, too. It was the first time we'd ever employed a lawyer, and we couldn't get enough of it. We basked in litigation. The judge ruled in our favor, and my mother—forty-eight years old at the time—came home from court, found my Queen album, and played "We Are the Champions" full volume.

Four years later we moved into our first house, and it was at this point in our lives that we collectively decided we'd had enough of neighbors.

The fact that my mother didn't rush outside to help Mr. Polaski didn't surprise me. Not at all. Not that we had anything specifically against the man. In fact, as far as I could tell, he was gentle and soft-spoken, probably in his mid-sixties, and polite, though I never ventured close enough to find out. His wife was another story. Any day of the week, she could be found standing in the street, wearing her robe and house slippers, flagging down neighbors and pointing (frequently at *our* house), her mouth in a state of perpetual motion. From the beginning we had made it known to her that we weren't interested in what she knew about those surrounding us—the failing marriages, the alcoholic husbands, the mob-connected families—and it was precisely *this*, our disinterest, that eventually caused us to become the object of Mrs. Polaski's public speculation.

"We keep her up at night," my mother said not long after we had moved in. "Amazing. We keep our distance, and she loses sleep over us."

My father was a roofer, always exhausted after work, his eyes bloodshot from the roof's debris blowing into them. His hands had open wounds from splattered tar, his nose speckled with white sunspots. He ate without looking up, and that afternoon, while spearing a wedge of pork chop with his fork, he said, "Yeah. Well. Fuck her."

And that became our controlling ideology whenever we thought of our neighbors: Fuck 'em.

That is, until the day I returned home from college. Mom and I were riveted. A man trapped on his own roof was better than anything TV could offer up that early afternoon. I sat there, catatonic, for nearly three hours, amazed that such things could happen, until Jenny, my girlfriend, knocked at the side door. I caught her attention and waved her inside.

"Jen," I said. "You've *got* to see this."

"What?"

"Come here."

After pulling her into a crouch, I took her hand, shaped her forefinger into a pointing position, and aimed it at Mr. Polaski.

"So what," she said. "Some guy's sitting on the roof. Big deal."

"His wife took away the ladder."

"Oh. Why didn't you tell me that in the first place?" she asked.

"This morning all he did was yell at her," I said, brushing my face against hers, sneaking two fingers between the buttons of her blouse, trying to slip one under her bra. "But now he's stopped," I said. "He's calculating his next move."

"How long's he been up there?"

"Five hours. Maybe longer."

Jen wiggled herself free of me and said, "Why don't you go help him, Jack?"

"Uh-uh," I said. "No way. The second I step foot on that lawn, his wife has a legal right to shoot me."

"She wouldn't do that."

"You don't know her," I said. "I'll bet she's loaded up and *waiting* for me step over the property line."

Jen peered up at Mr. Polaski. She gasped. She had a heart murmur, and her breath would catch at unexpected moments. It wasn't life threatening, but it had provided me with a good excuse before we were dating to rest my head on her chest and listen to the faulty, murky workings of her heart.

When we first began dating, Jen was a freshman in high school, and I was a senior; though now that I was in college, our age difference bordered on criminal. Here I was, on the one hand, quickly approaching legal drinking age, and Jen still couldn't drive a car. Yet this is what thrilled me, the deviance. The big joke in the dorm was that I couldn't keep away from jailbait. Whenever a grade school girl walked by, my friends hooted and yelled, begging me to run away.

They'll lock you up for that, Jack! Don't do it! For the love of God!

Jen turned from the roof now and said, "Listen. We need to talk."

"Sure," I said, though I knew this meant trouble.

I escorted her past my mother, to my bedroom—a tiny, make-shift quadrant of the attic with a sloped ceiling, bamboo paneling, and chalky tile above our heads. At first Jen wouldn't say anything. She pointed the crown of her head at me, the ghostly white part in her hair zigzagging like a scar from top to bottom. So I said, "What's up? What do you want to talk about?"

"Us," she said, and I nodded. I knew exactly where this conversation was headed. I didn't even have to listen. My job was to stand there and catch the key phrases, her words hurling toward me like a series of slow-spiraling footballs: *long-distance relationships . . . freedom . . . still friends. . . .*

When she finished, I leaned forward and kissed her, and to my surprise, she didn't pull away. I unbuttoned her blouse, and she said, "It's hot up here."

"Boiling," I said. I walked over to the window, and when I jerked open the curtains, Mr. Polaski's face, not more than ten feet away, greeted me. I'd forgotten how close my bedroom was to his roof, and I almost screamed when I saw him there. We made eye contact, and he nodded at me. Then he pulled a pack of cigarettes from his shirt pocket, shook the pack a few times, and extracted a cigarette with his teeth, the way tough guys do. We were so close, I could have opened my window, leaned outside, and lit it for him.

I turned around and Jen looked up at me, smiling, then she looked beyond me, at Mr. Polaski, and she let out a hair-raising scream. She was naked, except for her pink cotton panties. "Shut it!" she yelled, but something had slowed my reflexes. "Shut it!" Jen said again, covering herself, but when I looked back, Mr. Polaski had turned to face the other way. I pulled the cord that shut the curtain.

Jenny had already started putting her clothes back on. She had a lovely, childlike way of getting dressed—easily frustrated, huffing, exasperated when her ankle caught in the tapered leg of her jeans.

"Hey," I said. "It's okay. Relax."

"He gave me the creeps."

"You have to think about it from *his* perspective," I said. "He doesn't really have a choice. You know?"

She snorted. "This is your idea of a practical joke, isn't it, Jack?"

"He scared the hell out of me, too," I said. "You don't believe me? Feel my heart."

"I want to go," she said. "It's over between us, okay?" When I didn't say anything, she said it again: "*Okay?*"

"Sure," I said. "Okay. All right. Whatever."

I followed her outside, saw her to the end of the driveway, and watched as she stalked angrily down the street. She bounced theatrically with each step, fists clenched as though she were looking for someone, anyone, to pound on.

When my father came home from work, bleary-eyed, he mumbled something either to me or to my mother before heading to the bathtub where he would stay for at least a half hour. He used Lava soap to scrape the globs of tar from his skin, along with a tin can of milky white goop for washing away whatever else had attached itself to him during the long day. When he finished his bath, he shaved, then joined us in the kitchen, reeking of Old Spice, triangles of blood-stained toilet paper stuck to his chin and neck.

Dad began the conversation, as always, talking about his day at work, distinguishing between his fellow workers not by their names but by the insults he'd grown accustomed to calling them. One was *peckerhead*. Another, *numbnuts*. His boss was always *that no-good cocksucker*.

Mom waited until he'd finished dinner before letting him in on our secret, and when she finally did, she teased him with information. "You have to see this for yourself."

"Why?"

"You just have to," she said.

Dad followed my mother and I followed my father, and together we stood on the porch and stared up at Mr. Polaski. The sun had moved over his house, and he was buried in shade now.

Mom said, "He's been up there for eight or nine hours." She

looked over her shoulder at my father and said, "What do you think? Should we help him?"

My father narrowed his eyes, as if he saw perched on the roof every neighbor we'd ever had. He said, "What's he ever done for us?"

"Good point," I said.

"Besides," he said, "if we help him down from there today, they'll both be over here tomorrow wanting to play Bunko." Back in the kitchen, Dad fixed himself seconds. Pouring marinara sauce over stiff cobwebs of spaghetti, extracting meatballs and Italian sausage with tongs, he said, "It's none of our business."

And it wasn't. The three of us knew the truth, that this was the price one paid for maintaining a certain level of peace and privacy. Our experience had taught us this, and all evidence pointed in one direction: that good deeds caused only grief.

"You're right," I said. "Fuck 'em."

Perhaps the most startling thing I ever saw my father do happened when we lived in the condominium. This was a month or so after the verdict had gone in our favor. Mr. West, the debunked president of our condo, was on his way to the mailboxes; my father was standing at the bottom of a flight of stairs, on his way to our storage locker. I was inside our apartment, drinking a Tab, so I missed the first of what was said, but a few unpleasant words had already been exchanged, and when I opened the door I heard Mr. West say, "And tell that fat ass wife of yours that . . ."

And then his sentence trailed off.

It was true: my mother had a weight problem. She was a large woman. I took for granted how she looked; she was my mother, after all. But her weight was a private issue, and I knew the moment West said what he did that my father wouldn't let it slide. From where I stood, I could see both of them: West bent over a wrought-iron railing, yelling at my father, suddenly trapped by his own words; and my father below, picking up the nearest thing he could find, which just so happened to be the door to the laundry room, a door which, for reasons unknown, was off its hinges and leaning against a wall. My father lifted it over his head and began running up the stairs. Donald B. West must have realized just then that my father was capable of anything. He was being chased back upstairs by a man wielding a door. Right or wrong, my father had made his point, and Mr. West never again made mention of my mother in any context, good *or* bad.

Tonight, after dinner, Dad asked me if I would help him work on the car. Helping meant handing tools to him. What my father wanted was company, though he'd never have said so. I agreed, though I hated leaving behind Mr. Polaski.

Outside, Dad lugged his toolbox over to the front of my mom's Olds 88. He popped the hood. My mother dreaded these moments. She'd often said that my father used only two tools to fix a car—a hammer and a saw—and there was a grain of truth in this. Two years ago, my father tried replacing a coil for the heater in my Ford Fairmont. It was wedged somewhere inside the dashboard, out of his reach, and the longer it took him to get to it, the more frustrated he became, until, finally, on the brink of madness, he sawed a hole in the floorboard of the car, below the glove compartment. Naturally, it defeated the purpose of replacing the part—after that, a draft always blew through the seams of the patched-over hole—but my father had conquered the car, and that was all that mattered. Two years later, he still brought it up. *Remember that son of a bitch?* he'd ask and shake his head nostalgically.

Today he was trying to locate the source of an ominous sound coming from the car. There were always ominous sounds coming from the cars he drove. He would slow down to a crawl on the toll road, squint, and say, "You hear that?" And if I said no, he would begin describing it to me, while cars and semis soared by, honking and flipping us off. The sound we were searching for today was "something rubbing against something."

He listened to the engine for a solid ten minutes before motioning for me to kill it.

"Did you hear that?" he said.

"No."

"Sounds like it's coming from *here*," he said, pointing, "but I can't see anything." He rifled through his tools, found a standard screwdriver, and started poking around the engine. I watched without doing anything for a good half hour while my father pushed on belts, removed the air filter cover, and spun the fan with his hand. It amazed me, really, how he could continue working after a long day already spent in the sun, breathing in the fumes of hot tar. I'd helped him roof a few times, illegal side jobs when the union was striking, mostly work given to him from the owners of apartment buildings where we'd previously lived. An hour in the sun, and I was ready to pack it in, call it a day. My work ethic, by comparison, was pathetic. The sun made me nauseous; the fumes, sleepy.

My father wiped his hands onto his shirt and said, "The poor bastard."

"Who?"

He motioned with his head, tipping it toward our house, but meaning the house *beyond* our house: the Polaskis'.

"Oh yeah," I said. "It's pretty funny, isn't it?"

"Don't kid yourself, Jack," Dad said. "There's not a goddamn thing funny about it." His voice remained matter-of-fact, not at all scolding. He said, "There've been times I've gone to work so pissed off, I thought about walking *off* the roof. Now don't get me wrong. I don't think I could ever do it. But I've *thought* about it, by God. I've stood at the edge and looked straight forward and *thought* about it."

"You know, though," I said, "he didn't go up there to *jump*. His wife took the ladder away."

Dad bounced a wrench off his toolbox and said, "I know *that*, for Christ's sake. That's not what I'm talking about." He crouched, picked up the wrench, and ran his hand across the fresh dent in his toolbox. He stood and said, "Hey. Check this out. I've been saving them for you."

He led me to the back of his pickup and heaved two giant duffel bags up and over the tailgate. "Go on," he said. "Open them."

I untied the knot of string cinching the bag shut, though I didn't have to; I already knew what was inside. Soccer balls, baseballs, tennis balls, kick balls. Balls for every sporting event imaginable. All year long, Dad collected the balls he'd found on roofs (mostly from schools), and he hoarded them for months before finally springing them on me.

"Thanks," I said, and I dragged them to the side of the house. I wasn't an athlete, and so our garage was full of several Hefty bags full of balls. Occasionally, I took a bag of tennis balls to a court and knocked them with a racket as far as I could, one after the other, until the bag was empty. Once, I sold a medicine ball to a friend for ten bucks.

"Why don't you start 'er up again," Dad said. "I'd like to find that sound before it gets dark."

As I was sitting in the car, revving the engine, Mom, using her cigarette hand, motioned for me to come back inside. Dad's head was buried under the hood, so I slipped away unnoticed.

Mom popped a cough lozenge and said, "Look."

"Jesus Christ," I said.

Mr. Polaski was flat on his belly, one leg dangling off the side of the house. Slowly, carefully, he positioned himself so that he held on by the mere pressure of his palms against the shingles, both legs hanging off the edge. Then, one hand at a time, he reached down and took hold of the gutter, where he hung, building up the courage to let go. I could see clearly what was going to happen before it happened, but before I could say anything, the gutter broke loose from the house and Mr. Polaski fell to the concrete patio below. The gutter, still clutched in his hands, knocked him on the head.

Mom gasped, and I pressed my head against the screen. "Oh, shit," I said.

Mr. Polaski lay on the patio, silent. His eyes were open, and I entertained the thought that he was okay, that the fall wasn't nearly as bad as it looked. And I was about to say as much to my mother when the man began screaming. His right leg was twisted at a crazy angle, and he had a gash over his eye from where the gutter had hit him. I'd never heard anyone scream like that before, and I kept expecting Mrs. Polaski to come rushing outside to help her husband, but nothing happened. The central air unit continued chugging; the windows remained shut.

"Hey," my father said. "Where'd you go?" He moved closer, his breath warm against my neck.

Mom said, "I think we should call an ambulance for him."

Dad shook his head. "We don't know what the hell goes on over there."

"Look at his leg," she said.

"For all we know," Dad said, "he beats his wife and he's getting what he deserves. We don't have any obligation to get involved." After a moment of just standing around and staring at Mr. Polaski, Dad looked at me and said, "You ready to come back outside and give me a hand, or what?"

It was dusk now, but I kept circling the neighborhood, recrossing my tracks six times in less than two hours, each time passing Jen's house, looking for signs of life. Nothing. Not a trace. Each time I circled, I noticed changes the city had made while I was gone. The speed limit had been reduced from thirty to twenty, and on some blocks it was as low as fifteen. Stop signs had been put up where before there had been no warnings at all. A few streets had become one way only. It seemed to be a conspiracy, a way to detect and trap those of us who'd escaped—defectors trying to sneak invisibly back home for a week or two. But I was lucky. I'd caught the changes in time and adjusted accordingly.

The seventh time I circled the city, I decided to swing through the parking lot of the condo where we used to live, where my father had chased a man with a door, because I hadn't ever returned. The first time I drove by, window down, all appeared to be quiet, serene even, though I knew better than to believe that. Lights were on, TVs were mumbling, but the people inside, I'm sure, were brooding and plotting, taking their troubles to sleep with them, dreaming of violent, unrestrained revenge.

I drove behind the condos for a closer look, but when I pulled around the bend, I hit the brakes—a bit too hard—because I'd forgotten about the new development, and its scope took me off guard. Where there had once been fields now stood what must have been a hundred one-story duplexes, all housing for the elderly. The sight startled me: the brightness of it all; the concrete and shrubs; the wide, smooth roads twisting into dead ends or cul-de-sacs—my youth, paved over now and colonized.

One summer, between the fifth and sixth grades, I spent most of my spare time here, lurking around that field, doing nothing but torturing insects—grasshoppers, mostly—needlessly ripping their legs free from their bodies, pulling off their heads, or crushing them in such a way that, although maimed, they would continue to live. I must have seen myself as a kind of Dr. Moreau, and the field leading all the way back to the chain-link fence that separated our city from the industrial park was my island. Torturing bugs occupied the bulk of my time back then. It was like a drug, as intoxicating, an escape from whatever was going on in my life at that particular moment, and it took a year or so of plucking wings and tearing off antennae for the remotest sense of guilt to creep into my consciousness. I suppose the fact that they were silent while I conducted my experiments was what allowed me to keep doing what I was doing. It was a phase, common among boys, and when it passed I vowed never to do it again. Even now, if I happen to catch an insect inside my house, I'll take it outside and unfold my hand, more out of habit these days than guilt. But I'm sure the guilt is still there, lingering, though all of that was so long ago, and none of it seems particularly real anymore.

Mr. Polaski was no longer screaming when I got home. In fact, he wasn't anywhere in sight. It was possible he'd crawled somewhere in search of help, but if this were the case, I couldn't tell where he'd gone.

Mom normally left a dim light on for me, but the house was pitch-black tonight, and I stumbled from room to room, touch-feeling my way around. Then I touched what was so obviously somebody's head, and I thought, *Mr. Polaski. He's been waiting for me.*

My neck tightened, and I said, "What are you doing here?"

Mom said, "I'm sorry. I thought you saw me."

I caught my breath. I said, "Jesus, Mom. You scared me to death."

She flipped on the end-table lamp. The bag of lozenges was on her lap, along with a box of Kleenex. I could tell she'd been crying, something she was inclined to do. Growing up, I'd assumed it was out of boredom, or a certain hopelessness that everyone around here seemed to suffer from; but only now, after a year away, did it cross my mind that maybe, just maybe, it was a chemical imbalance, perhaps something controllable with medication.

"Are you okay?" I asked.

"Yeah," she whispered. "I'm trying not to cough. That's all."

I ran my hand over her damp, curly hair. I crouched next to her recliner and said, "What happened to what's-his-name next door?"

"Mr. Polaski?" she said, as if we were surrounded by dozens of men trapped on roofs by angry wives, and it was necessary to identify one from the other.

"Yeah. What happened?"

"An ambulance came."

"Really!" I said. "I didn't think the old witch would ever give in. Sorry I missed it."

Mom didn't say anything, and I could hear through the open windows in our house the whir of the Polaskis' central air-conditioning. It was night, the temperature had dropped significantly, yet the central air continued chugging.

I said, "It wasn't her, was it? *You* did it. *You* called for the ambulance."

Mom held the tissue to her mouth in case she began coughing.

"Take a cough drop," I said.

She shook her head and opened the bag to show me. It was empty.

"There must be more around here somewhere," I said. I checked the kitchen cabinets first but couldn't find any. In the bathroom, inside the medicine chest, I found prescription cough syrup, long past its expiration date.

I brought the medicine and a tablespoon to my mother, and I poured it for her, working hard to steady my hand so as not to spill any of it. She opened her mouth, and I slipped the spoon inside, pulling it out only after her lips had sealed around the spoon's neck.

She nodded and wiped her mouth with the napkin.

I said, "Why did you do it?"

"What?"

"Call the ambulance."

She said, "I kept thinking it could have been me out there."

I wanted to reassure her, to say, *That won't ever happen*, but I knew it might. Anything was possible. Only today my father had brought up the prospect of walking off of a building.

"Watch," I said. "Tomorrow night they'll both be over here wanting to play Bunko."

"Don't make me laugh, Jack," Mom said. "I might start coughing."

I kissed her, stood, and walked back outside. I picked up the two duffel bags of balls and dragged them into the backyard. I found an old baseball bat inside the garage, behind a shovel and rake. I emptied one of the bags, picked up a tennis ball, and hit it toward Mrs. Polaski's house. It flew over the chimney. I picked up another, and this time I hit the metal awning over her back door. I tried a golf ball next and missed it with the bat, so I picked it up and threw it instead. I pegged the central-air unit. With my foot, I spread the balls before me. There were softballs, ping-pong balls, and racquet court balls. There were blood-red rubber kick balls and leather soccer balls, which I nailed, one by one, with the tip of my shoe.

One nicked her door. Another bounced off her car. The sixth one broke her bedroom window.

This last direct hit inspired Mrs. Polaski to turn her light on. I picked up a baseball and lobbed it at her shadow, but the ball just thumped the curtain, then promptly died. I picked up a tennis ball and waited. When she stepped outside wearing her bathrobe, I threw it at her legs, missing on purpose, but causing her to side-step quickly out of the way.

"What are you doing?" she yelled. "Are you *crazy*?"

"I thought you liked sports," I said. I threw a golf ball as hard as I could at her car, a Cadillac the color of butterscotch. It ricocheted off the front right fender.

"That's it," she said. "I'm calling the police."

"No need to," I said. "It's too late."

"What do you mean?"

"I mean, it's too late," I said. "Your husband's already dead."

There was silence. I had finally captured the woman's attention.

"He died on the way to the hospital," I said. "Head injury, they told me."

"You're lying," she said.

I shrugged. "A fall like that . . ."

"Oh God," she said and covered her mouth.

"He needed your help," I said. "Surely you heard him. He was right there where you're standing, yelling your name. You *must* have heard him."

Mrs. Polaski fell to the ground. She let out a long, mournful wail. Then came the crying. She bawled like a child, unable to catch her breath between sobs. Gasping. On her knees, she leaned forward, arms outstretched, her face touching the ground. Softly, her entire body bounced to the staccato of her weeping.

I packed the duffel bags and dragged them into the garage. I shut and locked the door, then headed back to the house.

Upstairs, while gut-wrenching sobs floated up to my window, I lay in the dark and dialed Jen's number. It was already after midnight, but Jen picked up on the first half-ring.

"Hello?" she said.

I didn't say anything.

"Russell?" she whispered. "Is that you?" She laughed. "Quit playing games."

The line between us buzzed and crackled. *Who the hell's Russell?* I wanted to ask but didn't.

"You're a naughty boy," she said, then laughed and panted into the receiver. "Naughty, naughty," she said breathlessly.

Downstairs, my mother was coughing, Mrs. Polaski was crying, and a siren moaned somewhere far, far away. I listened to Jen talk that way for awhile—*Say something dirty*, she whispered, *say something really nasty*—and then I heard it, that catch in her breath, between words. For a second, nothing followed. No breathing. No words. It was only a second, but it seemed much longer. Ten seconds. Twenty. At last she sighed, her breathing stabilized, and when she spoke again—*Russell*, she said, *why won't you talk to me? What's wrong, sweetheart?*—I leaned over, returned the phone to the cradle, and shut my eyes.

Limbs

I found him buried up in the tree. You could say I stumbled onto him, though this is not literally true. I saw his shoe first, a Reebok sneaker. It sat next to the tree, flat on the ground, something curled and tucked away inside, hidden. A shadow stretched along the shoe's pad, but I couldn't see at first what cast it. In winter, brittle corpses of rodents littered the field, popping underfoot, and I suppose this is what I expected when I lifted the shoe: a shriveled field mouse, four tiny paws frozen to the fabric. But the shoe was much heavier than that, as heavy as a foot, though I'd never have guessed that a foot—or part of a foot—was actually in there. Even after I had turned the shoe upside down and watched the bones tumble out, it took some time before that final, necessary leap of logic made it possible for me to see the long, gray, knobby pieces for what they had once been: five toes.

I checked the shoe's size (thirteen—four sizes larger than what I wore), and I walked over to the tree, a weeping willow, and leaned against the trunk, considering one of two options: drop the shoe and forget about it, or bring it back to the house and show it to Ivy. But the very thought of Ivy made me want to wing the shoe as far as I could. I wanted to box the tree with bare knuckles and claw my face bloody. Ivy was the reason I was outside in the first place. I'd left the house to get away from her. I had walked until I reached the outer edge of our property, hoping to leave behind the sour taste of our argument. I couldn't even *look* at her right now. What, then, would she make of me returning to the house with an old shoe and the dregs of five disgusting toes? What would she think if I took my new souvenirs to the laundry room, locking the door behind me so as to study them in private, without her input?

To hell with this, I thought. *To hell with everything.*

For some reason—I'm not sure why—instead of dropping the shoe and walking away, I looked up. Frustration, perhaps. The universal gesture of a person in the throes of desperation. A reflex. Though it could very well have been a sound, too—a squirrel tightrope walking its way across a telephone wire. Or maybe I was checking the weather, though this is unlikely since I knew perfectly well what the weather was like: bone cold with gray snow-bloated clouds lumbering overhead. I'd been staring out the kitchen window earlier that day, watching the sky, staring so long that what I saw instead of clouds were a thousand ghost Rottweilers migrating above the tree line, our dead Rottweiler, Caesar, leading the pack.

It was March, below zero, which is why I couldn't smell the half-rotted corpse hanging in the tree; it was frozen solid. And it had been a long time since I'd wandered all the way out to where the four property lines joined together. The weeping willow marked that point exactly. What was left of the man's body simply hung there above me, buried in the tree. *Buried*, because it was obvious someone was trying to hide him, stuffing him out of sight, though not counting on the animals to pick away the meat, as they inevitably would—a possum, say, lugging away an ear, or a raccoon making off with a finger or two. More importantly, I say *buried* because I knew who he was. I knew the moment I realized a man was dangling in the limbs above me.

That night, while the police scoured the area, slicing floodlights over scent-trailing hounds, my neighbors Mitch Pitchlynn and Ken Bock came over to play poker. Friday night was poker night, and we saw no reason to let the arrival of a dead man discourage us from taking each other's money.

Mitch said, "I expect to get my ass kicked tonight. Playing cards with a man who found a dead guy doesn't strike me as a particularly prudent move, but I'm a gambler and I'll take my chances."

Ivy eased off the couch and crept furtively up behind me. She had come to inspect my hand, but I quickly folded the cards until they fit into my palm, then I turned them away from her.

"Well, boys," she said. "Do me a favor. Don't take *all* of my husband's unemployment money." She'd managed one last dig for the night—a low one, at that. Then she reminded Rachel that it was well past her bedtime.

"*Mom*," Rachel groaned. "It's not even *midnight*."

Rachel was twelve, our only child. I said, "Let her stay up. She can help her old man cheat. You'd do that, wouldn't you? Help your daddy cheat?"

"Dad says I can stay up." When Rachel crawled over to the back of my chair, reached around my waist, and dug her chin between my shoulders, I knew Ivy couldn't say *no*. We'd agreed long ago never to contradict each other in front of Rachel when it came to the ground rules of discipline. We'd discussed this months before Rachel was born, how such behavior would lessen the other parent's credibility. And yet I couldn't resist. If Ivy wanted to play a game of one-upmanship, I was more than eager to return the serve.

I dealt three hands around the horn before turning around to smile at Ivy, letting her know that we were, for the time being, even on digs, but she had already gone to bed. The bedroom door, I suspected, was locked.

Mitch reached over, squeezed Rachel's arm, and said, "If your daddy's got three of a kind, smile at me. If he's got four of a kind, blink your right eye. A flush, shake your head twice. A straight, wiggle your ears."

"A royal flush," I said, "crack him over the head with a hammer, because that's exactly what it's going to feel like when he sees my hand."

Rachel said, "What are you guys jabbering about?"

"Poker," I said, but my voice disappeared beneath the PA system's static outside, a reminder of the weeping willow and the dead man I had found.

Ken pulled a cigar from his bomber pilot's jacket. "Do you mind?" he asked.

"Why the hell would I mind?" I said.

"Not you, numbnuts. I'm talking to the kid."

"Why would I mind?" Rachel asked. I could tell she was enjoying all of the attention. It was the rarest of nights, one she would think about years from now, no longer sure which parts had actually happened and which she'd made up. Our backyard, normally pitch-black, was weirdly illuminated, as if a major motion picture were being filmed out there, and the sickly sweet smell of Ken's cigar must have stung her nose and made her dizzy. She rested her chin onto my shoulder and wrapped her arms tightly around me, pinning me to the chair's back. I shut my eyes, imagined getting electrocuted. Then I wiggled free to pick up my cards: three aces, two queens.

"Well," I said calmly. "Who do you think did it?"

"You have any doubts?" Mitch asked. "Old Vern White. No question."

I nodded. Vern had been my guess, too. "I hope they nail the bastard to the wall."

Ken peeked up from his cards, then back down. He said, "It ain't Vern."

"Fifty bucks," Mitch said, reaching for his wallet, making a show of it, as he was prone to do.

Ken shook his head. "No money on this one. I'm just saying he didn't do it. It's too easy. Don't get me wrong, I don't like the bastard any more than you guys do. I just don't think he'd bury some guy on his own land. It'd be a stupid thing to do."

After raising the bet twice, after pushing the last of my money into the pot, I slapped down my cards and declared, "Full boat," unable to stop grinning—unable, that is, until Mitch, frowning, slowly fanned his own cards to reveal four leering Jacks. "Sorry," he said, scooping the small mountain of coins and bills toward him.

I sighed. I tried not to think about the money. "Look at it this way," I said to Ken. "The *beauty* of it is that he buried a guy on his own property. Because it's not just *his* property. It's mine. It's yours, too. And Mitch's. You ask me, the man's brilliant. You see what I'm saying?"

They did. The tree marked the spot where all our properties touched, yet it signaled the division as well. The issue had come up only last year when Vern White shot and killed Caesar for wandering over the invisible border and onto his land.

"I caught him trespassing," Vern White had said when he called to say he'd shot our dog. "You want him, you should come over and get him."

Everyone had liked Caesar. Though lazy and overweight, he was loyal to the end, a good companion—a hundred-and-fifty-pound Rottweiler that yearned for nothing more in life than to be the family lapdog. How many times had Caesar balanced himself precariously upon my knees, blocking my view of everything except his own fur, while his tongue, plump and moist, swiped my face?

Not that any of this mattered to Vern White. The rule of thumb around these parts is to shoot first and ask questions later. That, at least, had been Vern White's modus operandi.

It had happened in April. Rachel was away at school. Ivy found a box we could put him in, one with a flap so we could drag our dog back over onto our land. I carried a crowbar in case Vern White came out to offer up a few words.

"Watch," I said. "He's going to shoot us, too. It's a trap."

"White trash," Ivy repeated through gritted teeth. "He's nothing but *white trash*."

When we saw what had happened—that Caesar had wandered only a few feet beyond the invisible property line, not even close to Vern's house—Ivy and I must have sunk into a kind of shock. I remember looking up into the sky and praying. I am not a religious man, but I pleaded to God that day, I *begged* God to let

Vern, that good-for-nothing cocksucker, step outside and walk over to where we stood so I could bash his skull in with my crowbar. Please God, I prayed. Please let the old son of a bitch come out here and say something, for all I needed was an excuse. And Ivy, who normally opposed violence, yelled for Vern to step outside as well. She taunted the man, calling him a coward, a white trash piece of shit, but Vern wouldn't show his face. He stayed inside, hidden. He must have sensed something in our voices, something he couldn't have guessed we'd possessed: the ability to kill.

But rage like that can last for only so long, and the next time we saw Vern was from a distance—which is how we always saw Vern White—and we felt utterly helpless. Much as we wanted, we couldn't really *kill* the man. So what *could* we do? He didn't have any dogs of his own; he wasn't married; his house was rigged with sensor lights; he kept his pickup in the garage. The man was close to eighty, so the best we could hope for was illness, something that would debilitate him, make him suffer. A stroke. A heart attack. Alzheimer's. But even that dim wish faded after a few months.

Then, in November, a man named Toby LeBeau disappeared. He was single, twenty-two. He held a B.A. in theater from Southern Illinois University. After graduation, he moved to Benton, into a trailer next to the Pinch Penny Laundromat.

Few in town could remember LeBeau. Even before he'd disappeared, the man was all but invisible. Employees of the two-screen Cineplex where LeBeau had been hired as a manager two months before his death were the only people who knew him at all. But even the ushers and projectionists couldn't add anything worthwhile to the thin stick-drawing profile the police had put together. *He kept to himself,* they'd told detectives, *you know: the quiet type;* though late one night at the Last Call, a few ounces of alcohol coursing through his bloodstream, one of the ushers conceded that LeBeau was sort of a pansy, and that he had taken his job far more seriously than he should have.

"It's a movie theater, for chrissake," the usher had said. "I mean, it's not fucking NASA over there. We're not launching *rockets* every two hours."

The three of us—me and Mitch and Ken—wallowed in speculation of the worst kind. We were no better than anyone else in town, basing our conclusions on tidbits of misinformation. On Thanksgiving Day, during football intermission, we came up with the idea of starting a pool. Using poster board I found squirreled away in Rachel's closet, we put together a grid and placed the names of local men inside, each man a potential murderer. Then, over the next few weeks, we passed it along to people we knew, five bucks a box, winner take all. I picked a man named Ralph Udell by closing my eyes and pointing, the way I tended to gamble, a strategy, no doubt, that explains why I lose more frequently than win. But the next time I decided to sock down a fin, I studied the grid more carefully, and I saw that Mitch had added my name to the board, along with Ken's, Vern White's, and his own.

"Jesus," I said. "There goes twenty bucks I could've won."

"What do you mean?"

"No one's going to bet on *us*. You could've put Gary Brooks's name instead of mine. Or Henry Raz's instead of yours. Raz was out of jail by October, wasn't he?"

"It's a joke," Mitch said. "You need to lighten up, pal."

Later that night, against my better judgment, knowing what she thought about these things, I told Ivy about the grid, and I told her about my name's being on it, along with Ken's and Mitch's and Vern's; and while I rambled on about how I thought it was bad luck, how I didn't like my name, even as a joke, to be included alongside the names of local thugs, Ivy dug through her purse, snapping and unsnapping billfolds, until she produced a five-dollar bill and held it toward me.

"Here," she said. "Put this on Vern White's head."

"Now, honey. Listen. Okay, true, he killed Caesar. But that doesn't mean he'd kill some kid in town. No one even knows who this Toby LeBeau character is. What would Vern's motivation be?"

Ivy kept her arm extended, the bill wilting from the tips of her fingers.

"Look," I said. "There's no sense throwing away five bucks."

"Who says I'm throwing it away?"

Of course, the more I thought about it, the more I began to believe that maybe it *was* true. Then, before long, I *hoped* it was true. The next day, I carefully penciled Ivy's name below Vern's, and I handed the five-dollar bill to Mitch. I said, "Money aside, I hope she's right. I hope the fucker killed LeBeau."

Mitch nodded, placed the bill into a shoe box. Without looking up, he said, "But you've got to admit, the money would be nice, too."

By the end of January, with LeBeau still missing and no one in custody, we had lost interest in the pool, so Mitch returned everyone's money. But on the day I found the body, we couldn't stop ourselves from speculating all over again; it was only natural.

"Maybe LeBeau was queer," Ken said. "His name's queer. Toby LeBeau. Faggot name if I ever heard one. And a lot of people around here don't like queers."

"Maybe *you're* queer," Mitch said.

Ken said, "I'm married, asshole. Remember?"

Mitch nodded, yawned, then folded. He reached over, touched my daughter's elbow, and said, "How do the braces feel?"

She had fallen asleep, curled near my feet, twisting herself around one of the card table's legs, and when Mitch touched her, she barely opened her eyes, a sleepy-lidded gaze as though she were staring up not at our neighbor but at her lover, and it nearly broke my heart. Truth be told, I was flat-out drunk by then— drunk and beaten down after a peculiar and unearthly day—and since there's nothing worse than liquor-fueled sentimentality, I nudged Rachel with my foot, harder than I meant to, and said, "Mitch wants to know how the braces feel, sweetie."

"They hurt," she said. She opened her mouth and ran her finger across the gleaming metal inside.

"Too many circus peanuts," I said.

"What?"

"Too many Pixie Stix."

She punched my thigh.

"Stop by tomorrow," Mitch said. "I'll make a few adjustments."

Rachel stretched and said, "I want to look outside again," so I flipped over my cards and walked to the window with her, and together we watched the floodlights snapping off one at a time while squad cars crept slowly away, their taillights, red and fuzzy around the edges, dissolving into the night's gloom.

It's violent country down here in Southern Illinois. Not L.A. or New York City violence where people get caught in the crossfire of gangs and end up shot in the head or blown to Kingdom Come for cutting off the wrong jerk on the expressway. No, the violence around here has a distinctly weirder edge to it than that. For starters, dismemberment is on the rise. It's not uncommon to open the *Benton Journal Star* and read about a limb someone has found in the Shawnee Forest. Not a tree limb—though there are plenty of those—but a leg or an arm, and sometimes a head (though technically speaking, I don't think a head counts as a limb).

A few years back, a doctor from Murfeesboro was arrested for killing two of his three sons for the insurance money. He used a shotgun. I worked with a woman who went to him regularly back in the 1970s, and she told me that what she remembered about him more than anything else was the hair on the backs of his hands, abnormally thick tufts sprouting from his knuckles, and how some nights she couldn't fall asleep from thinking about those bare hairy hands touching her thighs and belly in the privacy of a cold, sterile room, and how he had delivered her first child only two months after he'd taken the life of one of his own.

More recently, someone fished up a woman's head out of Rend Lake. The paper offered a description, though the words conjured up an image of what might have been anyone's head, really. After two weeks with no new developments, a drawing of the head finally appeared in the *Benton Journal Star*, though it wasn't, as one might expect, a computer enhancement of what the woman would have looked like alive. It was simply a crude sketch of what the head looked like after someone had reeled it in from a body of water: dead-eyed and bloated with hair stiff as seaweed.

Men at the local diner—a half-dozen retired miners—entertained themselves for days on end with the drawing.

"Hey, Fenton. Isn't this your *mother-in-law*?"

Or, "Hey, Baxter. *Who* says we don't appreciate art down here?"

Or, "Hey, Gus. Only *you* would go fishing and catch my ex-wife's head."

That Saturday I awoke on the couch, my body curled tight as a fist, my spine unnaturally bent in order to fit within the confines of the armrests. After the slow and torturous process of showering with a hangover, then getting dressed, I found Rachel and walked her over to Mitch's.

Mitch lived by himself in a large, draughty Gothic Revival farm house. An only child, he returned home from college after his parents were found huddled together in the front seat of an idling Chevy station wagon, its windows rolled down while the garage door remained shut and stuffed along the bottom with old beach towels. Mitch cashed in his parents' stocks and opened a novelty store, Benton Joke-O-Rama, a place I rarely visited— embarrassed, I suppose, to be seen among the aisles of fake barf, sex board games, and greeting cards that featured morbidly obese people wearing next to nothing or nothing at all.

Today, though, Mitch would be all business. He treated his dentistry with the utmost professionalism, though I suspected it was on account of its being illegal, and that his seriousness was a compensation for the diploma he didn't have. After his parents' double suicide, Mitch dropped out of dental school. He did what most of us did: he opted for complacency. But he knew enough about teeth and owned most of the basic tools to take the occasional side job, and since Ivy and I didn't have dental insurance, he was thoughtful enough to offer us his services at fantastically low cut-rate prices.

He greeted us at the door, already dressed in a white smock, a surgical mask loose around his neck.

"Come in," he said and stood aside, waiting to close the door. "Hey, Cruthers. I never noticed until this very moment. Your teeth."

"What about them?"

"They're sort of set apart."

"They're fine," I said.

"That's not the point. Wide-set teeth are a sign of good luck. It means you're going to travel."

"Where the hell did you read that?"

"I don't know," he said. "Nowhere. It's a superstition."

"Well," I said, "you're wrong. I'm unlucky by nature and I'm stuck right here. In *Benton*."

"Hmm," he said. "Maybe they're not set apart enough. I could take care of that, if you like." He nodded thoughtfully, put his hand on Rachel's back, and said, "Well, princess. How about letting me look around inside your mouth for a while?" He led her away to a bedroom he'd converted into a makeshift examining room, equipped with a genuine dentist's chair he had bought from a bar in town that had gone bankrupt. The chair had been the bar's special feature, set up so the bartender could lean you all the way back and pour a pineapple kamikaze down your throat. I liked going into Mitch's room just to see that chair again, one I had sat in many times, tipped back, my hair hanging almost to the floor while blood and alcohol rushed to my throbbing head.

Rachel plopped down onto it, the cushion hissing under her weight. She said, "Dad. Could you take a hike?"

"Oh yeah. Sure. No problem."

Mitch winked and shut the door between us.

I headed for the bar in the parlor. "Hair of the dog," I muttered. Dust-covered picture frames lined the halls, haunted by the sepia relatives Mitch could no longer identify. Eighty-year-old wallpaper, decorated with cabbage roses, curled at the upper seams, revealing chipped plaster beneath. Cobwebs hung artfully from the corners, and the floorboards creaked with each step. Then, as if the late 1800s had violently collided with the 1970s, you stepped into the parlor and found atop the fireplace mantel Mitch's collection of cheap trophies from his childhood: dozens of tiny bowlers, baseball players, and martial artists loitering together, each athlete frozen in his own universal pose. Many treasures were nailed to the walls, including a macramé Aztec calendar, a giant hand-painted plaster "M" for Mitch, and a framed poster of W. C. Fields wearing a stovepipe hat and peeking up from a deck of cards. Presiding over it all was Mitch, of course: Mitch, the high school stoner, trapped inside the picture frame but peering blearily out as if from the frosted window of a time machine. Generations meshed unhappily together here, and for this reason alone, Mitch's house made the hair on my arms stand straight up.

I walked over to the particle board bar wedged in the corner and removed a KEEP ON TRUCKIN' mug from a pegboard hook. I was about to pour myself a gin and tonic when I found our grid of suspects rolled up and tucked away. I flattened the poster board and ran my finger across the names. I would remind Mitch to reactivate our bets, to hold people, if at all possible, to their first choices, since Ivy had a lock on Vern White. She would stand to collect roughly five hundred bucks, money that would come in handy now more than ever.

I was adding up the names of legitimate suspects, hoping to get a better assessment of Ivy's odds and potential winnings, when I hit my name. I'd have blown past it, too, if not for the other name penciled in below mine. Taggart West. I rubbed my forefinger across the name's soft imprint. "Taggart West," I said. "Who the hell is Taggart West?" A man I didn't even know had put five dollars on my head.

I rolled up the poster board, walked to the examination room, and jerked open the door without knocking. Mitch was holding what looked like ordinary pliers against my daughter's teeth.

"Jesus Christ," he said. "Don't scare me like that." He removed the pliers, lowered his surgical mask, and said, "You okay, Rachel? Did I hurt you?"

Rachel shook her head, but she was glaring at me, as if it were her bedroom door I'd jerked open without sufficient warning.

Mitch said, "What the hell's wrong with you?"

My heart was pounding so hard I could barely breathe. I flattened the poster board onto Mitch's tray of dental equipment and said, "Who the hell's *this*?" stabbing Taggart West's name repeatedly with my finger.

"Let's see," Mitch said, and he leaned toward it, as if a close scrutiny of the handwriting would bring an image to mind, a face to match the scrawl, but I knew Mitch was faking it, that he knew damn well who Taggart West was.

"Oh yeah," he said, straightening up. "Yeah, yeah, I remember. *You* know Taggart. He works at the Currency Exchange."

"Bald-headed?" I said.

"Yeah."

"Eyes too close together?"

"That's the one."

"Well," I said. "I never liked the bastard. Seems to have a short fuse."

"Now, Cruthers," Mitch said. "It's not like there were a lot of names left by the time I showed the grid to him. He wasn't going to pick *me*. I was standing right there. You want to see something *really* screwy, look at what Ken did. Put five bucks on himself.

Said he didn't like the idea of people betting against him. Claims something like this could jinx him for good."

"You ask me," I said, "he's got a point."

"Screwy," Mitch repeated.

"Honey," I said to Rachel. "What do you say? You want to put five dollars on Mitch?"

"What for?"

I shook my head. There was no sense stirring up pointless trouble. "Ah, to hell with it. Looks like Ivy's gonna walk away with the whole ball of wax, anyway. That is, of course, if you re-activate everyone."

Mitch wiped Rachel's mouth with a dishtowel. "That feel better?"

"I think so."

"Too tight?"

Rachel shrugged.

"Let me know tomorrow," Mitch said. He removed his smock and washed his hands, a civilian once again, back to the Mitch who sold novelty vibrators and garlic-flavored chewing gum. The dentist act was over. He smiled and said, "You ever notice, Ken seems to fixate on homosexuals?"

"Fixate? I don't know if I'd go so far as to say *fixate*."

"Sure he does," Mitch said. "Last night we're throwing around motives, and what does Ken come up with? Maybe LeBeau was *queer*."

"The guy's lived here his whole life," I said. "Imagine that. You and me, we went away to college at least. We've traveled around. But Ken . . . I doubt he's ever been out of the *state*. We're what, forty miles from Indiana? An hour from Kentucky? Two hours from St. Louis? St. Louis might as well be in France as far as Ken's concerned."

Rachel had already left the room. For all I knew, she'd gone outside to check out today's developments, pressing her belly against the yellow crime-scene tape that had been wrapped around a generous circle of trees. It was possible she was outside flirting with cops, though I hoped to God she wasn't. In the past few months Rachel had begun to bud into something I hadn't prepared myself for, teasing not only the boys at school but our friends and neighbors as well. There was something calculated about the way she moved around a room, or the way she kept her head low while peeking up at, say, Mitch or Ken. I kept reminding myself to warn her—for her own good (I knew, after all, how men thought)—but the timing was never quite right, and when the other men weren't around, she slipped back into being a child again, totally incapable of subtle nuances and subterfuge, and I felt silly for even thinking about bringing it up.

"My point," Mitch said, "is that maybe, just maybe, Ken's a repressed homosexual. You know. Still in the closet."

I let out a long groan. It wasn't like Mitch to make simple deductions. There was no evidence pointing in that direction, other than Ken's paranoia that everyone residing outside of Benton was probably a fruitcake of one kind or another. I knew the point I was about to make wasn't a point at all—it was a flimsy defense—but I had my reasons for bringing it up, so I said, "He's married. Remember?"

Mitch hesitated, narrowing his eyes, then said, "Cruthers, Cruthers. You disappoint me. The fact the man's married doesn't mean *dick*, and you know that."

I *did* know it, but I had wanted to see his reaction. I was fairly certain Mitch was having an affair with Ken's wife, Maggie. I hadn't told anyone; it was only speculation. The truth was, I didn't care one way or the other. I preferred to be left out of whatever covert liaisons surrounded me. But I was curious. On two occasions, at suspicious times of day, I had seen them together: Maggie in the passenger seat of Mitch's LaBaron, Mitch driving. One time, they were heading out of town. Another time, they were heading back in.

The first time, all I saw was a flash out of the corner of my eye, the way you catch a body part in passing, and only later, after you think you've forgotten about it, the part connects itself to a person, and you say to yourself, *Ah ha!*—but the moment you think this, the image begins to fade, eclipsed by doubt, as if the conscious is passing the subconscious, the way the moon covers the sun, leaving you in that weird bright darkness of unknowing.

The second time, I knew for certain what I saw. On top of that, I was sure Mitch had seen me as well. I was leaving the Tru-Value on the outskirts of Benton, clutching a newly purchased caulking gun, and when I saw him, I started to point the gun at him, but then I saw Maggie so I didn't. I stepped back into a patch of shade, and as the LaBaron passed, Mitch looked toward me, a sideways glance, though his head still faced the road beyond him.

Mitch could have told me anything and I'd have believed him. A word or two, and I'd probably have forgotten all about it by now. But it was Mitch's refusal to offer up a voluntary explanation that prompted various sordid scenarios to roll through my head. An affair was certainly a realistic possibility. Ken, after all, worked long days in the coal mines—relentless hard work with no time to slip back home. Mitch, on the other hand, ran his own business. He set his own hours. He came and went as he pleased. He was a handsome man, too. A real charmer. And though Maggie wasn't the best-looking woman in Benton, no one could deny the sexual aura that seemed to surround her. *Earthy* was how Mitch had once put it. The only makeup she ever wore was black eyeliner; her hair was strawberry blonde, naturally curly. She was thirty-four that spring—two years younger than Ken, one year older than me and Mitch. And I'll confess: If I wasn't married, if I were a single man who lived walking distance from a woman whose husband spent half his life underground, I might have been tempted myself.

But Mitch, our best poker player, revealed nothing. He leaned back in his dentist's chair and said, "Maybe you're right. I was just throwing out a theory, that's all."

The week before I found Toby LeBeau, I had begun thinking more and more about Mitch and Maggie, and of the two occasions I'd seen them together. I'd been unemployed for three months, laid off from my last job at National Pharmaceuticals where I had worked in the gut of shipping and receiving: long mornings spent filling orders, dull afternoons knifing open boxes and doing inventory. Lunchtime, I would eat slices of smoked ham or turkey and stare into the homemade chicken-wire cage that held the Styrofoam peanuts we used for packing. I would stare intensely at a single point inside the cage, falling into a deep trance, and I would sit there like a zombie for the rest of my break until the *I Love*

Lucy theme song, floating through the ductwork, all the way from the boss's office, signaled the top of the hour, time to get back to work. It was the most relaxing part of my day, the hour I most looked forward to, because my only responsibility was to exist. That was all: *exist*.

Then I was let go, the result of cutbacks across the board; and here, in Southern Illinois, unemployment is high and getting higher all the time. So each month I would go to the Job Services office in West Frankfort, sit, and talk with a counselor, and each month a check would arrive to get me through. But my employment history had been sketchy, a few months missing here and there, and I knew that soon, very soon, the checks would stop coming, and that our lives would take a sharp turn in an unpleasant direction.

During the first few weeks of my unemployment, however, Ivy and I experienced a brief, but intense, period of rejuvenation. We had temporarily recaptured the intimacy we'd somehow lost a dozen years ago, satisfying cravings we hadn't revealed to each other since our early days of courtship. With Rachel away at school, Ivy and I attempted to make love in every room of the house—broom closet, attic, and breakfast nook not excluded. Only the crawl space under the house proved problematic, the glow-in-the-dark eyes of an opossum scaring us naked out of our sleeping bags and back into our house, where we belonged. Even more startling than this newfound fountain of sexual energy were the things we said to one another. Ivy's opinions, I discovered, had changed dramatically over the years, and I clung desperately to the idea that we were new people—strangers, even— and that the old boredom of routine and familiarity would finally melt from our days and nights. But three weeks into my unemployment, we'd begun to wear on each other, and slowly, regrettably, we sank back into our old, corroded lives.

To pass the time, I started watching a lot of television. Soaps, mostly. At first I laughed at the overblown acting, the grand gestures; but soon, before I knew it, I was sucked in, leaning closer to the TV, raising the volume, turning my head to catch the subtleties in an actress's voice. And it was here, during these early morning hours of contrived infidelity, that I had begun to think more of Mitch and Maggie, trying to sort through the fact and fiction of my memory. And it was half an hour before I found LeBeau that I decided to bring them up to Ivy in a round-about way.

"At what point," I said, "would you say that a husband or wife has been unfaithful to the other?"

Ivy bit her lip, her own peculiar way of cementing her thoughts, a prelude to speech. Behind her, the credits for *As the World Turns* scrolled up the screen, much too fast for anyone to read.

"Go on," I said, coaxing her.

She smiled. "Why're you asking?"

"Curiosity," I said.

"Is that all? Curiosity?"

I killed the TV with the remote. "Now, wait a minute," I said. "You don't think *I'm* screwing around, do you?"

"No, no," she said. "It's just an odd question. That's all."

"Well," I said, "it's hypothetical."

"Okay." She crossed her legs, resumed smiling. "Ask me again."

"Where do you draw the line," I said, "between fidelity and infidelity? Where's the point?"

"So what you're saying is that there aren't any shades of gray. There's just a single, solitary act dividing good from bad."

"There's got to be a point," I said, "where you cross the border. Sooner or later you're going to hit that point where it's definitely infidelity, and what I'm wondering is where you think that point is."

Ivy bit her lip again, one of her last remaining tics from grade school. She was only a year younger than me, but she looked maybe four or five years younger—twenty-eight or -nine—and biting her lip never failed to knock a few more years off. She said, "I don't think it works like that. I don't think it's a physical act. It's whether you're in love with the person you're messing around with. *Then* it's infidelity."

"Oh, horseshit," I said, then smiled, trying to keep everything lighthearted. "Now let me get this straight. A woman sneaks away from her husband and meets some schmuck at the Benton Motor Lodge. They roll around in the sack for a couple of hours, right? And according to *your* definition, the woman has still been faithful to her husband?"

"If she doesn't love the guy. Yeah, sure."

"You're not *serious*, are you?"

"Of course I'm serious. Why wouldn't I be?"

"Okay. Let me put it another way. Let's say it's *me*. It's *not* me, this is purely hypothetical, but let's say it *is* me. I leave you alone at home and go meet up with some woman at the Motor Lodge. We get a room, shut the door, and get down to business. Now here's what I want you to imagine, okay? Sex. Real nasty sex. I'm not in love with her, and she's not in love with me, but I'm going down on her. Are you picturing all of this? Are you imagining it? Remember: you don't know this woman, I *barely* know her, but I'm going down on her and I'm driving her wild, and when I finish up, she goes down on me. But right before she finishes me off, she climbs up on top and we start screwing. We screw—I don't know—three, four times. Then I take a shower and come back home to you, my *wife*. Now, if I'm understanding you correctly, and I think I am, you would *not* consider me unfaithful. Am I right?"

Ivy said, "And this is all hypothetical."

"Of course," I said. "But that's beside the point. What if it wasn't? *That's* what I'm asking. Put yourself in that position and make the call."

"So what you want is a physical act. A clear-cut moment of infidelity."

I nodded. The tone of our conversation had suddenly shifted. In fourteen years of marriage we'd never before defined for each other this line of demarcation, and suddenly I wanted to know.

"Okay," I said. "Let's start from the beginning. A kiss. On the mouth."

She laughed. "Yeah, right."

I wasn't smiling.

"A *kiss*," she said. "Of course not. That's silly."

I said, "I suppose I'll go along with that. Another kiss, then. This time it's hot, though. Tongues and whatnot."

Ivy shook her head. "No." She was losing her sense of humor as well, meeting my eyes when she answered.

"All right. I'll give you that. Probably harmless. Okeydokey." I looked down at my hands, and for some reason, they struck me as remarkably thin and bony. A set of weak, inconsequential hands. "Let's see," I said. I looked back up. "Groping. Clothes on."

"Clothes on?"

"Yep."

"No," she said.

"Hmm. Interesting. Okay. Clothes *off*." I smiled. I winked at her. I knew I had her. I was certain.

"No," she said.

"No?"

She shook her head.

I considered stopping right there, asking her *why*, but I decided to skip ahead and up the ante, backtracking if necessary, figuring where we went wrong.

"Oral sex," I said. To lighten things up, I added, "Clothes off," as if it mattered.

"On how many occasions?" she asked.

"Once," I said. "Not that I think it makes any difference. One time, twenty times—but let's say once. Just *once*."

"And they're not in love?"

"*Nada*. Not one fucking bit."

"You're getting angry."

"Why would I be angry?" I said. "We're just talking, right?"

"I don't like your tone," she said.

"Well," I said, "I don't like your answers. Seems to me I can't *help* my tone. So let's hear it. Oral sex. Clothes off. One time. Yes or no?"

"No," she said.

I stood up, nearly upsetting the coffee table with my knee. "You have GOT to be joking. Tell me you're joking."

"You're scaring me," Ivy said.

"*I'm* scaring *you*? Jesus H Christ. We're married fourteen years, and today—*today*—I learn that you think a blow job doesn't constitute infidelity. And I'm scaring *you*?"

She remained seated, legs and arms crossed, and said, "It's hypothetical. It's nothing."

"It's *not* nothing, and you know it. What we're talking about here is the basic difference between right and wrong. It's that simple."

"I don't want to talk about this anymore," she said.

"Well, maybe I do, goddamnit," I said. But the truth was that I didn't. I needed to slow down what was going on inside my head, to separate the thoughts that were jumbling together. What I needed was to cool off, so I snatched my jacket from the coatrack and left the house.

The subzero temperature instantly helped. Freezing cold is good for that. It forces you to think about your physical self. It forces you to recognize that thin line between pain and frostbite, the point at which the body begins to go to hell in no time flat: snot leaking from your nose; knuckles, cracked and bleeding; the way you can actually feel the contours of your skull, and how the ridiculously thin protection of skin seems to sear against bone itself. It's all you can think about, the limitations of the body, and before long, every other thought falls away.

I trudged out into the field behind our house. We owned a pretty good swatch of land, though I rarely wandered beyond where I mowed in the summer, a semicircle large enough for the barbecue grill, picnic table, and horseshoes. There was no need to go any further, especially after Vern White had killed our dog. The trees were arranged in such a way that at certain angles you could see all the way to Vern's house, while at other angles you could block him out altogether. A dozen acres separated us.

That afternoon, I ventured out into the chaos of petrified weeds and stiff arctic stalks. With each step, something crunched beneath my shoes, and the further I walked, the more frequently I startled animals: a snowshoe rabbit, a tomcat, a squirrel. Though my decision had not been a conscious one, I headed out toward the weeping willow.

My hands were tucked deep inside my pants pockets, my face aimed at the ground, shielded from the direct blasts of wind. I was thinking about my ears, how the wind relentlessly pounded the drums inside, how the edges wouldn't stop throbbing, when I noticed the shoe. A few minutes later, while leaning against the tree, I looked up and saw Toby LeBeau. And I couldn't help myself: I laughed. I shouldn't admit that I laughed, but I did, I couldn't help it. For the past six months I'd half expected to be the one who found him, the way *most* people in town had entertained the idea of stumbling upon him, becoming a hero by nothing more than happenstance. I had played any number of scenarios over again and again in my head: LeBeau partially sunk into the marshy side of a road; LeBeau mangled in a Dumpster; LeBeau resurfacing somewhere along the perimeter of Rend Lake just as I happened to be driving along, admiring the view. And here he was, the man himself, as though I'd won some sort of macabre lottery, the gift dangling above my head, already picked apart by animals. And I couldn't help laughing, thinking of all those dumb-shit cops with their shovels and crews of workmen digging up the ground day after day, and the fact that no one ever thought to look up instead of down.

Sunday, things still weren't back to normal between us, but Ivy offered me her leftover waffle, a soggy emblem of hope, along with a half-eaten sausage link, all of which I eagerly accepted.

"This is perfect," I said. "It really hits the spot."

To prove it meant nothing to her, that she would rather donate food to the enemy camp than throw it in the trash, Ivy ignored me. She stood at the sink and blasted water over dirty dishes. When I finished eating, I walked behind her, but she tensed up—I could see the cords in her neck, her entire body folding into it-self, the way a pill bug curls at the slightest touch—so I left her alone.

Outside, a few cops stood guard around the tree, but the investigation was at a standstill until Monday. I leaned against my pickup, watching the cops who hung around the tree and flicked cigarette butts onto my land. I could feel them looking at me, and I considered walking over and asking how the investigation was going but thought better of it.

Then, on Monday, Ivy and I learned from the morning news-paper that we had become suspects. Not just the two of us, but Mitch Pitchlynn, Ken and Maggie, and Vern White as well.

Mitch and I thought it was hilarious—the very idea!—and so in celebration we bumped our card game up four days early.

"Oh yeah," I said, dealing a round of seven card. "We all had motives, didn't we? Ken thinks he was queer. Typical hate-crime material. Mitch says the guy never came into his gift shop. Lack of patronage seems a good enough reason to kill a guy, don't you think? And me—well, that's easy. For the entire three months that he managed the Cineplex, they played that *Mutant Ninja Turtle* bullshit. Three months! And whose decision was that? LeBeau's, of course. Only movie theater in town, and he didn't have sense enough to realize someone would banish him from the face of the earth for not changing the picture more often."

It was easy to joke about the dead—we didn't know the guy, after all—but Ken wasn't laughing.

"Hey," I said, reaching over, tagging his shoulder. "What's wrong?"

He said, "I don't care if he was queer or not."

"But don't you get it?" I said. "You keep bringing it up. It's obviously eating away at you. So there's your motive." I winked at him.

"I don't want to be a suspect anymore," Ken said. He sounded like a child who'd tired of a game that had turned sour.

Mitch said, "C'mon, Ken. You have to admit, it's sort of exciting. We're in the spotlight, pal. All three of us. People think we're dangerous. Hell, I bet we've already got groupies. I read in the paper last week, this guy on death row, he murdered fifteen women, and you know what? He gets love letters from chicks all over the country. Do you believe that?"

Ken laughed, but when Mitch looked at me, he saw I wasn't smiling. He was trying to read my expression, as if anything I knew about him could be seen by looking into my eyes, the way you would look into a View-Master and watch a story unfold each time you pull down the lever with your forefinger. I looked away before he could actually see anything, and after a few more hands of poker, I called it an early night.

"Sorry, guys," I said, "but I'm beat. Too much excitement."

On his way out the door, Ken said, "You think we're being watched?" He was wearing his bomber pilot jacket and smoking a cigar, but he looked more like a grade school kid trying his best to pass for a grown-up, something straight out of an old Our Gang movie—a chubby ten-year-old puffing a stogie.

Mitch said, "You can bet your hairy ass we're being watched. Probably got their infrared goggles on us this very minute." He gave his middle finger to my backyard and said, "Here's one for the police file, boys."

The next morning I was fiddling with the deck of cards Mitch had left behind, working on my repertoire of fancy shuffles, when I noticed that the back side of each card had been tampered with. Nearly infinitesimal marks had been made with a razor, a code for the person who had put them there—the most likely suspect being Mitch, since the cards were his.

But surely it was a mistake. Surely Mitch had not been cheating us all along. I would ask him in due time, and he would provide a perfectly reasonable explanation, but until then I would not mention it to Ivy. Having used my unemployment money to gamble with, I was not in a good position to argue with her. So I stashed the cards away, if only to defer Ivy's scorn at me for playing Mitch's patsy.

Later that morning, freezing rain turned everything to ice: the trees, the grass, the rocks, our picnic table, our car. The backyard had metamorphosed into an ice forest, as brilliant and unreal as anything from one of Rachel's childhood picture books. But it was dangerous, too, so we stayed inside and played Monopoly. We drank hot cocoa and fell asleep off and on throughout the night while the TV spoke to us, its volume low and seductive.

Sunday, when I stepped outside, I spied two people near the weeping willow. I couldn't at first make them out. From this distance, they could have been anybody. It was early afternoon, and the temperature had risen so fast the ice had turned to fog. I felt as though I were standing in a cloud, trying to make out the features of people standing waist-deep in another, more distant cloud. With each step, I seemed to float closer toward them, an eerie sensory illusion, I realized, but I felt airy and light-footed all the same, as if in a dream. I continued floating along until I recognized them, then stopped before they saw me. It was my daughter and Mitch Pitchlynn.

Rachel was laughing, and Mitch was touching my daughter's shoulder. While Rachel looked up and pointed into the weeping willow where the body had been, I crouched closer to the ground so that only my eyes and the top of my head remained above the fog. Mitch was smiling and talking. He was wearing a tan field jacket with many pockets and a corduroy baseball cap—a handsome man with a skill for wooing women. Ivy had said once that it was his eyes. *They lure you in*, was how she'd put it.

I was about to quit acting the fool, to stand up, walk over to Mitch, and say hello, when I realized that Rachel was rising into the air. It was as odd as anything I'd ever seen: my daughter, standing erect, arms above her head, rising from the earth. Then I saw Mitch's hands, his fingers clasped together, and Rachel's foot resting in Mitch's palms as he lifted her above him to the first sturdy branch leading to the place where Toby LeBeau's body had been hidden.

For a second, maybe as long as two, I was paralyzed. And then I yelled: "Goddamn you. Get back here. *Now!*" It was a voice I'd used often enough with Caesar. Probably the exact same words, too. Rachel looked startled—Mitch, merely confused, as though unsure where the voice was coming from or who was speaking.

"Rachel," I yelled. "I'm talking to *you!*"

I must have crouched even deeper into the fog, unable to see anything except my own hands and legs, but I could hear Rachel jogging, her shoes slapping the ice crystals, and I managed to spring forward and catch her just as she was about to pass. A tackle, though I didn't mean for it to be so rough. We both fell, and she screamed. I covered her mouth. "Shhhhhhh," I said. "It's all right, honey. It's me." I let go of her. "Are you okay?" I asked. "I mean, did he hurt you?"

"*You* hurt me," she said. "I think I sprained my ankle. What're you doing out here? Are you *crazy?*"

"Shhhhhhh," I said. "Keep your voice down. Let's crawl back to the house."

"What's wrong?" she said. "Is someone after us?" She peeked above the fog line.

"Quiet, sweetheart. Let's just go back to the house."

Together, we army-crawled to the mowed part of our yard.

Then I picked her up and carried her the rest of the way, into the house.

"What did he say to you?"

"Who?"

"Mitch," I said.

"What do you mean, *what did he say*?"

"Did he *lure* you over to the tree," I said. "What were the two of you doing?"

"We just met there. On accident." When she slipped off her shoe and sock, I saw that her ankle was already swollen. "This really *hurts*, Dad."

"We'll get you some ice in a minute," I said. "I need to ask some questions first." I paused, detecting a familiar echo in what I had just said: I sounded like any number of the cops who'd been pestering me these past few days. I kissed Rachel's cheek and said, "Listen, hon. We need to be careful. Don't play around with Mitch unless I'm there. And don't go over to the tree by yourself. Once all of this blows over, everything will go back to normal."

"I wasn't *playing* with Mitch," she said.

"Okay, all right," I said. "*Whatever* you were doing then." I stood and walked to the refrigerator. I broke apart a tray of ice and wrapped a dishtowel around five sticky cubes. I twisted the towel and brought it to Rachel. Kneeling, rubbing my forefinger over the soft balloon of ankle, I held the compress against her pale skin, but I couldn't help thinking of the shoe I'd turned upside down, Toby LeBeau's bones tumbling out.

"Why was he lifting you into the tree?"

"It was my idea."

"Sure it was. But why?"

"I wanted to see how it felt. I wanted to stretch out and pretend I was dead."

I stood and walked to the window. The fog was thicker, and I wasn't sure if Mitch was still near the tree or if he'd gone home. "Don't ever do that again," I said, and though I was talking to Rachel, I was thinking of the way Mitch had touched her shoulder and what I would say to him the next time we met. "Okay?" I said. "*Okay*?"

"Al*right*," Rachel said. "Jeez."

The whole time Rachel told her side of the story—how I'd tackled her in the fog; how when she fell, her foot twisted all the way to the right—Ivy simply glared at me.

"What the hell did you think was going on out there?" Ivy asked.

"I don't know. It gave me a chill, though. You know?"

"No," she said. "I *don't* know. Mitch is our friend. He's *your* friend, for God's sake."

I shrugged, and for the rest of the night Ivy wouldn't speak to me. She tended to Rachel: replacing ice, taking her temperature, fetching paperback novels about woebegone teenagers in and out of love. The next day, Ivy pointed to Rachel's ankle and said, "Look at it. It's worse."

"Is it?"

"Just look," she said. "I think it's broken."

I had an old pair of wooden crutches in the attic, too large for Rachel, but she used them anyway. She liked to swing high and land on her good foot, though each time she landed I cringed, fearing more trouble.

At the hospital, I filled out an information sheet on Rachel, but when I failed to produce an insurance card, the receptionist looked scornfully at me.

"I must have left it at home," I said, shuffling through my wallet for good measure.

Rachel sat in the lobby, fascinated by everyone who came in. When I sat down next to her, she leaned against me and whispered into my ear, "I think that guy over there got shot in the head." She motioned to a man sitting across from us. He had a large gauze bandage taped above his eyes. The tape circled his head five or six times.

"I don't think so, honey," I said. "Maybe a concussion, but he wouldn't be sitting out here if he'd been shot in the head. In New York City, maybe. But not here."

A nurse entered the waiting room with a wheelchair, which delighted Rachel. If she was going to suffer, she would suffer in style. I could already see her reporting back to her friends at school, embellishing the agony. She was at an age where pain was a valuable commodity, in that the more you had, the more enviable you were.

In the examination room, the nurse asked what had happened. I was about to answer, to keep our story simple, when Rachel pointed at me and said, "He tackled me."

I smiled. I choked out a laugh. "That's not *exactly* what happened," I said.

A doctor was standing off to the side, gingerly fingering his stethoscope. Rachel had succeeded in getting his attention. We were behind a semiprivate partition, an absurdly bright rectangle of space. A plastic curtain separated us from another bed where someone lay moaning.

"Dad's right," Rachel said, continuing. "Actually, he was *hiding. Then* he tackled me. I didn't even know what hit me."

Heat rose to my face, though I fought to remain calm. "She's exaggerating, of course," I said. "Kids!"

The doctor stepped forward and held his hand out for Rachel's chart. He was in his fifties, had a neatly trimmed beard, and was accustomed to holding out his hand and getting what he wanted. It was obvious he didn't want to be here, that the ER was, in fact, the *last* place he wanted to be.

He looked at me and said, "And you're her father? Frank Cruthers?"

I nodded.

"Cruthers," he said. "I know the name." He kept his eyes on me, and without coming right out and saying so, he was letting me know that *he* knew that I was a suspect in a murder investigation. It seemed my name wasn't ever going to disappear from the daily newspaper, especially since I was the one who'd found LeBeau's rotting carcass.

"If you don't mind, Mr. Cruthers," he said, "I'd like to speak privately with your daughter." He touched Rachel's knee and said, "Is that okay with you?"

"I don't care," Rachel said. "Whatever you guys want to do. I'm just along for the ride."

I sat in the waiting room, alone with the man who Rachel thought had been shot in the head. I berated myself for not coaching Rachel, for not explaining to her how touchy they were in hospitals about child abuse, and how easy it was to misconstrue something innocent for something vile.

An hour passed. Then another. Fifteen minutes into the third hour, the nurse rolled Rachel to the automatic doors and told me she was ready to go. Nothing was broken, the nurse explained, but sprains could be nasty, sometimes more painful than a break. She handed over a prescription and ordered me to pull my car to the wheelchair ramp. "For insurance purposes," she said.

I scanned the parking lot, certain it was a ploy. Why else were they making such a big deal of sending me out alone to fetch my car? The police would apprehend me here, take me in for further questioning. Mitch would go down to headquarters and say, *It was pretty weird. One minute she was running. The next, she was gone. It looked like the fog had swallowed her, but now it makes sense. Of course. It was Cruthers!*

But the police never surfaced. I was safe. Once Rachel situated herself inside the car and we were back on the road heading home, I felt strangely exhilarated, as though I'd successfully pulled off an elaborate caper. Briefly, in the hospital's waiting room, my life had slipped into that gray area where anything at all might have happened, but now, miraculously, I was free, and whatever threat of danger I'd been feeling seemed far, far behind us.

Ken came over to my place right after work, his face streaked black, eyes red. The clothes he wore were sooty. Together we walked out into the backyard, though not all the way to the weeping willow. He said, "You haven't told the police anything I've said, have you?"

"What do you mean?"

"You know. The queer business."

"No," I said. "Of course not. Why?"

"I don't know," Ken said. "I get the feeling they're zeroing in on me. Even in the paper, my name's the one that comes up the most."

"Really? I thought mine did."

"Uh-uh. I've been keeping count," he said. "Maybe Mitch said something. That I'm anti— you know, anti*queer*. Truth is, I'm not. I just brought it up that day. A theory. That's all."

"Listen," I said, and to put his mind at ease, I said all sorts of things I didn't necessarily believe anymore. "I don't think they think it's us," I said. "It's Vern White, or it's somebody we don't even know about. Jesus, Ken, the whole police force is antigay, for that matter. If LeBeau *was* gay, they'd have closed the case already and moved on to something else. You see what I'm saying? You're all bent out of shape for nothing. If you're innocent, you're innocent."

Ken rubbed his forehead, unintentionally streaking the coal in such a way that it looked like war paint. "What do you mean *if?*"

"Forget it," I said. "You're taking everything way too literally. To be honest, you're starting to scare me. And you're one of the last friends I've got."

Over his shoulder, in the distance, his wife, Maggie, stood on their back porch, wearing, of all things, a cotton summer dress. I'd seen it months ago at a barbecue: lightweight and floral with bright, cheery colors. Her arms were bare, though it must have been twenty degrees. Worse with the windchill. Yet there she stood, arms crossed, while the wind, blowing east, lifted her hair and the hem of her dress. Even this far away I knew her thoughts were of Mitch Pitchlynn. The dress, I suspected, was probably the one she'd worn the first time Mitch had snaked his hand up between her legs.

I wanted to shake Ken and say, *Open your eyes, pal,* but the very thought of telling him what I knew tired me beyond belief, and the only energy I could muster was to slap him on the back. I wagged my head and said, "Why don't you go home and get some sleep, pal. And quit thinking about LeBeau. He's dead. Okay?"

My unemployment checks finally stopped appearing in the mailbox. Apparently, I had received all the money I was entitled to receive, and there would be no more. Aware that this would happen, I took measures to prevent totally running out of cash. For starters, I'd quit paying the bills over a month before. I'd decided to see how long we could float along as debtors. For spare money, I cashed a check for fifty dollars—the maximum amount—at the local grocery store, then continued cashing checks for the same amount each day, depositing the subsequent funds into my account in an attempt to stay one day ahead of the bank and grocery store. There's a name for what I was doing— *check-kiting*—and I considered finding more grocery stores where I could kite even more checks, but I never got around to it.

I told none of this to Ivy, of course, not even that the unemployment checks had run out. To admit to these failures would mean admitting to larger, more serious failures, the likes of which I didn't yet know. In the meantime, I kept hoping something would pan out, though *what* that something might have been I couldn't have said.

I canceled Friday's card game, and the game after that, the following Friday. I avoided Mitch as much as I could.

Day after day, we continued appearing in the newspaper as suspects. At first, people who knew me took it in stride: Cruthers, a victim of bureaucratic red tape. Cruthers, a scapegoat for an incompetent police department. But as the days stretched into weeks, I detected a shift in their allegiances. Little things, really. Diverted looks. Small talk cut uncharacteristically short. There was no sense in defending myself. I'd have looked paranoid. I was, after all, innocent. So I stuck closer to the house. Besides, I didn't have enough spare money for a cup of coffee.

One night after dinner, while helping Ivy clear the dishes off the table, I looked out the window above the sink and saw Mitch walking toward the house. I hadn't seen him since the day he lifted Rachel into the tree, and I was afraid he was heading our way to cause trouble.

Rachel said, "Look at my foot, Dad. It's like new." She started hopping up and down on it.

"Rachel," I said. "Go to your room!"

"Why?"

"Don't ask questions," I said. "Just do as you're told."

Ivy gave me that look, the one she'd been giving me all week, her death glare. "What's wrong with you?" she asked.

"He's almost here," I whispered, looking over Ivy's shoulder, into our backyard. I turned and grabbed Rachel by the arm.

"Ouch," she said. "You're *pinching* me."

"C'mon," I said. Then I whispered what I really feared: "He may be armed."

Rachel tried wrenching herself away. "Let me go," she said, a whine creeping into her voice.

"Let her go," Ivy said more forcefully.

The doorbell rang. I tightened my grip on Rachel, pulling her toward me. I dragged her into the hallway, though once there, all reasonable solutions to the problem eluded me. Her bedroom was upstairs, too far away. To get to the attic, I'd have had to pull down the staircase, which would cause a racket. In light of the circumstances, I opened the door to a hall closet and nudged her to get inside. "Just a couple of minutes, sweetie," I said, pleading, but as soon as she realized her fate, she began crying. "Go on," I said, trying my best to sound as hopeful about the situation as I could. "Please, honey," I said. But when I heard Mitch's voice, I simply shoved Rachel inside and shut the door, blocking it with a footlocker.

I met Mitch in the living room. Out of breath, I said, "What's up?"

"Thought you'd get a kick out of this," he said and proceeded to tell me about a basement sale across town and the harpoon he had bought for next to nothing.

"A harpoon," I said.

"Jesus Christ, Cruthers, you should've *seen* the shit this guy had there. He said he'd always wanted to go whaling. Do you believe that? Said the only reason he was selling it was he got tired of tripping over the damn thing."

"What do you need a harpoon for?"

"What do I *need* it for?" he asked. "Hell, I don't know. Conversation piece, I suppose." He opened his mouth to say something more when Rachel ran into the room, shrieking at the top of her lungs, her face contorted from crying. The makeshift barricade had failed and she stood now against her mother, hugging Ivy tight and bawling uncontrollably.

"What's wrong, baby?" Ivy asked.

"*Daddy*," Rachel began, her voice breaking into sobs with each word. "*Daddy put me in the closet*," she said.

I looked at Mitch and smiled. "We were playing a game. Something in the closet must have spooked her." I took a step toward Rachel, but she let out a blood-curdling scream, as if I were going to murder her. "Honey," I said and almost started crying myself. I met Ivy's eyes, then turned to Mitch. "Let's go outside," I said. Mitch followed but didn't say anything, so I said, "We play this silly game. It's silly, really. Too silly to explain. Something in there must have gotten to her." I shook my head and tried to laugh. "I can't imagine what the hell it was, though."

Schmidty, the lead cop investigating the murder, stopped over the next day and asked if he could talk to me. "Outside," he added.

I said, "Sure," though I felt instantly sick to my stomach. I suspected Mitch—or Ivy, even—had called the police and reported me. I pictured Schmidty putting me in a fancy wrestling move, his flabby body no longer as versatile as it had been during his glory days on the mat at state finals, yet still powerful enough to do serious and permanent damage to someone such as myself.

He took a pack of Lucky Strikes from his shirt pocket, shook it, and, using his teeth, pulled one free. He lit it and said, "Look. What I don't get is this. LeBeau was in that tree for three months. *Three months!* You mean to tell me that a man lives in a house and doesn't walk out into his backyard for three months at a time?"

"Why would I?" I asked.

"Hell, I don't know. A man normally goes outside and checks out his own land, makes sure it's okay. Men are like dogs. We piss on things that belong to us. It's our way of telling people to keep their grimy hands off."

"I guess I've always been the sort of guy who pisses *inside* his house," I said. "The outdoors don't appeal much to me."

Schmidty's squint got tighter and tighter as he sucked on his cigarette, as if the more he inhaled, the less room there was inside his head. When he shut his eyes completely, smoke began to pour slowly out his mouth and nose, thick blankets rolling as if from under the door of a room on fire.

"I remember you," he said finally.

"Oh yeah?"

Schmidty suddenly opened his eyes wide and said, "We went to high school together."

"Yes, we did."

He poked his forefinger into my solar plexus. "Drama club," he said, then turned his head and spat.

"No. That wasn't me."

"Chess club?"

"Wrong again."

"So. What was it?" he asked.

"Nothing," I said. "I just went there. That was all. I put in my time, and then I was gone."

"I've got yearbooks," he said. "You better not be lying to me."

"No, sir," I said before trudging back to the house.

A creditor called later that morning, asking about my delinquent VISA bill. Ivy was in the next room, close enough to hear, so I curved my hand around the mouthpiece and stood at the far corner of our mudroom, hoping to shield all sound.

"I've been going through a rough time," I whispered.

The woman said, "What? I can't hear you."

"I said, I've been going through some tough times."

"So when can we expect your payment?" the woman asked, bored. "Can you mail it today?"

I hesitated; I didn't know what to say.

"Was that a *yes*?" she asked.

"No. Look. I'm not sure . . ."

"Mr. Cruthers," she said, but I hung up, ending the inquisition.

The next morning I happened to look out the window and saw a man tooling around the house. I stepped outside, and though I meant no harm, I picked up a lead pipe in the event I would need to defend myself.

"Can I help you?" I asked

The man turned slowly, still looking down at the clipboard he was holding, and said, "Is this 414 Potter?"

"You bet," I said, forcing a smile, trying to seem neighborly.

"I've . . ." He glanced up, saw the lead pipe. He cleared his throat. "I've got an order here to shut off the electricity," he said.

I laughed. "I didn't order that."

"No, sir," he said. "*We* did. Looks like you're three months behind."

"*Three* months?" I said. "I thought it was only *two* months." I looked at my house, as if it could cough up an explanation for this mishap, then I caught sight of Ivy, who was holding a spatula and watching us.

"A few more days," I said, without much conviction.

"To be honest," he said, "it should have been shut off after two months. Somehow you slipped by us."

"There you go!" I said with renewed hope. "Everyone makes mistakes! Don't you see? *You* guys made a mistake, but no one gets in trouble. Right? Well, now, *I've* made a mistake. So why does my electricity have to be shut off? Why should *I* be the one who gets punished?"

He eyed my lead pipe and said, "Okay. I'll cut you a break."

"Thank you," I said. "Thanks!" I was so relieved, I wanted to hug him. My life was crumbling around me, but I had managed to stave off this one small disaster. I said, "I can't tell you how much I appreciate this."

"Okay, okay," he said. "Just write me a check for the past two months, and I'll talk to someone in accounting."

"Two months?" I turned again to the house. Ivy hadn't moved. I tossed the lead pipe aside. "I thought you were a burglar," I said. I couldn't look at the man anymore. I stared at my shoes, conjuring the ghost memory of bones spread along the ground, an omen of worse things to come. "Go ahead," I said. "Do your job."

Back in the house, I sat in the kitchen, sipping coffee, and stared out toward the weeping willow. No one had removed the yellow police tape. It circled several trunks like some long-ago tribute to American hostages overseas. What few lights were on inside the house suddenly blinked off. I was watching the second hand of an electric clock when everything stopped, and it struck me in that instant that death might be like this, a peaceful moment of suspended time before the tunnels of light or fire beckon.

The past few days, I had assumed Rachel was in her room, slowly working off her anger at me, teaching me a lesson by refusing to acknowledge my existence. But as morning inched its way toward noon, a string of worst-case scenarios bubbled up from the dark corners of my imagination, each scene more debilitating than the last.

I found Ivy in the living room, but she ignored me. She rubbed moisturizer into her palms, over her knuckles, twining her fingers together and cracking her knuckles.

"Where's Rachel?" I asked.

Ivy's hands gleamed inside a funnel of sunlight, the moisturizer accenting wrinkles. "Why?" she asked.

"*Why?* She's my daughter. *That's* why."

"She's staying with a friend," Ivy said.

"What friend?"

"That's none of your business."

I sat next to Ivy, my leg against hers. I said, "Look, sweetie. It's not just Mitch. It's everyone. We don't know these people, not really, and to claim we do is foolish. A guy was murdered, and somebody—I don't know who—put him up in that tree. On *our* property. For all we know, it could have been one of our friends."

"Oh, come on. Get real," she said.

"Listen," I said, gently, touching her hand. "Let's face it. What do we really know about Mitch?"

She moved her hand away. "I think you should spend less time persecuting your friends and more time concentrating on how to pay the bills on time."

"You're changing the subject," I said.

"Changing the *subject*? How can you say that? We're sitting here in the *dark*."

"Okay," I said. "Let me give you an example. Mitch cheats at cards."

"Oh *please.*"

"Seriously," I said. "He left a deck of cards here and I was messing around with them when, lo and behold, I saw that they were marked. Our *friend*, who you're so worried about me persecuting, has been robbing me—robbing *us*—for God only knows how long."

"I don't believe you," Ivy said. "They're probably from the joke shop. He probably didn't even know they were marked."

"Hah! Well, then, how about this? Did you know that Mitch is having an affair with Maggie Bock? Well? Did you know that?" I laughed. "You *didn't* know that, did you?"

Ivy stared at me for a good, long time. Then she narrowed her eyes and said, "You're lying."

"Why would I lie? I saw them together. Twice, in fact. Mitch even looked at me, but he won't admit he saw me. We act like nothing happened."

"You're making it up," she said, "to make some sort of twisted point. Or to justify your behavior."

I couldn't stop smiling: I had her. There was nothing she could say. I was privy to information she didn't know, and now that I'd sprung it, she couldn't deny I had a point. I said, "You can't believe it, can you? I couldn't either. But that's exactly what I've been trying to tell you. I mean, what do we really know about *anyone*?"

Ivy stood abruptly and walked away from me. I had thought gossip would bring us together, perhaps return some intrigue to our lives, but it had backfired, and violently so. Ivy was fuming. In the kitchen, she ran water full blast into the sink, though the dishes were clean and drying in the rack.

"What's wrong?"

"Nothing's wrong," she said.

"Come on," I said. "Just tell me what's wrong."

"Leave me alone," she said. "Okay?"

"Look," I said. "I know you like Mitch. Hell, *I* like Mitch, too. Liked him, at least. But when you think about it, he's a bit of a slimeball, don't you think?"

Ivy said nothing.

"I don't get it," I said. "All I'm trying to do is protect us. Why're you so pissed off at *me*?"

Ivy said, "I'm tired of listening to you talk about what you *think* you know. You know what? You don't know anything. Nothing. Your head—it's so *thick*."

"Just what the hell's *that* supposed to mean?"

The water continued gushing from the faucet while steam rose and darkened the window, but Ivy said nothing more. She was done with me.

I found my most recent electric bill, tucked it into my pocket, and stomped out of the house. I'd hoped I could barter with the business office, make a promise, sign some papers, *something*, surely there was *something* I could do. I was not a bad man.

Each time a large, oily-looking black bird swooped too low, I picked up a rock and threw it, a warning to keep away. Downtown, without meaning to, I ended up in front of Mitch's store, Benton Joke-O-Rama—a name, I realized, that lampooned an entire town and its people. What Mitch was saying was that *we* were the joke, and that he would gladly take our hard-earned money in exchange for a can of fake snot and a glow-in-the-dark condom.

I cupped my palms to the window and peered inside, and at the first glimpse of Mitch, I was reminded again of Rachel in the fog, Mitch lifting her into the tree; and I felt the same pulse of nausea I had felt that morning when I was certain these were going to be the final minutes of my daughter's life if I didn't do something right then and there. Why else was he lifting her into that tree? And the more I mulled it over, the more I was convinced that Mitch had known LeBeau, and that if he himself didn't kill the man, he had at the very least played some role in LeBeau's demise.

When Mitch spotted me, he motioned for me to come inside. I started walking away but stopped at the sound of his voice: "*Cruthers.*"

I should have kept walking, but I didn't. I turned toward him. I could feel my own blood pulsing through me. I felt it running through my neck, inside my head, against my eardrums.

Mitch said, "Howdy, pal," before taking the whole of me in: my posture, my expression. He grinned sheepishly and said, "Bad news?"

"I want you to stay away from her."

Mitch moved closer. "Easy there, boss. Slow down. What're you talking about?"

"I don't want you to ever fucking touch her again, or I'll bust you up. You hear me? I swear to God, Mitch, I'll rip your goddamn head off."

Mitch squinted, as if narrowing his eyes could improve his hearing.

"*You* know what I'm talking about," I said. "Just stay the fuck away."

"Jesus, Cruthers," he said. "What did Ivy tell you? Whatever she told you, pal, it's not true. Why don't you tell me what she said so we can talk about this. Okay?"

"*Ivy?*" I said. "Who the hell said anything about *Ivy?* I was talking about *Rachel.* I was talking about the day you lifted her into that tree."

Mitch opened his mouth—he wanted to backpedal, to re-tract—but when nothing came out, not even so much as a sound, he shut his mouth and smiled, slowly wagging his head. Mitch, of course, had caught his own mistake before I did. He was wagging his head because he had cornered himself without my help, and now he couldn't figure any quick and reasonable way out. I, on the other hand, was slow on the uptake, but as soon as Mitch's accidental admission of guilt finally materialized, it dissolved just as fast into a red-hot core, and I knew I had to get away from Mitch. I couldn't think it through—what had happened, what I needed to do—so I turned away from him and headed once again to the electric company to negotiate my bill, but on my way, I stopped off at the Alibi for a drink.

The Alibi used to be the Déjà Vu—former home to Mitch's hydraulic dentist's chair—before the Vu went belly up. It had been my favorite bar, in fact, back in the days when I would analyze with scientific precision why one bar in town was superior to another bar. The only inhabitants today were two men I didn't know, proof that I had not set foot inside this building for years, and the topic under consideration was the new Thai restaurant that had opened up in Carbondale, forty miles away. The men, deep into their discussion, did not at first acknowledge my arrival.

"I hear it's cheap as shit," the customer said. "And good."

The bartender said, "Yeah. Well. Count me out."

"Ever had Thai?"

"Around my neck," the bartender said. "Never on a plate."

"I'm told they serve octopus on rice," the customer said. "You like fresh *Octopussy*, don't you?" He waggled his eyebrows conspiratorially.

"Call me old-fashioned," the bartender said, "but I still prefer plain ol'."

At that, they turned and grinned at me, welcoming me into their fraternity of innuendo. I took the last of my cash out of my wallet and slapped it onto the bar. I grinned back, trying my best to play the role of common-man-out-for-a-drink, but I was unable to stop thinking of Mitch: Mitch Pitchlynn mounting my wife, Mitch the freewheeling bachelor screwing Ivy—*screwing her*—from every direction imaginable while I was away at work, ridiculously filling corrugated boxes with Styrofoam peanuts, hoping to keep delicate electronic parts from getting smashed during transport.

"Shot of Jack," I said, "and a beer chaser."

The bartender obliged. And he continued to oblige until my money ran out, at which point he gave me one on the house.

"Cheers," I said, knocking it back. Then I stepped outside on rubbery legs and peered unnecessarily up at the sun. It was still bright out, too bright for me to be so drunk, and everywhere I walked I caught eerily curved and misshapen reflections of myself. Then, suddenly, the tip of my left foot jammed into an uneven slab of concrete, and I found my torso propelled forward while my legs tried frantically to catch up. Just as I was coming back into sync, I heard the roar of sirens whisking toward me, and I anticipated being arrested for public intoxication, but all three vehicles quickly hummed past, their ear-piercing drone growing and vanishing, like a cloud of bees heading for a warmer climate.

By the time I reached the joke shop, the lights were off and the SORRY, WE'RE CLOSED sign had been placed in the front window. I walked around to the alley and tried the heavy door without luck. When I saw that Mitch's car was gone, too, I kicked the door once, hard, then headed home.

I had not anticipated finding Mitch at my house—in fact, my house was the *last* place I expected to find him—yet there he was. He was standing on my front porch, and Ivy was standing next to him, Rachel behind them. It was as if the three of them now constituted a family, and I no longer belonged. It crossed my mind that Rachel was in on this as well—perhaps she had known all along about her mother and Mitch—though on closer inspection, all three seemed curiously detached from one another, staring off into the distance, oblivious to my presence. Not until they heard the clomping of my shoes up the side porch's steps did they snap out of their respective trances to turn and look at me.

"Cruthers," Mitch said. "You won't believe this."

"What won't I believe?" I asked, approaching him.

"He's drunk," Ivy said. "Look at him. He's drunk."

"No, tell me, Mitch. *What* won't I believe? You'd be surprised. I'm open to the possibility of any fucking thing these days. Go ahead. Let's hear it."

Mitch said, "It was Ken."

"Oh really," I said. "So it wasn't you. It was *Ken.*" The idea was preposterous, an insult, and to show them I was no fool, I calmly reached over and took hold of Mitch's throat. I pressed my two thumbs into his windpipe as hard as I could, shoving Mitch backwards the whole time, across the porch, stopping at the wall of the house. Ivy and Rachel were both screaming, but they were now in the very back of my mind. They might as well have been yelling at me from the far end of a tunnel. Killing Mitch was my sole objective, and everything else faded away. It faded into pulsing dots across my field of vision, into tiny gyrating squares and triangles. And it continued to fade, my view of the world becoming increasingly dark, until we both fell onto the porch and I noticed two policemen running toward our house.

Since when had the police ever responded so quickly to a call? How could they have appeared mere seconds after I had begun my chore?

Then I saw beyond them, past Mitch's house, all the way to Ken's, where three squad cars had congregated—no doubt the same three that had buzzed past me earlier—and Ken, handcuffed, stood with his chin resting on the car's roof. Two officers had pulled their guns and were ordering me to raise my hands—*"Raise your goddamned hands, sir. NOW!"*—but I was mesmerized by the sight of Ken, who was still wearing his work clothes, and who, it seemed, was watching us with equal amazement, perhaps even thinking that I had attempted, but failed, to rescue him.

"Okay, okay," I said, raising my hands.

Mitch lay at my feet, coughing. Rachel was weeping. Ivy, I could tell, was afraid that I wasn't smart enough to understand how precarious my situation was, and how the balance of my life might rest with my next move. But even then, at what would for all practical purposes prove to be our final seconds together as husband and wife, I was capable of surprising her. I showed her how a reasonable man would act given half a chance.

I own a few acres of worthless land on the north side of Benton, right off I-57, the expressway that leads north to Chicago and south to the exit for Carbondale. I had bought the land not long after Ivy and I married, with the thin hope that the city would one day want to build a ramp for the Rend Lake tourists, and that they would need property to do so. I had heard exorbitant prices quoted for land purchased under such conditions, and so I forked over my savings account (a paltry sum) on the off-chance that these plans would eventually pan out, but no one ever expressed any interest, and rumors of a ramp have all but disappeared.

Two years ago I put a camping trailer on the land, a twenty-three-foot Holiday Traveler equipped with a stove and fridge, three thin beds, and a miniature restaurant-style booth for eating. There was a toilet and a narrow shower, too. In the two years that I owned it, I had developed a romantic notion of what roughing it would be like, even though I had never stayed in the trailer for more than an hour at a time. After a month in jail for assault, however, I decided to make the Holiday Traveler my new, permanent home. It was cheap, so why not?

What I had failed to take into account, of course, was the devastating blow of reality. For starters, my only source of water was a single garden hose wedged up through a window. To flush the toilet, I needed to fill a bucket with water and dump it down the bowl. A shower required pouring water into a portable solar pouch, hanging the pouch up in the tight confines of the shower stall, then crouching under the weak drizzle, hoping it lasted long enough for me to wash the suds from my hair. Only one burner on the stove worked. The oven required lighting, but I was afraid to strike a match because of the overwhelming fumes from the kerosene heater. Upon my arrival there was no electricity, and during my first few days in the trailer I kept forgetting to pick up candles while in town. Mice, meanwhile, had nested under